Dark Shimmer

Also by Donna Jo Napoli

Alligator Bayou

Daughter of Venice

The King of Mulberry Street

Dark Shimmer

DONNA JO NAPOLI

WENDY
LAMB
BOOKS

Text copyright © 2015 by Donna Jo Napoli
Jacket art copyright © 2015 by kid-ethic.com
Map art © 2015 by Shutterstock

Visit us on the Web! randomhouseteens.com

Educators and librarians, for a variety of teaching tools, visit us at
RHTeachersLibrarians.com

Library of Congress Cataloging-in-Publication Data
Napoli, Donna Jo.
Dark shimmer / Donna Jo Napoli. — First edition.
pages cm
Summary: A retelling of Snow White from the evil step mother's
point of view as fifteen-year-old Dolce grows up on islands in a
Venetian lagoon where she learns how to make mirrors, but when
her mother dies she is taken in by a widower and his daughter
while she secretly continues making mirrors and slowly goes mad
from mercury poisoning.
ISBN 978-0-385-74655-7 (trade) —
ISBN 978-0-385-90892-4 (lib. bdg.) —
ISBN 978-0-375-98917-9 (ebook) —
ISBN 978-0-553-49418-1 (pbk.) [1. Fairy Tales.] I. Title.
PZ8.N127Dar 2015
[Fic]—dc23
2014039740

The text of this book is set in 11-point Baskerville.
Jacket design by kid-ethic.com
Interior design by Shannon Plunkett

Printed in the United States of America
10 9 8 7 6 5 4 3 2 1
First Edition

Random House Children's Books supports the First Amendment
and celebrates the right to read.

For Wendy Lamb,
who shimmered around me
from the very first thought
to the very last word

Dark Shimmer

Part I

HOME

CHAPTER 1

Blood

I'm swimming through the lagoon in a giant circle around our island, free and graceful. My body isn't my enemy in the water. And nothing can hurt me here—there are no nasty creatures in these waters, though men say they exist far away, in deep ocean waters. Here it's shallow. Most of the time I could simply stand if I got too tired to swim. And for the few deeper spots, I could float on my back. But I won't get tired; I'm the best swimmer of any of the kids.

I turn my face toward the lagoon. In this direction I can look out so far, the sky meets the sea. I'm not even sure where one ends and the other begins. That's comforting. Mamma likes to say that even though we live out here, separated from the rest of the world, the water and sky remind us that we're linked to everything.

My eyes go back to the island. Dawn slides slowly across it, making it shine yellow-gold. The fishing boats will be going out soon, but I've already passed the point where they come and go, so it doesn't matter.

From here I can see the field, and the canal beyond it. Two swans swim in the canal, calm as stones. It is lined with houses, almost all empty. Lots of people lived here once. Thousands. So many, there were two convents and sixteen cloisters. The buildings are in ruins now. There was even a bishop here. He sat in the big stone chair outside the church of Santa Maria Assunta.

There are only sixty-four people here now. But Mella is with child, so we'll soon be sixty-five if she's lucky. Sometimes women aren't lucky in childbirth. We're not many here, and that's how we want to keep it. This island is our refuge. Whenever men get in a boat to go trading, they tell the people they meet how our children die from marsh fever all the time. Otherwise, the people who originally owned the houses here might come back . . . and then we'd lose everything.

I swim past the marsh. Mosquitoes hover over it, a black cloud stark against the dawn sky. The air over the marsh is putrid— *mal aria*. Most people who breathe it get a fever so high, they're in bed for weeks. Some even die. But the mosquitoes thrive on that air.

A man slogs through the grasses, bare-legged, with a cloth wrapped around his loins. It's Giordano, of course. He's the only one who can withstand that air and the only one who works so early. I change my stroke so just half my head emerges from the water. My hands and feet don't break the surface—no part of me makes a splash. He's unlikely to see me. We're not allowed to swim alone, not even me, though no one really cares if anything bad happens to me. No one except Mamma.

Giordano flails his arms at the mosquitoes. He's already clumping back out to drier land. He picks things from his legs and throws them in a bucket. Leeches.

People use disgusting, slimy leeches for healing. Someone

must be sick. Maybe Mella had her baby in the night and something has gone wrong. Oh, I pray not. I pray Giordano is gathering the leeches to sell to physicians on the other islands.

The only thing I know about those islands is that the people who live there make glass and are rotten, like people on the mainland. Everyone here says life there was awful, and they wince. Only on our island are we safe. We children aren't allowed to go out in a trading boat. Those wretched people might snatch us. They steal children and make them their slaves. We're not even allowed to look toward other islands. We can look only north and west, to the forests on the mainland. Hardly any people live there.

I'm on the final stretch of this long swim; just around that bend I'll see home. Mamma and I live in a room in one of the old convents, San Giovanni Evangelista. Now I see the bridge we cross to get to our home. Looking at it from here, it occurs to me that our home is on its own island. Ha! We have our own island. It's as though Mamma is queen and I am princess, like in one of Giordano's tales of the land he used to live in. Princess! If I said that to the other kids, they'd laugh in my face. Though not really in my face . . . they can't reach anywhere near my face.

I swim faster. I can't wait to call Mamma my queen. She'll laugh, happy.

"Hey!" calls a voice from behind me.

A boat! I won't look. I swim fast, faster than I've ever swum before. If it's coming after me, I can't hear for the pounding pulse in my head. I'm lost if they get me. Mamma will never even know what happened to me. *Fast. Please, Lord in heaven, let me be fast.*

I'm onshore in minutes and running toward home. I race along the rocky path, cross the little piazza—the campo—and go sprawling on my face, slamming my forehead against the ground.

"What's the matter with you?" It's little Tonso. His brother, Bini, stands beside him.

"Run!" I wave them off. "Strangers are coming!"

Tonso screams, "Where?" They dash around a corner.

I roll over and dare to look back. No boat has followed; no hateful strangers chase.

My knee split open in the fall. But I'm all right. I pick pebbles from the gash. I'm all right, I'm all right.

The boys creep out on bowed legs white as sticks without the bark, especially Tonso's skinny leg, the one that never grew right. They peer in all directions.

I stand up. I'm older than these boys, but not by much. Still, they're half my size.

"I don't see any strangers," says Tonso.

"A boat came by."

"You're lying," says Bini.

"I am not! They nearly caught me."

"You? Who'd want you?" says Tonso.

Bini nods. They think I wouldn't even make a decent slave.

My ears buzz. My cheeks burn. My whole body is aflame.

I walk a few steps past them, my back tall, then break into a run, no matter the pain in my knee. I go straight to the church of Santa Maria Assunta. It's empty. I race down the center of the nave and don't even glance at the skull of Santa Cecilia, the martyr. I stop under the main apse. I strip off my wet smock and turn my face upward.

Light streams in through the rose-colored glass window. Maria the Virgin holds the baby Gesù high and looks down on me from the glittering gold background. A host of apostles stand below her, in a ring around the bottom of the dome. I wonder what they think, whether they can look ahead to that babe's death. Mamma says only priests know, and there are no priests on our island anymore.

I turn in a circle holding my hands out, palms upward. Palms matter to God the Father, so they must matter to Maria the Virgin. Gesù's palms bled. Not when he was a baby, like in the window's mosaic, but when he was grown. When they killed him. Mamma tells me all about Gesù.

"Maria, look at me, see me, please," I say, but softly. She can hear me, even up there. That's part of being divine—hearing everything, seeing everything, feeling everything. I'm spinning now, faster and faster. "Stop me." I slap my palms on the very top of my head. "Stop me from growing. Stop me from being a monster."

And I fall. I always fall when I spin like this. I put my lips to the marble mosaic. "Help me." I press one cheek against the chilled stone. "I'm twelve years old and taller than any man here. I tower over the women. You can see it. You can stop it. Help me." I clear my throat. "Help me." This isn't right. Someone has to listen. "Help me!"

"What are you doing?" It's Giordano.

My fingers scrabble across the floor for my wet smock, but he's already swooped it up. I squat, knees to chest, arms holding all of me together tight. "Give it back."

The tips of his shoes graze my toes. "Don't worry. No one wants to look at your ugly body. No one ever will."

I know that. Why else would I cover up? I glare. "You have a fat, old face."

"Your mother named you Dolce—'sweet'—out of hope, I guess. You're far from sweet." He drops the smock on my head.

I scramble into it as he walks around me.

"I saw you running. Those long legs of yours afford you one advantage."

"I'd give them up in an instant to have yours." I don't know why I said that. It's true, but it's wicked. Mamma says I have a healthy body . . . and ingrates are the worst sort of people.

Giordano tilts his head, and his eyes drift upward to the Virgin. He sighs. "You know what, Dolce? This is the first time I've ever felt sorry for you. Your mother would have done better to leave you on a doorstep in the big city before she moved here. But she'd lost six babies already by the time you came along. . . . She felt cursed. She wouldn't listen to reason. Did you know that?"

Of course I knew that. But he's almost acting nice. Doesn't he realize he's saying Mamma would have done better to kill me? That's what abandonment would have meant. No one wants me.

"So here you are. A freak among us." He laughs, and his big apple cheeks look ready to burst. Everyone has apple cheeks but me.

"It's not funny."

"No. Not for you, I suppose not." He rubs the back of his neck. "I was a freak when I first arrived. A freak even here. I spoke different—the way they speak way down south on the mainland. I ate different. Eh, you know, everywhere you go, you're a stranger. But you can't just sit in a hole your whole life, can you?"

I scream inside my head. All Giordano had to do was learn to speak like here, eat like here. He has no idea what it's like to be a real freak.

"Look at all that blood on your leg. You fall all the time. Listen, you want to make people like you?"

"It's impossible."

"What would you think of making mirrors? Venerio needs an assistant. He's getting too old to keep up with the workload. It's a nasty job. If you do it, then he doesn't have to recruit some other kid."

"Nothing I do will make the kids like me."

"Maybe not. But if you helped, the kids would be relieved, and at least Venerio would act like he liked you."

"I don't care if Venerio likes me or not."

"You'd have a way to fill your time, learn a little. And he'd give you something to bring home for dinner each night."

"I can catch fish on my own."

"Not fish. *Moscardini.*"

Mamma loves those tiny octopuses. She hums as she eats them, laced with salt. My heart opens at the thought of presenting Mamma with a gift. I nod. "Thanks."

"I'll let Venerio know," calls Giordano from behind me.

I walk home, feeling eyes watch me. I step through our door. The kitchen fire sputters loudly. The smell of cod and anchovies permeates the room, a surprise in this season.

Mamma takes one look at my knee and rushes over to put her arm around my waist and draw me close. I have to lean down to kiss her cheek. "I'll put the fish aside," she says. "My *baccalà* can wait. I'll go get liver, my beautiful daughter. Liver and lungs can fix anything. Don't you worry, Dolce. Don't you worry one bit. You are my treasure. Your face—so fair."

She always says that. A sense of pain and tenderness fills me. I don't understand why Mamma loves me, but I love her so much for loving me.

CHAPTER 2

Work

I'm in a hurry, but I weave my way through the yellow flowers anyway. Sunflowers, they're called. Some explorers recently crossed a vast sea, discovered hot islands, and brought these flowers back to this part of the world. I love them. They grow taller than me, and they seem to be constantly smiling. With seeds all over their faces, big striped seeds that crack in your teeth.

When I emerge into our work area, I see my wildcat friend, Gato Zalo. He sprawls on his back, tummy to the sun, blissful. Inside my chest, I feel the color of his fur blend with the color of the sunflower petals, golden and sweet, as though I've become the clearest honeypot.

Not even a whisker twitches. I squat and put my hand on Gato Zalo's ribs. He twist-jumps to his feet with a hiss and looks around.

"It's just you and me."

He walks off with a flick of the tail, unforgiving. I'm supposed to touch him only when he offers himself; those are the rules he established. Well, that's all right. It's work time. Besides, all it takes to lure him back is a pile of fish heads.

I like to feed Gato Zalo; it makes him happy, and it cuts down on the number of birds he kills. I love the birds. They eat the insects that would destroy our gardens. And nothing eases loneliness better than the trill of birds. Even the short, harsh cries of the terns that breed in the marshes are a respite from being solitary for hours on end. That's another good thing about the new sunflowers—doves come to eat their seeds.

I lean over a transparent sheet of glass. It's made on one of the other islands. Venerio told me glass used to be made on our island, years and years ago. The very rich had glass windows instead of oiled paper ones.

I'd better get busy. I've been working for Venerio for two weeks now, and I learn fast, but this is the first time I'm working alone. Venerio had a coughing fit yesterday, so today he is trusting in me while he rests up. The glass I'm supposed to turn into a mirror lies long and narrow on the ground. It's about the length of my forearm and the width of my hand. Last year Venerio made only small mirrors; you could carry them in one hand. But now the glass is larger. Carrying this one takes two hands, even for me. If we'll be working on bigger and bigger glass, that's good, because my size will be an advantage. And bigger glass means my job will take longer. Both things are good—both will make everyone realize they need me.

People have been nicer to me since I began working for Venerio. The mothers, I mean. Some of them even smile when our eyes meet. None of the kids are nicer to me, though. So I have no choice but to glare at them; otherwise they'd steal my food and taunt me even more.

I place my hand on the sun-warmed glass. I know how they

make these larger pieces. Venerio told me. He likes to boast that when he was young, before he got the tremors, he used to blow glass. To make the glass, they burn sea plants and then pour water over the ashes and mix in sand and cook it till it melts into a clear liquid. Then they dip one end of a long metal pipe in the liquid and hold the pipe high and blow into the other end. The molten glass grows into a huge bubble. Then the blowers swing the pipe so that the bubble hangs heavy and low and stretches into a long, hollow pod. They cut the ends off while the pod is still bubbling hot and then cut along one side and flatten it out. And there you have it—a long, flat sheet like this.

Our men pick up the glass sheets from the glassblowers' island and bring them here for Venerio and me to turn into mirrors. As pay we get whatever we need—sometimes money, sometimes food, household furnishings, different fabrics, tools.

They make mirrors on that other island, too. But our job is special. We experiment with the mirrors we make, trying different methods to get the backing to stay on. Few others experiment like we do, because of the cost of the materials. But we don't care about costs. That's because no one gets the metals as cheap as we do. Venerio has friends far away, on the mainland. They mine tin from Monte Valerio and quicksilver from Monte Amiata, and send the metals across mountains and meadows and across the wide lagoon, to us.

The tin arrives in small sheets as thick as the top half of a thumb. Our boys pound it with a roller for days until it's only a tenth that thick. There is a short stack of sheets waiting for me.

I place a thin sheet of tin on the glass. It's smaller than the glass, so I pick up flakes of tin from the pile of pieces that have broken off in the rolling and add them carefully at the edges until every speck of glass is covered.

Now I carry the glass over to the slab of limestone that Venerio has scrubbed clean. I blow on the top of the stone, just to make sure. Then I remove the tin from the glass piece by piece, arranging them on the limestone exactly as they were on the glass. I'm good at this. I have sharp eyes and a steady hand, not like Venerio.

No one's allowed to be around for what comes next except me and Venerio. This is the part that turns his toes and fingers pink, I'm sure, because the boys who roll the tin have ordinary-colored toes and fingers. Someday my toes and fingers will turn pink, too, I bet. That's all right with me, though. It's the mark of my profession. I grin. I have a profession, and I'm good at it.

I open the iron flask and pour the shimmering quicksilver onto a soft goatskin cloth. I quick plug the flask so the remaining quicksilver won't disappear into the air. It can do that. I left the plug off my first day on the job and Venerio beat me with a stick so I wouldn't forget again. And I won't, though it would be easy to, because quicksilver gives off no smell to remind me to plug the flask.

I rub the soaking-wet cloth over the tin until the quicksilver covers it evenly, dabbing at the loose flakes ever so lightly so nothing moves. A little quicksilver runs off the edges of the tin, but it's supposed to. It's important that every bit of tin gets covered, and that's the only way to make sure. This coat of quicksilver is a little thicker than the coat I tried last time. Venerio and I vary each part of the process, one at a time, so we can find the most efficient formula for making these mirrors. I'm determined to be the one to find that formula.

The tin and quicksilver merge into one as I watch. I hold the glass over it and look through, lining it up perfectly. I set the glass on top of the tin, edges matching. The fingers of my right hand are dirty with quicksilver; I've left prints on the glass, but that's no problem. The only quicksilver that will stick is the part that touches the tin, because the quicksilver eats through the tin and together they form something new and hard that sticks to the glass. I wipe off the prints with my clean left palm. I spread a strip of wool over the top of the glass, to protect it from scratching, and I layer it with bricks. Sweat drips from my forehead onto the bricks. It's not that hot today; it's the concentration . . . that's hard work.

I rub my hands clean with another piece of wool. Then I sit down and look at my work. Venerio will be the one to uncover it in three days. He'll lift one end of the mirror just a little, and then the next day raise that end a little higher, each day higher and higher, till the mirror is vertical. That way, whatever excess quicksilver didn't disappear in the air will run off into the box waiting just for that purpose. Then Venerio will cut away any tin that sticks out—but there won't be any, I'm so careful—run a chisel around the edges, wipe it all down, and paint the back to keep my work from flaking away.

The result will be good. But probably not perfect. Not yet. Next time maybe Venerio will leave it for four days. Or maybe he'll use more bricks, make it all heavier. We'll keep trying until Venerio declares it can get no better.

I worked hard and finished sooner than I expected. But I mustn't be seen walking home too early; people should think it took me hours and hours to set a mirror by myself. Let them be in awe of how hard I work. I sit on a low pile of rubble, and the sun feels good. I keep thinking about the idea of Mamma and me living on our own island. You can see tiny bubbles rising from the water below our bridge now and then, so people say a devil lives there. But it's not a devil, it's a guard. Royalty have guards. Mamma always calls our home a castle, after all. It doesn't matter that it's rotting and crumbling. I'm still a princess.

That makes me better than the other kids. It's crazy, but who cares? Being better than them in a crazy way is better than being worse than them in every way.

But, oh, I have a trade. That makes me better, too. And being a monster made it happen. Ha!

A breeze comes off the water. It ruffles the edges of the wool that stick out from under the bricks. My mirror cooks under there, like rolls in an oven. I won't own that mirror, I won't even ever look in it—after all, mirrors just show how ugly I am—but it's mine all the same.

I stand and stretch to get the kink out of my neck from working bent over for so long. Then I slowly head into the center of town.

Voices come from the other side of the wall beside the path, from Bartolomeo's garden. I stand on tiptoe and peek over the wall. The pink oleanders are odorless, unlike the heady red roses. You'd never know from their mild aspect that chewing any part of them can kill you. Bartolomeo is a physician, and he uses the oleanders to fix women's problems and calm the heart. Poking up through the bottom branches are purple flowers on long stalks. That's monkshood. A mountain plant, it can grow in shade. Bartolomeo brought it here from Austria. The leaves are hairy and poisonous to the touch. But monkshood lowers fever and stops the horrible coughing that torments old people in winter. This is Bartolomeo's medicine garden. I call it his horror garden, and I love it. No one's allowed in without him. Bartolomeo doesn't like me any more than anyone else does, but he takes me into his garden often because he's flattered by how closely I listen to him.

The voices hush for a moment, but here they come again.

I peer beyond the bushes and see Mella. Druda, Bartolomeo's wife, huddles beside her. Bartolomeo is nowhere to be seen. So they're here secretly. Mella's shoulders shake with sobs. Druda puts a hand in the center of Mella's back and waits. They talk, but I can't make out their words.

The visible sadness brings tears to my eyes. If Mella were alone, I'd go to her. She needs a kind word.

Mella steps away and I can see . . . a baby. Druda takes the baby from her arms. Mella lets out a cry of despair. She grabs for the child.

For an instant I see naked flailing. What? I bite my tongue to keep from calling out.

Druda quickly wraps the baby up and walks off.

Mella drops to her knees and holds her face in both hands. She rocks forward and backward, moaning.

She's alone now. But I don't go to her. My insides have turned rock hard. Finally, she stands and smooths her dress and leaves.

I lean back against the wall and my eyes burn. It occurs to me that this wall is absurdly high. If someone wanted privacy, they could have made a wall that came up to my chest. That height would have served perfectly. It's as though this wall is trying to keep out taller beings—monsters like me.

I walk on. When I reach the church of Santa Maria Assunta, I go inside, straight to the casket of Sant'Eliodoro, and look down through the glass top. He's wrapped like a dried-out caterpillar in his cocoon of clothes, nothing of him visible but his old brown skull, turned the wrong way, as though he's trying to suffocate himself. His clothes . . . they're squashed into a heap, so who knows, really, but they seem . . . long enough for someone tall . . . maybe taller than me. I always figured they dragged on the ground behind him. I leave, shaking inside.

Soon I'm standing beside Mamma in the kitchen. She drops *moscardini* whole into wine and water in which potatoes and garlic are already boiling. She stirs, then scoops everything into our bowls. All the while, she talks on and on, but I don't listen. I can't.

Mella's baby was different.

That night I lie awake and look up at the stars through the open window. I can see the constellation of the harp. It's usually dim, but right now it glitters bright. I imagine it playing. I've never heard a harp, but Mamma says it sounds like angels singing, and that's easy to imagine. I sit up and listen hard. *Please, angels, sing to me. Loudly. Drown out my thoughts.*

A couple of weeks ago, on the tenth of August, we celebrated the feast of San Lorenzo. The people here love him best of all the saints. Hundreds of years ago, some Roman prefect demanded that San Lorenzo give the church's riches to him. So San Lorenzo brought the poor, the lame, the blind, and the afflicted before that prefect, declaring these were the true riches. He was killed, of course—all saints die horribly, it seems to me. Everyone here loves to tell his story.

I would scream right now if Mamma weren't asleep. They're all a bunch of liars. They praise San Lorenzo when they don't agree with him at all. They don't value the afflicted. They hate the afflicted. They hate me.

And even though Mella cried so hard, she let Druda take her baby.

The quiet, familiar sound comes: a boat slides past along the canal. I run out to see who it is. I race beside the canal to the end and stare at the boat till its lamp is out of sight.

Slow footsteps come up behind me. But I know whose they are. I don't turn around.

"Dolce?" says Mamma. She touches my hand. "What are you doing out here?"

"Watching."

"Watching the lagoon? Bad things happen in the lagoon at night. Come back home."

"Where are they going, Mamma?"

"Who?"

"A boat passed."

"Oh. That." She comes to stand beside me. "The big city."

"At night?"

"Mmm."

"How come?"

"They're taking Mella's baby there."

My teeth clench so hard my ears hurt. "Why?"

"For adoption. He'll be better off there."

"Why?" My voice gets loud, but I don't care. "They're hateful in the city."

"It's Mella and Lorenzo's decision. It's their baby. Dolce, come back inside. Come to sleep." She takes my hand and pulls me behind her.

I give up. My arms ache from emptiness. I should be holding something. I can't think what, though. I stumble through the dark, fall onto the bed, roll so my back is to the open window, plug my ears with my fingers, and shut my eyes firmly. I am cut off from everything.

Except my thoughts.

All babies have big heads and short arms. But Mella's baby wasn't like other babies. Head smaller. Arms longer. Eyes . . . I don't know how to describe them . . . just different. Even his hands were different, with skinny fingers that scrabbled the air, all equally separated. Oh, Lord. Mella's baby is like me. He's a monster.

A monster wouldn't be adopted by anyone. And the lagoon is all around us.

Bad things happen in the lagoon at night.

I will never let anyone rip my babies from my arms.

I will never have babies.

CHAPTER 3

Foot-Fishing

"I know you're following me." Giordano looks ahead as he speaks, but for sure he's talking to me. He carries a bucket in each hand.

I stay behind him and let him think he's clever for noticing me. Inside my head I laugh at him for not noticing Gato Zalo, who tracks us both at a distance. Giordano would shout and chase the cat off if he saw him. He'd try to kill him. Everyone says our island is best without predators.

It's not fair. I don't know how Gato Zalo wound up here, but he's got as much right to be here as anyone else. As soon as I can, I'm going to leave him a treat.

I dare to look back at my cat friend. He's gone, as though smeared to nothing in the damp air. I'm bereft.

This moment feels thin, like being alive but not quite. Most of the island is still asleep; usually the fishermen go to work right about now, but the tide is out, so it's too shallow for the boats this morning. Giordano is the first soul I've spied. Exactly the one I hoped to find.

"Come on up here and walk with me."

I run to his side.

"If you don't speak, not a single word, you can help me."

Why would I want to help him? My goal is for him to help me.

We move through the soft gray air as though floating in a memory. We're heading south. I keep my eyes down so I'm not tempted to look across the water to the next island. We arrive at a *fondamenta*—a stone wall wide enough to walk on that separates the land from the sea. Giordano sets the buckets on the wall, then jumps down into the water. It comes only to his hips. At high tide, he'd have to swim in this spot. He grabs one of the buckets and holds it above the water as he slogs off. After a few steps, he stops and looks back at me expectantly. I jump in. He keeps looking at me. I grab the other bucket. He nods.

We wade slowly, with me several steps behind. The bottom grasses are spongy underfoot with a slight film of slime. Silver clouds of tiny fish bloom, and dart away to safety. I'm tempted to dunk my bucket to catch them. They're delicious raw, soaked in lemon juice with onion and parsley chopped fine. But the bucket is heavy; I'd never be fast enough to catch them. And Giordano might get mad. He has a plan for these buckets.

All at once the grasses end, and the half-muddy, half-sandy bottom shows starkly through the clear water, even in this weak light. Giordano holds up a hand: halt. I stop and look at the shells scattered here and there on the bottom. The best clams, the tiny ones with the stripes, are just below the surface. I could dig them up easily. They would be scrumptious with oil and pepper over long strands of pasta.

I can't seem to think of anything but food. I skipped the evening meal last night. My stomach was all ajitter over seeing Mella's baby, even before I knew they were taking him away. I clutch the bucket to my chest so I can sort of hug myself.

And I do the forbidden: I look out at the island directly ahead.

A spire rises high. It looks like an ordinary place. Appearances can be so deceptive. Why did marsh fever plague our island but not the others, so that many people live there now, but only a few of us live here? Sometimes I wonder if the Lord is punishing us.

But that's wrong-minded. We're here because it's safe. That's what everyone says. We're here because nearly twenty years ago a group of us was smart enough to take over this island and make it ours.

Suddenly, Giordano rips the bucket from my arms. Did he guess at my wrong thoughts? Will he tell Mamma where I was looking?

He holds a bucket high in each hand and leaves me standing there. My arms hang empty, useless. I squat in the water till I'm chest-deep and let my hands glide through it like when I'm swimming. The air above the water turns rosy with dawn.

It occurs to me that the grassy areas throughout the lagoon could hide any number of things. I don't want to step on anything . . . anything tossed in the lagoon at night . . . anything dead. I swallow a lump of sadness.

Giordano is clumping through the muddy sand. He stops, turns around, and points at me, then at the water. I look down. Crabs have emerged in his footprints. Ha! I hurry from footprint to footprint, snatching them and throwing them into his buckets. Foot-fishing!

We work like that till both buckets teem with crabs. The water is now up to Giordano's chest; the tide is rising fast. At last he nods and hands me a bucket. The buckets are so full, I have to keep pushing crab legs back inside, and still a few crabs escape, *plop, plop.* They slide through the water, scuttle under the sand, gone. We slog back to land and set the buckets on the *fondamenta* and I climb up.

Giordano goes back out in the water. He fetches a net he must have set there yesterday evening. He slogs over to sit beside me.

"Can I talk now?" I ask.

Giordano picks seaweed from his net. He glances up, then goes back to work.

"Did you live right near the king?" I ask.

"You did a decent job this morning, Dolce." He picks the seaweed fast. "Venerio says you're a good worker at the mirrors, too. You're strong."

"The king . . . ?"

"I complimented you. You're supposed to say thank you."

"Thank you. I want to know about the king."

"What king? This is a republic." Giordano gives a little laugh. "Are you talking about my homeland?"

"Yes. Did you ever see him? Did you see the queen? The princesses?"

"I did."

"Really?"

He tosses me one end of the fishing net. "Pick. The ones like this"—he holds up some leafy seaweed nearly like lettuce—"they go in the pile here. The rest are junk." He throws a lacy seaweed back in the water.

"I know which ones you sell to the glassblowers." I get to work. The pile between us grows fast. "Tell me about your homeland."

"You don't want to move there, if that's what you're thinking. There are wars all the time."

"Is that why you left?"

Giordano lifts one side of his mouth as though I've said something funny. "I left to be with my own kind."

"I thought you said you were a stranger when you came here."

He shoots me a glance and looks down at his task. "What

is it you want to know, Dolce? Why are you asking about that kingdom?"

"Does everyone love the king?"

"Hardly. He's got a whole army to protect him."

"Just him?"

"Well, no. The entire kingdom. But it's always the kings who manage to start the wars, so they're the ones people try to kill."

"So no one likes him?"

"They revere him, I guess. He's rich. Powerful."

"And what about the princesses? Do people love them?"

"Those haughty spoiled brats? They walk like this." Giordano moves from the hips up, as though strutting, stiff-backed. Even though he's sitting, I can tell the gait he's mimicking. "They don't talk to commoners except to bark orders."

I blink. "You're lying. Princesses in stories are lovely."

"Stories aren't life, Dolce."

I find a tiny live shrimp in the net and pop it into my mouth. It crunches sweet and salty. "But even if they walk like that, no one would kill them, right? No one would dare."

"No." Giordano stares at me. "Why are you talking about death today?"

"Everyone should be."

"What do you mean?"

"People kill ones they don't like."

"That's murder you're talking about, child. Good people don't do that."

"That's not true. I saw that baby go off in the boat in the middle of the night . . . off into the lagoon."

"Mella's baby? Is that what you're talking about? No one murdered Mella's baby. He'll be adopted."

"I don't believe that."

Giordano shrugs. "Suit yourself."

"I face the truth. No one here likes me."

"The mothers like you."

I shake my head.

"They do, Dolce. I heard them talking. They've taken to you lately. Some of them are sorry you've been so left out. They talk about how odd you've become, but they know you're not bad. They look at you differently now."

"Only because I'm making the mirrors. They think it'll be my fingers and toes that go pink instead of their sons' fingers and toes. I might be saving their boys, so the mothers can see potential for me. Who knows? Someday I might be someone who could die in place of their boys."

Giordano wipes sweat off his upper lip. "You have a dramatic streak."

"But you're not saying I'm wrong."

"You go talking like that, and you'll find yourself isolated for good."

"That's all right with me. I'm supposed to be isolated. I'm a princess."

Giordano laughs.

I stand. I could kick his buckets of crabs off the *fondamenta*.

Giordano catches my foot in midair. "Go away, Dolce. Go be a princess. Pink toes suit a princess."

I walk away haughty. This is my princess walk. I don't need anyone. I am a princess. And no one will dare try to kill me.

CHAPTER 4

Eating

The sun is low on the horizon. It'll set in minutes. It's funny how the sun seems to rise so slowly but set so quickly. "Mamma, we need to hurry."

"Another minute." Mamma greedily throws two more crabs into the bucket I'm holding. She finally stops and grins at me. "Enough."

We slosh back to shore, then walk home, our shifts dripping. It's dark by the time we go through the door. I build the fire—that's my job—then change into dry clothes.

Mamma's already plopping crabs into the pot, one by one. Her clean shift smells like dry grass. I love the smells of autumn. I kiss the top of her head and watch the gray shells turn orange in the flickering firelight. "You're an expert at foot-fishing."

"There isn't much to it, is there? Anyone could be an expert. I'm glad Giordano taught you his secret. And I'm glad the tide was so low tonight that I wasn't afraid to do it myself."

"You don't have to be afraid ever, Mamma. I can teach you to swim."

"You're the mermaid, Dolce, not me. I'm content on land." She laughs. "Except when I have a craving for crabs. Then nothing else can satisfy me, and look, I go right into the water."

I don't have cravings like that. Except maybe for people to like me. Or to love me. Mamma makes life seem so simple, craving things she can have.

Mamma pinches my arm playfully. "My perfect daughter, you've made it so that I can satisfy my whims any time I want."

Perfect. Sometimes when Mamma says things like that, I'm so happy. But right now I'm too hungry to be happy. My stomach growls. "I guess I should throw roots into the water for me."

"I can't lure you with crabs, not even when I caught them?"

"I hate them."

"Who can hate crabs?"

"They take forever to pick through. How many are there in this pot? Fourteen? Fifteen? And still I bet you won't be full when you finish."

"You have to take pleasure in the whole thing, Dolce. You talk while you pick out the flesh. You tell stories. You—"

"What if you're alone?"

"What?"

"What if you have no one to talk to?"

"Then you plan. You figure out what you'll do in the day ahead. Or you just dream. You're a good dreamer, Dolce. I see you sitting sometimes, back against a wall, sun on your cheeks. You know how to dream."

Mamma watches me when I don't realize it. I bet she's the only one who ever looks at me when they don't have to. "You know what I'm dreaming of right now?" I ask.

Mamma thrusts her head forward and raises an eyebrow. Her cheeks pucker in expectation. "Close your eyes."

"Why?"

"Don't be stubborn, Dolce. Just do it."

I close my eyes. A moment later the vinegary smell under my nose is unmistakable. I open my eyes and quick take the plate of sardines Mamma's holding up.

She laughs. "I browned the onions slow, like you like, so the sweetness comes out strong. But I added something new."

I sit on the floor with the marvelous dish in my lap. "Raisins? And what are these?" I pop a little white thing into my mouth. "Pine nuts. Did you add pine nuts?"

"Raisins and pine nuts cover stinky onion breath. I want my fair daughter to smell as sweet as she is. I cooked it this morning, so it's had all day to grow succulent." She laughs again and scoops crabs from the pot. "As succulent as these crabs."

We sit there, eating and telling stories late into the night, and I make sure to eat my sardines at the same pace Mamma eats her crabs. Just to keep her company. She'd do it for me. I am the luckiest monster in the world.

Part II

EVERYTHING CHANGES

CHAPTER 5

Swimming

"Dolce! Come quick!" The voice is distant.

I don't even have to look to know it's Tommaso. He's ten and likes to follow me around, even though I'm fifteen. Sometimes his chatter makes my headaches come, and, oh, Lord, they pound me senseless. But most of the time I listen so I can learn about everything that's happening without having to get near the others.

I'm working on a new mirror. A finished one is propped to my right. I have one propped to my left, too. I don't look directly into them, of course. I look from the side and I watch the grasses behind me shake in the breeze and see the branches of the far-off apple trees laden with fruit. These mirrors calm me.

Tommaso runs up to me and leans over, catching his breath. "You have to come."

His manner frightens me. But I pretend that I don't care. I am a princess, after all.

Besides, I'm busy. The quicksilver on this sheet of tin didn't form an even layer. Lately my hands shake as bad as Venerio's.

I'll have to wipe it all off and apply it again. I must live up to my reputation. My mirror technique has indeed been adopted. Everyone on the glassblowers' island uses it now. So I need to make my technique even better—faster, somehow. Venerio says that's important, otherwise we'll be out of a job soon—and he says it angry, sometimes furious; he's become a grouch. So I'm working on the technique. I'm the best there is.

I put two fingers on the spot between my eyebrows and massage in a circle to fend off a headache. A shadow comes at me from both sides. I can barely see it, but it's there.

Tommaso touches my shoulder. I'm leaning over the low limestone, so it's easy for him to reach there. Still, I can't remember the last time anyone touched my shoulder. Or my face. His fingers make me shiver. I have a fleeting image of clasping them and pulling his hand across my eyes, my cheeks, my lips. The poor boy would be shocked.

Maria the Virgin didn't answer my prayers, no matter how many times I begged her. I kept growing. I'm enormous now. The tallest men don't even come up to my ribs; most don't reach my waist. If I ever have a husband, he'll have to stand on tiptoe to kiss my breasts, and even then I'll probably need to lean forward. But of course I know I will never have a husband. No one will ever choose me. And I'd never have children anyway.

Sometimes I press my mouth into the dirt and scream.

I've been a princess for three years now. No one acknowledges it, but I walk like princesses on the mainland walk. Like Giordano showed me. Except now and then my legs give way and I wind up sitting on the ground, muscles atwitch. I have some sort of weakness.

And I know Venerio has it, too. We're the ones who touch the quicksilver. I'll be like Venerio someday, guiding some other person whose hands are still steady while mine do a frantic dance in the air.

But I don't let on to anyone. If a person should happen upon me after I've collapsed on a path and asks what I'm doing, I yell it's no business of theirs where I choose to sit. No one knows what happens in my head or in my body. Besides, I'm fifteen; I'm no child.

Tommaso's hand brushes my hair aside and rests hot on the back of my neck. I press my lips together. My arms long to circle this innocent child. What I wouldn't give for a brother, a sister.

"Dolce," he whispers, his mouth to my ear, "it's your mamma."

I bolt upright. "Where?"

"Follow me."

"Where is she?" I shout.

"They carried her to Druda's."

I'm running, racing. These absurd long legs have some use.

My head goes all swimmy and pain throbs behind my eyes. *Please, please, don't let me collapse now. Please keep me strong.* I cut along the canal and burst into Druda's house. Margherita and Druda step away from the mattress where Mamma lies.

Mamma sees me and opens her mouth, then gags. I quick turn her onto her side just in time—she vomits onto the floor.

"Mamma." I rub her back and croon in her ear, "Mamma, I'm here. What do you need?"

She moans and curls around her stomach. Sweat bathes her.

"I don't understand. What?"

She mumbles.

I look at Druda and Margherita. "Do you understand?"

"She ate crabs." Druda shakes her head sadly.

"What's that got to do with anything?"

"Didn't you see? Dead fish washed up on the beach this morning. All this hot weather . . . it's the curse of the algae. No one should eat crabs or clams or mussels—none of that till the poison passes." Druda lifts her hands to the ceiling as though in prayer.

I could slap her. "Stop that! Mamma's going to be fine!"

"She can't even move, Dolce."

Mamma pants shallowly. And I think . . . *Yes!*

I streak out of Druda's house straight for Francesco's chicken yard. I chase the hens, take a flying leap, and catch one by a leg. She flaps and scratches and I almost don't have the heart to kill her. Still, wrong things happen all the time. And what choice do I have? I wring her neck, crying hard. I race back to Druda's kitchen and chop that hen in half. Her lungs and liver are hot and fat. I go to Mamma's bed and tear off a bite of liver with my teeth and press it into Mamma's mouth.

Druda gasps. "Have you lost your mind, Dolce?"

"Liver and lungs," I say to Mamma. "Liver and lungs can fix anything."

Mamma gags, then coughs and coughs till she goes limp.

I rub her back. "Eat the lungs at least." I push a piece into her mouth, but her head rolls back.

"Let her be, Dolce." Druda speaks softly.

"Leave her in peace." Margherita makes the sign of the cross, then lifts the cross around her neck to her mouth for a kiss.

"Get out of here!" I scream at Druda and Margherita. "Get out, get out!"

The women run.

"Mamma, they think you're dead." I pull her onto my lap and hold her close. "Please don't be dead. Please. Please."

Her eyelids flutter. She opens them and looks at me, as though surprised. "Dolce? You're still here?" Her voice is nearly inaudible. Then her eyes close and her head falls and her whole body goes heavy.

I hold her a long time. Eventually, someone pries me from her. I slide to the cold stone floor. It feels good against the backs of my legs and under my hands. So many people have walked over it for so many years that the surface is smooth as skin. I could stay here forever.

But people bustle about as though they know exactly what to do, as though they've been waiting to do it.

I stand, scoop up the lungs and liver, and go outside. I won't watch as they wash my mamma's body.

I walk to the grasses and leave the chicken innards for Gato Zalo. I keep walking, all the way to the *fondamenta*. This is as far as I can go. My whole world is behind me now. And it's empty. My life will consist of work, and of Gato Zalo for however long wildcats live. A buzz starts in my ears.

Mamma. No. This can't be.

I jump into the water before I even realize what I'm going to do. It's the end of summer; I'm wearing my thin smock. I tie the hem in knots at the sides. This way I can swim.

"You're still here?" Mamma's question. She was incredulous. "You're still here?"

Where else would I be?

Where else should I be?

I release myself to the water and swim.

It's early afternoon. I have the sense of impending death—my own death. But I've had that sense before; it means nothing. It's Mamma who has died, not me. From crabs she caught foot-fishing. I am screaming.

I swim hard. The next island comes close fast. I didn't think it would be this easy. That island was always far, far, far. How could it be this close?

I'm not cold, but my teeth chatter. A spasm shakes me and I go under, swallow salt water, come up sputtering and crying.

Mamma is dead. My mamma. The queen of my island. The queen of my life.

And I'm in the sea. I have no one on the island behind me anymore. But I have no one on the island ahead of me, either. I have no one anywhere.

Have the people on these islands ever heard of me, of the monster? Would they kill me on sight? Or torture me? I've heard of torture; the world outside my island is full of masters of torture.

I might as well die in the sea. Just sink.

But my arms circle through the water, pulling me forward. My arms won't let me drown.

Now I can make out many houses, and a big church. There are lots more houses beyond those, more churches. Lots of people.

I keep swimming. Soon I'll pass this island. There will be a next one.

Another spasm racks me. I go under; my feet reach and reach, but I can't touch bottom, it's so deep. How did that happen? Fear forces my arms above my head. I surface and roll onto my back and float. If I stay this way, the water will carry me to the island without my having to decide anything.

The coward's way.

I swim around the east side of the island. I hear a bell toll the noon hour, calling the faithful to prayer. I imagine everyone rushing here and there. I can't face that many people.

I need someplace smaller. Where people might need me, talk to me, where someone might even like me.

Look at that: I want to live. How strange. Mamma is dead, so the best part of me is dead. But the rest isn't. Not yet.

I swim and swim. My arms ache, my legs ache. The first island is far behind me now. I'm not sure I could make it back there even if I wanted to. After a while my arms and legs move without my telling them to. It's as though I could swim forever, as though I could die and keep swimming.

Ahead, a tuft of green emerges from the water. As I swim, it grows taller. Trees. Another island. I don't see houses.

Deserted?

I need to get out of the water. A deserted island is fine with me. I can live off wild greens till I figure out what to do next. I can cover myself with branches at night.

The closer I get, the more clearly the trees sketch their outlines: tall cypresses. Mamma calls them holy.

Mamma is dead. I should never have taught her foot-fishing.

No one will share meals with me again. No one will sing with me at night. No one will be so happy when I bring home special foods. No one will tell me I'm beautiful.

Mamma is dead.

And I'm swimming to an island that looks to be deserted.

But what does it matter if there are no people? I'm alone no matter what.

I swim hard again. A cramp seizes me. I go under, and my feet hit the bottom. I make it to shore, stumble past rocks and pebbles to sand and grasses.

Then I fall, and cry myself to sleep.

CHAPTER 6

Others

Alone heron strolls among the clumps of grasses. His head is the rust red of ripe chestnuts, his black neck stripes move like eels in night water, the hump made by his back and folded wings echoes the curve of a belly full with child. The purplish-blue cap on his head marks him as king of this island. I love him instantly.

He picks his way on those grand stick legs. Pecks at something. He's been at this a long time this morning. I bet he's quick enough to catch a fish. *Go on, bird, be flexible. If you're hungry, eat what's at hand. Survive.*

I watch from the spot where I fell yesterday. Warblers sing behind me. Little bitterns squeal. Gulls cry. This must be a bird haven. Mamma would call me lucky. Oh, my mamma. I bite the side of my hand in grief.

Ai! My lips are dry. My whole mouth is dry. I've been salted, like cod for winter. Lord, I hope there's sweet water somewhere on this island—a rock shallow where rain collects, a mud-hole, anything.

A lizard thrashes in the heron's long bill, disappears down his throat.

"Yay!"

With a hoarse scream, the heron takes to the air, but my eyes are on the girl who just shouted. She comes running from the cypress trees, hair ribbons trailing behind her, flapping her arms. I gasp. Those arms—they stretch far above her head. She's all out of proportion.

She dances around, skirts flouncing. Then she spies me. Her face lights up and she runs over. "Who are you?"

I move slowly. I don't want to frighten this monster of the long arms and legs. She might not know there are others like her. I smile to allay fears that will surely arise as she takes in the whole of me. Finally, I'm on my feet, unfolded, towering above her. *Please, child, don't run away.*

"What are you doing on the beach? Watching the bird? Do you love birds? I do. Why are your skirts tucked up around your legs? Did you sleep here?" She tilts her funny head—it's small for her body, just like mine was when I was her age, and we both have small foreheads. She cocks her spindly arms and rests her fists on her hips. "I don't have a scarf on because we're on the monks' island, and anyway, I'm little. You, though, you should cover your hair. You're too old to be like that." She blinks. "Well, make your skirts decent and come on. The monks will give you a bed." She runs toward the trees, as fast as I ever did.

I stare after her.

She stops, comes back, and smiles. "Can't you speak? Or are you just shy? My aunt is shy. At least around men. Papà says that's why she'll never marry. She says he's wrong—she wouldn't want to marry an old man who wants her just to take care of him. Here, let me help." She steps close and yanks at my skirts.

Swimming with my skirts tied together made the knots harden. The girl works in silence at one knot, then the other, cheeks bunched, lips protruding. She doesn't mind being close to me. I must keep breathing. This is such hard work for both of us—her untying, me breathing. Finally, my smock falls and the girl jerks it straight. She's much taller than Tommaso, but I'm sure she's younger than him, maybe seven?

The girl surveys me. Her arms hang below the top of her legs. She's just like me. I stare.

"You're a mess." She wrinkles her nose, a prominent nose; the middle of her face isn't sunken. "Seaweed is clumped in your hair and you stink like dead fish."

Is that all? She doesn't mention my size. Is she crazy?

"But I don't care." She holds out her hand. "Come."

I watch her take me by the hand, though I'm ready to bolt. Her hand is hot and soft and large. As large as an adult's, but with long, slim fingers. It's so much like mine was at her age that I have to suppress a yelp of amazement. The girl tugs at me like Mamma did. No one else has held my hand for years, not since I was really young. The fact of her hand around mine makes my heart expand.

Only now do I feel the effects of all that swimming yesterday. Arms, legs, chest, back, neck, buttocks, all of me aches. And I'd eat anything right now. I'd chew on a rock. Thirst rasps me raw. I'd give whatever I have for sweet water. I roll my head in a circle one way, then the other. I can feel a headache coming on, a vicious one. *Please, please, don't. Please let me enjoy this child a while longer.* What I wouldn't give to stretch—stretches can stave off the headaches sometimes—but I don't want to appear even larger. I don't want this girl to drop my hand in fright.

We pass through the cypress trees. The island is not all forest, after all. Ahead, a meadow. With a building. A cloister. It's kept up; this must be where the monks live. Maybe they've taken this girl in as a charity case.

We approach an arch. Reluctantly, I pull my hand free and fall behind the girl as we pass through the archway, to stay ready for whatever might happen, whoever might appear. Other people won't accept me the way this monster child seems to.

We walk along a portico that forms the perimeter of a court-yard . . . with a cistern in the middle! I run and put my hands on the edge and stare down into it. No bucket, no bucket. But there's a bowl carved into the stone base for birds, and that's brimming with water. I get on all fours and scoop with a hand. The water is so clean, so lovely, I dip my face into it until eyes, cheeks, ears are submerged. This is bliss. I pull back enough to lap like Gato Zalo does. Sweet water. My head feels lighter. Maybe the pain won't come, after all.

The girl laughs.

I slosh up one last mouthful. She's still laughing. And she's right. I'd never do this back home. I turn to face her and fall on my bottom. She laughs harder. And I'm laughing now, too, laughing as though this isn't the end of the world. Laughing like Mamma, as though I've always known how.

Bong. Bells ring. Could it be midday? I look around. I can just see the point of the bell tower above the roof of the cloister. A person hangs on the thick bell rope, a person who will not welcome me like this girl has.

"What is the meaning of this? Who are you?" A man comes at me from the side. He's huge!

I curl in on myself and look at him sideways. I've never seen anyone so large.

He's one of my kind. And the girl is my kind.

Two, three, four other men follow him. The one who spoke is dressed in saffron-colored breeches and shirt and a black vest. The other men wear long, faded black shifts with a rope at the waist. All huge. All my kind.

An island of monsters.

I circle my arms around my knees and tuck my chin into my chest and close my eyes and rock. This cannot be real. I am delirious. The mirror malady, the illness that's gradually stealing all my strength, must be addling me. Will I die now, alone?

"What's the matter with you? Get up at once!"

"Stop that! You're frightening her, Papà."

I open my eyes and peek at the group from between my knees. Children don't talk to their fathers like that.

The girl comes to stand between me and her father.

"Step aside, Bianca."

"No. You have to be nice to her. She's shy. Mamma would have wanted you to be nice to her."

The man's face softens. All at once I understand that the girl's mother is dead. Just as mine is. A knot forms in my chest.

"And she can't answer you anyway," says Bianca. "She can't speak."

"I can speak." This is a dream of delirium. I might as well reveal myself. I stand and let my arms drop to my sides. If I could stand up for myself on my island against real adversaries, I can stand up against imagined ones. I move so that Bianca and I trade places. It is me who intervenes between father and child now. In my hallucination, I am her shield.

"Where did you come from?" says the father.

"Across the water."

"Where?"

"My land. My realm."

"What are you talking about? Who are you?"

"Princess Dolce."

"You're a princess?" says Bianca. She looks up in wonder. "Why are you dressed like that?"

"I escaped."

"Tell me more," says the father.

"You must know. You know everything that's in my head. Hallucinations are that way."

The father opens his mouth in obvious confusion. His nose is like his daughter's, standing out sharply from between straight cheeks. I put my hands on my own flat cheeks. I desperately want to reach up—imagine that! me, reaching up—to place my hands on his face. Why hold back?

I put my hands on the man's cheeks. He makes a quick intake of breath. His skin feels real. Funny thought. What do I know of men's faces?

"She slept on the beach," says Bianca. "She's dirty. Can I help her bathe?"

"I'll prepare water," says one man.

"I'll prepare bread and figs," says another.

"Neither of you can wash her," says Bianca.

"Of course not," says the first man. "We will leave her in your care."

Bianca gives me an imperious look, then turns and walks away. I don't want to stop touching this vision of a man. I search his eyes. This is a good dream, for I can see he's not sure he wants me to stop touching him. I drop my hands and follow Bianca.

"We're not through talking yet," says the father.

Bianca and I stop and look back.

"Shouldn't you address her as 'Princess'?" says Bianca.

"We're not through talking yet. Get clean. Eat. Rest. But then we talk. Princess."

CHAPTER 7

Clean

Faint light comes through the lone window. Bianca holds a saltcellar in one hand and a cup of tan-colored liquid in the other. "For your teeth."

I reach for both.

"No, the salt first. Then you rinse with the flavored water. You dip your finger in the water to start, though, so the salt will stick to it."

I rub my teeth clean. It feels good. Then I rinse and spit into the cup. "What flavor is that?"

"Cinnamon." She laughs. "Don't you know cinnamon?"

I shake my head.

"Do you like it?"

I nod.

"Well, good. Take that dirty smock off. Everything, take off everything."

How can the child be so presumptuous? But I do as told.

"Sit on the stool. See the sponge on it? You know what sponges are?" She smiles.

I nod. But I don't smile back.

"I brought that sponge from home. It's good, don't fear. The monks don't use it."

I sit on the large sponge that covers the seat.

She puts another even larger sponge on the floor. "For your feet."

I put my feet on it.

Bianca dips a small sponge in the basin of water. The steam carries the strong scent of rosemary. I hunch forward over my thighs and she rubs my back. The hand sponge is soft, like warm lard. "This is how Aunt Agnola does it to me," Bianca says. The warm water rolls down the sides of my breasts and over my ribs. It drips from my nipples. Some sinks into the sponge; some puddles on the floor. "Lift your hair. Good. That's good." She rubs the back of my neck, the backs of my ears.

Now she kneels in front of me and rubs my feet, top and bottom and between the toes. I feel like a pampered child. And it's a pampered child who is pampering me. My head spins. She grabs my hand and scrubs it. Harder. Then the other hand. "I thought the pink on your toes would come away. But no. It's like the pink on your fingers. Is that part of being a princess?"

I shake my head. "It's part of making mirrors."

She pauses and studies me. "Here, take the sponge. You do your front. Aunt Agnola says girls must do their front on their own. But don't forget the cracks. The crack behind, too. Aunt Agnola rubs under her breasts. You mustn't forget there, either."

I clean myself under Bianca's beady eyes. There's no disgust in those eyes. I grow bolder and sit straight.

"We can do your hair now. Do you want help?"

"Do you want to help?"

"Yes. I get to soap up Ribolin's fur when he has a bath. It's fun. Ribolin is Aunt Agnola's dog. He sits on her lap most of the time. He has a funny red penis that comes out when we bathe him. I feed him gizzards, so he likes me."

I don't know what a dog is. "I like gizzards."

"So do I. Ribolin growls as he eats them, and he'll nip if you try to touch him."

"Like Gato Zalo."

"Is that your cat?"

"Gato Zalo doesn't belong to anyone."

"Papà says it's a mistake to play with strays. They're dirty, they carry disease, and they bite. We can get you another cat. There are lots of good cats in Venezia."

"Venezia?"

"That's where I live. You didn't think I lived here with the monks, did you?"

"I did. You're all huge. I figured you chose to live together."

Bianca laughs. "You say funny things."

I clean my underarms. "So why are you here with the monks, then?"

"I like to go along with Papà when he visits monks, because they live in such out-of-the-way places. But I'm always ready to go home again." She picks up the bar of soap beside the water basin. "The water has rosemary in it. The monks don't have flowers in their garden. When we go back home, though, we can use rose water. Or we can boil any flower you want. The soap is mine. Smell it." She holds it to my nose. "Guess what it is."

I sniff. Then shrug.

She smiles. "I was hoping you wouldn't know it. I love to give surprises. And you're so easy to surprise."

"What is it?"

"Oranges. We boil orange blossoms. Have you ever seen them?"

I shake my head.

"The fruit is sort of like lemon, but ever so sweet. Apples are better, though. My mamma said apples can cure you of any ailment. But oranges are good. Their color is halfway between yellow and red. The blossoms are white, though. Be glad I have this soap. Lower your head."

I lean forward till my hair falls into the basin. "Why are you being so generous?"

"Isn't that how we're supposed to be?"

I tremble.

"Are you ill?"

"No. I'm glad."

"Oh." Bianca lathers up my hair while I go on shaking. "Do you know the six things most important in the world? Bread, wine . . ."

"Oil, salt," I chant with her, "something to go with the bread, and soap."

She laughs. "So your kingdom has the same saying?"

"Maybe they have the same saying everywhere."

"I doubt it. Papà says the world is full of scoundrels and fools. He's educated."

"Are you?"

"I'm a girl." She pushes my head up, and my sopping hair hangs in my face. "Are you educated? Do girls have tutors in your kingdom?"

"No," I say, though I can form letters. I've sat in front of inscriptions on the sides of buildings and copied the letters in the dirt with a stick.

"Oh." She rinses the soap from my hair and offers me a white linen towel. "I'm glad you don't strip your hair with lye and color it all red or yellow. Aunt Agnola does that. She wishes she were pretty. She likes rhubarb best. She thinks it makes her look like a flower, all pink-red."

I towel my hair roughly.

"Mamma had black hair like yours."

"You mean like yours," I say.

"Yes, but really like yours. With black curls. Papà likes your kind of hair."

I stare at her.

But she's rinsing the soap off her hands. "Let me comb it?" She turns to me with a shy smile.

"Why do you even ask, after all the other things you've done for me?"

"Aunt Agnola says combing hair is an act of love. Family love. She combs mine. She won't let anyone else do it."

"Is she your mamma's sister?"

"Mamma's dead."

"I'm sorry." I sigh. "My mamma died yesterday."

"Oh. I'm sorry, too."

I nod and we look at each other.

Finally Bianca says, "Aunt Agnola is Papà's sister. She should have gone to a convent long ago, long before I was born. Like my aunt Teresa and all unmarried women. But I'm lucky she didn't, because when Mamma died, she was there to take care of me. Now look." She pulls a comb from the pouch that hangs at her waist and puts it in my hands. "This is my comb."

The two rows of bone spines are joined in the middle by a carving of birds with curved beaks and plants with red buds. "It's glorious."

"I know. It was Mamma's. All her best things were saved for me."

"You must be rich."

"We don't have princesses in Venezia, but we do have nobles."

I feel woozy. I take a deep breath.

"You have to eat before you nap. The tray of food will be right outside the door. You can eat while I comb your hair, and then we can nap together. In my room."

"All right."

She fetches the tray and sets it on the table. "Go on."

I take a bite of bread, a bite of fig. It's sour bread, crusty outside and soft inside. The fig is at its ripest. I chew each bite tens of times, savoring every morsel.

Bianca takes the comb and stands behind me. She teases apart knots expertly, like Mamma did. And now she combs.

I wince. "You comb hard."

"My mamma said hard combing makes hair glossy. Aunt Agnola combs hard too. You have to press till the scalp wakes up." She finishes, then unfolds the pile of black cloth at the foot of the mattress. "This is a clean monk's robe. They don't have clothes for women at the monastery."

I slip on the faded robe. It smells of sunshine, and hangs so long it crumples around my feet. Clothing that is too long for me. Will marvels never cease? I roll up the sleeves. Inside this robe I feel shrunken, a shadow of myself.

Bianca laughs. "You look silly. I wish I could show you, but they have no mirrors here. Monks don't care what they look like. Some monks don't even talk. We visited ones near Monti Sibillini who used only their hands to understand each other, and I got to see snow on the mountaintops. Have you seen snow?"

"A dusting. But only rarely."

"That's how Venezia is, too. I wish it would snow more. I love snow. My mamma loved snow. She saw snow in the Dolomiti mountains, right before she gave birth to me. That's where my name came from. Anyway, the monks here are Franciscan. They sing with the animals, especially the birds. People say the monks understand the birds. Do you believe that?"

I shrug. "Why not?"

"Papà doesn't believe it. Aunt Agnola doesn't come with us to visit monasteries." Bianca leans toward me. "I'll tell you something . . . but don't tell Aunt Agnola, ever. Promise?"

"I promise."

"Papà is glad she doesn't come. He says these visits are our chance to be alone. But she mustn't know or her feelings would be hurt."

"I understand."

Bianca nods earnestly. Then, "Oh, I have an idea. I'll be your mirror." She stands stiff in front of me. "Ask me what you look like."

"I don't look directly into mirrors."

"Why not?"

I shrug.

She steps very close. "I told you a secret. So you tell me one. Why don't you look into mirrors?"

"They show what I don't want to see."

"I'll be a good mirror," says Bianca. "Go on, ask me what you look like."

"What do I look like?" I whisper.

"A fuzzy head. Hands with pink fingers. I see what you are."

I swallow. "And what's that?"

"Treasure. And I found you!"

My ears couldn't have heard right.

"Are you tired? My bed is ready—with clean linens." She folds her hands in front of her waist. "You'll let us nap together, won't you? All clean and cozy."

I smile and follow her down the hall to her room.

Somewhere outside I hear horns blow.

What a strange and lovely thing is this dream of mine.

CHAPTER 8

Plain Talk

"Tell me about yourself."

Bianca's father has spoken, but every head at the table turns toward me. Black eyes—monks and Bianca and her father alike. Shining, attentive eyes.

The table is outside, among pines and olive trees. The benches we sit on are rough pine. I run a fingertip along the spot beside me till I find a sharpness. I press hard. The setting sun paints the sky red beyond the rim of cypresses. The aroma of the sardines we just ate envelops me still. I float in this wonderland.

The father clears his throat. "You must speak."

Bianca yanks on his sleeve. They exchange a look.

"Say something," says the father, in more of a plea than a command. "Some clue." He hesitates. "Please, Princess."

I rest one hand on top of the other, palms upward. Blood drips from my right index finger where the splinter pierced it. "I float among monsters."

Eyes shift, alarmed.

"We are not monsters," says a monk, at last.

"Of course we are," says another. He lifts a finger. "Everyone is . . . in comparison."

"I'm not," says Bianca. "Papà's not. And you are not. Monks can't be monsters."

"We aren't monks," says a third monk. "We are *frati*— brothers. We are the little brothers of San Francesco. Monks seclude themselves, for lives of contemplation. Franciscan brothers work among the people to help the needy, the poor, and the sick."

"You're not among the people," says Bianca. "You're out here on this island."

"We are not secluded, though. You've heard us blow the horns every day. That's an invitation to the faithful. They can renew their beliefs here, with us."

"Who comes?"

"Nobles, like you. And holy men from everywhere. Even the pope, in 1466. He recommended us heartily, so for the past thirty years this island has had visitors."

Bianca's face squinches with perplexity. "Why build a church so far away in the first place?" The child is dogged. I silently cheer for her.

"San Francesco came here and founded this chapel hundreds of years ago. The island of Torcello was too crowded and noisy. So he made this chapel as a sanctuary for anyone who seeks it." The brother leans toward Bianca. "Maybe San Francesco came because of the birds. Have you noticed the birds?"

"That's how I met Princess Dolce," says Bianca. "We were watching a heron."

The brother looks at me. "You understand birds."

Everyone looks at me now.

"Why do you call us monsters?" asks a brother.

"Not just you," I say. "All of us. We are huge. Clumsy. Misshapen."

"A good description of mortals," he says.

"You talk like someone who might be drawn to convent life," says another.

The idea astounds me. Mamma talked with reverence of a holy sister who treated her well when she was a girl. "Would a convent take one such as me?"

"You can't go to a convent." Bianca shakes her head. "You're mine."

"Bianca!" Her father puts his arm around her shoulders. "Whatever are you saying? Princess Dolce must do what she is called to do."

"Aunt Agnola told me that women go to convents when they have no one . . . when no one wants them. Princess Dolce has no one. . . ."

"You don't know about—"

"She told us! She said she escaped. She has no one and nowhere to go. That's what she thinks. But she has us. We want her." Bianca stands, comes around the table to my side, and wraps her arms tight around me. I twist so that we face one another. Her head presses against my breasts. I stroke her hair. I don't understand why this child wants me, but all I can do is want her back.

Her father looks at me, aghast. "I apologize for my daughter. She's not usually like this."

"My mother died," I say softly, over Bianca's head. "I miss her so much."

"I'm sorry. Very sorry. Bianca's mother died years ago," says her father. "Bianca was so small, she can't remember her."

"She remembers the color of her hair."

The father's eyes glisten. "Well . . . We recently moved into a new home. Perhaps leaving her old home still upsets Bianca. She never acts like this."

Bianca turns her head to look at her father, but doesn't release me. "You saw her smock. She must have dressed as a poor girl to hide so she could escape. She was so thirsty, she drank from the birds' cup. She is lost. She is alone. And we are here."

"Your imagination has always been rich, my daughter."

"Look! She's real."

Bianca's words bring me up short. This child's heart beats against my own. Her hair tickles my throat. Maybe this is no dream. Maybe I'm surrounded by monsters.

I cannot breathe. I cough and cough. I can't stop coughing long enough to suck in air.

"Sea onion," Bianca says to the brothers. "Sea onion, fast!"

I fall off the bench with my knees tucked up, coughing so hard that my head hammers.

Something is shoved into my mouth. I know this . . . the bulb of the sea onion. I chomp down on it. I hold my hand in front of my mouth to keep the bulb in when I cough. Slowly, gradually, the coughs subside. I lie limp on my side.

"Do you want to go to bed?" the father asks.

I shake my head.

"Bianca, go with the brothers now. They'll tell you Bible stories and put you to sleep when you're ready. I'll take care of Princess Dolce."

"But she has to sleep with me."

"She'll sleep in my bed."

"Your bed is narrow. There's no room for the two of you."

"Of course not. I'll take a cot. There has to be an extra cot."

"I'll prepare one," says a voice. "Come, child."

I hear them leave.

"Let me help you." The father bends over and extends a hand.

I look away and push myself up to sitting. My chest and throat feel raw inside. Birds have alighted all over the table. They eat our crumbs, our remnants. "The birds. They're joyous." I laugh. I laugh just like Bianca.

The father drops his empty hand. "You do talk like a religious soul. Even a mystic. Is that why you cut your finger?"

I look at my finger. The blood has crusted. I lick it clean.

"Are you going to tell me about yourself?" he asks.

"You first."

He flinches. "Would you like to walk along the water as we talk?"

We walk to the cypress trees and pass through them to the shore.

"What do you want to know?" asks the father.

"You know my name."

"My name is Marin. My family name is Cornaro. Will you pretend you don't know it, since you're a foreigner?"

"Pretend?"

"You speak Veneziano. You are not foreign born."

"I didn't say I was."

"You called yourself a princess. We have no kingdoms here."

"Who are you to say whether or not I have one?"

"Is this some kind of sophistry?"

"I don't know that word."

The father stops. "Do you trick us?"

"No. I have found it helpful to live inside my head, my realm. There I am a princess, rather than a monster. It's simple."

He studies my face.

I study his. "Do you like how you look?"

He blinks. "I'm considered to be . . . fine-looking."

"Among monsters, perhaps. But what do you think of your-self?"

He stands taller. "I think I'm handsome."

"I suppose that's good. Maybe I could learn to think I'm pretty."

"Pretty? You're beautiful."

I laugh. I'm getting quite used to laughing. "Who's pretend-ing now?"

"You sound sincere."

"I am never otherwise."

"Shall we walk on?" He steps carefully on the shells and peb-bles. "Can I ask questions now?"

"Not yet. You know why I am here."

"No I don't."

"My mother died. Without her, my island would have been unbearable. So I left. That is the full story of my life."

He has stopped to stare at me again. "It can't be."

"It is. And you?"

"You want the full story of my life?"

"I want to know why you came to this island."

He walks again.

"I want my library to be the finest in all Venezia. Monasteries house old books. Beautiful things. Ancient Latin manuscripts. Sometimes Greek. I purchase them."

"What did you find on this island?"

"Nothing. I expected that, though. The Franciscans take a vow of poverty. No hidden treasures. So I came mostly because I heard it was a beautiful spot. Tranquil, peaceful."

"Bianca called me that."

"Called you what?"

"A treasure. Something she'd heard you say, obviously."

"My daughter is perspicacious."

"Another word I don't know."

"How old are you, Princess Dolce?"

"Fifteen."

"Are you married?"

It's my turn to flinch. "Who would have me? Besides, my mamma said girls shouldn't marry until they're past eighteen."

"Francesco Barbaro—have you heard of him?"

I shake my head.

"He wrote a treatise on marriage. He says marrying a young girl is best, because it gives a man a better chance to mold her personality."

"What if she wants to keep the personality she already has?"

"Ah!" He laughs. "Is it true you have nowhere to go?"

"Bianca said that, not me. I will find somewhere to go. I have to believe that."

"Come to Venezia."

"Big cities are full of tormenters."

"What on earth could you mean?"

"Everyone says it. And while I don't believe everything everyone says, I do believe my mother. She hissed when she spoke of cities. Venezia is horrid."

"I live in Venezia. And I am not horrid."

"But surely they are horrid to you. You're like me, after all."

"They are by no means horrid to me. And they will not be horrid to you. I won't stand for it."

I fold my arms across my chest. "You want to be my protector?"

He takes a deep, noisy breath. "Come look at this sculpture." He leads me away from the beach and back through the cypresses to a small clearing with three thick logs leaning against each other. Maria the Virgin has been carved into one of the logs. Into the next, angels. Into the third, a dove. "Do you like it?" he asks.

"They're beautiful. Who made them?"

"Probably one of the brothers." He scratches the stubble on his chin.

I imagine his roughness and my neck goes hot. I look at the sculpture. "Carved wood left outdoors like this . . ." I shake my head. "It will rot fast."

"But in the meantime, anyone can enjoy it."

"You smell like wet earth," I say.

"Dirt?" He looks alarmed.

"Like mushrooms. Or a fire that's just gone out."

"That's myrrh."

I nod. "It's nice."

His face goes solemn. "Bianca has become attached to you."

"She is dear." My voice breaks.

"I don't understand you."

"I use plain talk. It's you who is hard to understand."

"I've never known anyone from the *popolo*—the ordinary people. No one except servants."

"I've never known a noble."

"Even in a *frate*'s robe you're fair."

My mouth goes dry. "My mamma used to say that. She believed it."

"I am more than twice your age. Do you think of me as an old man?"

I shake my head.

His hand comes toward me. He touches my cheek so gently, it takes a second to know that's what has happened. I cry.

"Tears? What do you feel now?"

The image of Mamma talking about crabs . . . how sometimes nothing else could satisfy her, and when a craving came,
she was willing to go into the water she feared so much. I look in
this man's eyes. Everything feels simple. And dangerous.

"Please tell me."

"I crave you."

"Plain talk." His voice trembles. "I could get used to plain talk."

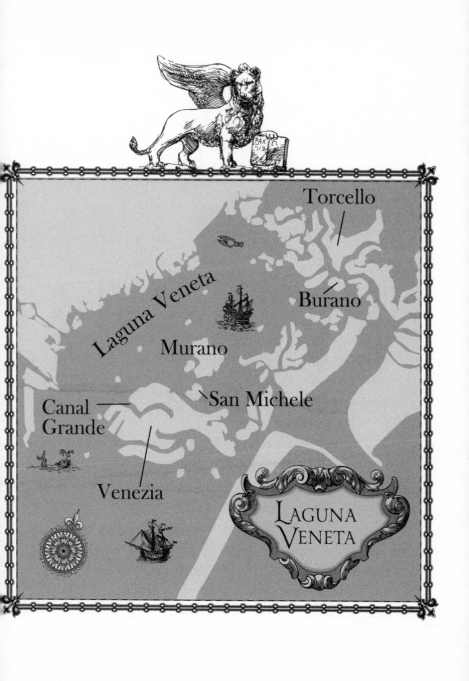

CHAPTER 9

Freaks

Marin stands at the bow with spread legs as the long, narrow boat glides toward the island he calls Murano. It's the glassblowers' island. Antonin, another giant who arrived this morning to take us away, stands at the stern, using a long oar to propel and steer us. Bianca sits beside me under the little canopy. None of them seems anxious. I press my lips together.

I am still in a brother's robe—Marin threw my smock in the fire before I could protest. But this robe has advantages: if necessary, I can pull the hood up and sink down inside as small as I can manage. The others have no way of hiding, though. No one can fail to notice their hugeness. I am ready to fight, for their sake and mine, but it seems we'd be much safer if we all had a way of hiding. I stare as the lighthouse ahead grows larger.

Bianca laughs. "Have you never been in a gondola as skinny as this one?"

I look at her. "A what?"

She points at my hand. "You're gripping the side so tight. But this gondola is very steady. Aunt Agnola says it's as safe as any old wide gondola, and she's afraid of everything. Let go."

I fold my hands in my lap.

Bianca puts her hands on top of mine and sits sideways facing me. "I was so excited when Papà had this gondola made. All the noble families are getting the new shape. And lots of ladies can fit under the canopy at the same time. Antonin will ferry you to afternoon parties with Aunt Agnola and me and the Contarini girls and their mamma. They live near us. If you walk, you have to cross three little bridges to get to their palace. We love to hear things like that about the city since we're never allowed to walk the alleys. The Contarini boat has sea horses engraved in the iron at the front. It's much fancier than ours. The girls love to say that."

I fix my eyes on hers. "Do you want to pinch them when they say that?"

She whispers, "Sometimes I think of pinching." We look away, trying not to giggle.

"No! Of all the things that could go wrong . . ." Marin looks right at me. "Pull your hood up, hide your hair, and hush. I'll do the talking. And, Bianca, fold your hands in your lap. Not a peep, child."

My hair is hidden before he finishes speaking. Coming quickly across the water is a small skiff. This is it. The tormenters. They will hurt us now. My knees press hard together. I gather Bianca in my arms and think of Mamma. She always said to be brave, stand tall . . . if there's nowhere to run . . . otherwise, run like mad; no one could catch me.

I dare to look ahead, to face our enemies. The skiff has two rowers and a third man in the center, all standing. A sword hangs from the belt of the man in the middle.

Oh, Lord, they are monsters, too! Why harm us? Outcasts need each other.

The skiff comes up and the front rower throws a rope to Antonin so he can pull the boats together. "Sire, what business have you in Murano?" asks the swordsman.

"What business is it of yours?" says Marin.

"We are *sbirri*, representatives of the Republic. We inspect all boats entering and leaving Murano. The secrets of our industry must be protected, as you well know."

"We are here to make a purchase."

"Glass?"

"No."

"A mirror? Show us the money."

"Not a mirror. Ladies' clothing."

The man frowns. "Only that? Why come to Murano for a tailor?"

"Exigency." Marin looks at me. "Would you mind lowering your hood?"

My hands shake, but I do as told.

Marin points at me with his chin. "My lady's gown was ruined. The good brothers were kind enough to lend that habit. But she needs new clothing before we return to Venezia."

The swordsman looks at me a moment, then bows. "Pass freely."

The front oarsman collects the rope and they row away.

"Scoundrels," mutters Marin when they are out of earshot. "The Republic hires criminals to patrol the lagoon. Thugs. If I'd given any indication we had large sums of money on us, they'd have found a way to extort some. I should have demanded their names so I could report them."

So Venezia hires monsters to patrol the lagoon. Tormenters

must abound there, but clearly there are kind people, too. People who befriend monsters.

"You called Princess Dolce 'my lady,'" says Bianca. "She is now, isn't she?"

Marin's mouth hangs open. He looks from her to me and back again. "We will make formal introductions in Venezia, of course. But Dolce has already accepted my invitation to stay with us." He looks at me and smiles.

Bianca bounces on her bottom. "I knew it."

I did, too, of course. But what it all means is more than I can fathom.

Bianca presses against me. "Aunt Agnola is good. I love her, you know I do. But a mamma is different. You'll be my mamma. Won't you?"

I put my arm around her again. "I will be good to you, as good as my mamma was to me." We nestle into one another, and the moment feels like a prayer. As though Mamma is listening, approving. And I wonder suddenly if the Lord gave me Bianca to make up for stealing Mamma.

Soon we step onto the pebbled shore around the lighthouse and climb up stairs onto a path. Marin leads the way. I mustn't show my fear. I learned that over and over on my island.

Everyone we pass is our size. I stop and stare. This is an impossible world. Have the monsters formed a colony on Murano, like birds?

Marin makes inquiries in a candle shop, and soon we are at the door of a tailor. Marin explains he wants a fine dress for me. Something in silk, in a brilliant color.

"Come in, come in," says the tailor. He leads us through a foyer and up the stairs, into his workroom. He bows to me. "Choose what you like. I can have anything ready within a fortnight.

If you please, take a look at these fabrics." He waves his hand toward rolls and rolls of silks, wools, linens, in every color.

"No," says Marin, "you don't understand. We need the dress now."

"Now? I could perhaps have it ready in ten days at the soonest, but—"

"Now. Before the afternoon. We return to Venezia this eve, and she must be wearing it."

The tailor shakes his head in dismay. "Impossible."

"Surely you have dresses that you could adjust for my lady." Marin hands the tailor a small purse.

The tailor takes the purse hesitantly. He weighs it in his palm. "Of course."

"And we'll need someone to arrange her hair."

"Of course."

"I'll go buy jewelry." Marin turns to me. "When you're ready, we'll have a little refreshment. Then leave for Venezia." He heads toward the stairs.

I run after him and clutch his arm. "Please . . ."

"What?" He bends toward me. "Don't be alarmed, Dolce." His voice is so soft. "Fears plague you. I see that. But whatever wrongs were done you, they have ended. You are with us now."

"Now?"

"Day by day, Dolce. That's how life moves." His eyes hold mine fast. "I'll be back soon. What's your pleasure? Pearls? Gold?"

"I . . . I don't know."

"Then I'll choose just one necklace. In Venezia you can choose for yourself."

My fingers uncurl slowly. Marin races down the steps.

"I'll need you to take off that robe," says the tailor.

"She has nothing on underneath," says Bianca.

The tailor opens a drawer, takes out a white shift, and hands it to me. "Slip this on, Signorina." He turns his back.

I put on the shift. "Ready," I breathe.

"All right, then. I have two gowns that could do quite well, with a stitch here or there. Silk, of course, as the fine sire requested. One is purple, the other indigo. Do you have a preference?"

"Indigo," says Bianca.

I touch her cheek. "Why?"

"I like the word."

I look at the tailor and nod.

I stand in the light from the window while he pins the dress, then takes it off me and sews, then puts it on me and pins again. He's precise. The silk is soft. I feel suspended, unable to guess at what might happen next.

Finally, the tailor steps away. "I believe that does it. Take a look." He picks up a mirror from the table. The mirror reflects perfectly. It's because of me that Murano has such mirrors.

I gaze at my image.

"You are indeed fair, dear Signorina," says the tailor. "And indigo was a fine choice. It's nearly as dark as your hair."

Fair? I look hard. I am me, still and always. Clothing changes nothing. I look at the tailor's face. He seems utterly sincere. I shake my head and look out the window. I feel a pang in my heart. "Bianca! Look!" I point. Venerio's short boat passes along the canal. He rows. Francesco stands in the middle. Has Venerio found someone to replace me? Does anyone miss me? Maybe the boy Tommaso. But he'll forget me soon.

Bianca leans out the window and follows my finger. "Dwarfs. I like them. Don't you?"

"Dwarfs?"

"Haven't you ever seen them before?"

I nod.

"They're funny. They always make me laugh."

The tailor comes to stand beside us. "Ah, those are the ones from Torcello. It's fever-ridden, that place. No one else wants it, so we might as well leave it to the freaks. They come here now and then, for supplies. They appear to be demented, poor things. Simpletons at best."

I clap my hand over my mouth to hold in the sick.

Bianca tilts her head from side to side. "Demented? But you're wrong. They're capable of lots of things. They make good servants."

"I suppose that must be true. They say if you visit Torcello, they'll run you off. The men are strong. But every now and then someone still tries to sneak over there to snatch one of the children to sell."

I stagger to the nearby cutting table and press a hand on it for support. The room swirls.

"Are you all right?" the tailor asks.

I put both hands on the table. My chest heaves. "Do you . . . do you, Bianca, do you have dwarf servants?"

"No. Hardly anyone does, really. There aren't enough of them. If you don't like dwarfs, you better not show it. Papà says all people have dignity, no matter how ill-formed or unable."

"Yes," I say. "That's true." I cry into my hands.

CHAPTER 10

Serenissima

The gondola slips through the water, and I'm listening to Bianca talk of Aunt Agnola's dog Ribolin when the bell sounds. It's distant but deep as it echoes across the lagoon. Bianca goes silent. We hold hands and peer through the fading light.

"Venezia," says Marin in a hushed voice as we round an island. "This view never fails to steal my breath. She deserves her name as *serenissima*—the most serene."

The city looms in silence, set against a pure blue, cloudless sky. Early moonlight shimmers off the water and the walls, white and pink and amber. It feels like a promise—like magic. Serenity pervades.

But as we approach and forms become distinct, that sense of calm evaporates. There are so many buildings, so close together, so many towers, that my skin goes gooseflesh at the thought of the vast numbers of people those buildings harbor. By day, this city must swarm like an anthill or a beehive. Narrow alleys run between buildings. I imagine them crowded, bustling. I grip Bianca's hand tighter.

I see no trees. Are they hidden behind walls? People can't live without trees and fields.

Antonin maneuvers the gondola through a small canal, where we glide under footbridges that connect to alleys on both sides and sometimes an open campo. I look around and try to memorize every detail. But it's all so strange, so many stones and doors, so many roofs and chimneys. The canal feeds into a larger one, a gigantic one. I see no people out and about, but I hear music from open windows where lanterns glow—a stringed instrument, like Francesco plays, and something else, which I don't recognize. I turn my head toward every noise. Laughter comes from behind us. Yowls and shrieks burst from a side alley. Are there wildcats here?

The gondola turns sharply and goes right under a building! It's a private waterway, a private dock. We stop. This is it. This is Marin's home, and I didn't even look at it from the outside, I was so caught up in noises. My breath comes short.

We get out and climb stone steps set at intervals that are right for my legs. Footsteps clack above us. Two plump women holding candles, a skinny young man hardly older than me, and a tiny four-legged animal appear at the top of the steps. I will never get used to seeing people my size. Bianca throws her arms around the wide waist of the younger one, who must be Aunt Agnola. The woman hugs Bianca back and looks at me questioningly over her head. I hang back, two steps below the landing. Funny, now I'm far shorter than them.

Marin clears his throat. "We have a visitor. A guest. Signorina . . ." He looks down at me with startled eyes. I can't think why.

"She's not a guest." Bianca takes my hand and pulls me up to the landing. "She's Princess Dolce. And she's family."

The animal sniffs at my feet. I stay perfectly still.

"Let's just call her Signorina Dolce among ourselves." Marin rubs his palm across his mouth. "This is my sister, Signorina Agnola."

I smile at Agnola.

She looks at me with the same startled eyes as Marin. She seems to hesitate. Then she comes forward a step and bends toward me, head lowered.

I look where she looks. The animal, of course. "This has to be Ribolin," I say with careful cheer. I dare to touch an ear. The dog pushes against my hand. I scratch him. He wriggles with pleasure. How funny. "Bianca has told me about him. What a delight."

Agnola straightens and gives a laugh. "I'm so glad you like him. You're a person of discernment. He's a good doggy." She turns to Marin. A look passes between them that I don't understand. "Let me introduce the servants. You don't have to be formal with them," she says gently. "You don't have to curtsy. A head bob will do." She looks at me intently and bobs her head. "This is Lucia La Rotonda, our cook."

The round, older woman bends toward me, and now I understand; this is what's done. My neck goes prickly. I bob my head. Lucia La Rotonda straightens and looks at me expectantly. So I bob my head again.

Agnola smiles approval. "And this is Carlo, our kitchen boy and general handyman."

The young man who has been standing awkwardly at the rear comes forward and bends low. I wait for him to straighten this time and then I bob my head. I look at Agnola. She gives an almost imperceptible nod.

"You must be hungry after all that travel. You're later than you said you'd be, but we waited on the meal just for you." Lucia

La Rotonda waves a hand toward a table. It stands at the rear of the room, which turns out to be cavernous. The floor shines in the candlelight.

We sit at the table and it's just like the table on San Francesco del Deserto, the brothers' island; it's made for people my size. So are the chairs. I look around. The lamp sconces are at the right height for me. The framed paintings are at the right height for me. My head is level with Marin's and Agnola's. We look into each other's faces without looking down or up. I feel light-headed. Marin says a prayer, the same prayer the brothers said, the same prayer the people on Torcello say, a simple thanks. The familiarity of it anchors me: this is all as it should be; I could belong here.

But then I look down at what Lucia La Rotonda has just placed in front of me, a spoon and an oddly shaped object. I want to ask her what it is, but she's already rushing away. I look at Marin; he's rubbing his mouth with his palm again, worried about something. I look at Agnola.

She smiles just the slightest. Her eyes go to the odd thing and back to my face. "Forks have become the rage in Venezia. We are a stylish town. Visiting dignitaries laugh at us, but I have to admit, it's better than scalding your fingers." She picks up her own fork. "No one would think of eating pasta without one these days. Don't you think forks are fun?"

Forks are not fun. They are less agile than fingers by far. But at least the food is good. And I'm hungry. I eat my fill and rip off a crust of bread to wipe my bowl, then stop and check first. The others are wiping their bowls. Thank heaven. I clean mine to a polish.

"And now," says Marin as he rises from the table, "I trust my dear Agnola to settle you for the night."

Agnola nods. "She'll share my bed."

"I want her," says Bianca.

"Not tonight," says Marin. "Dolce will sleep with Aunt Agnola."

Bianca bites her bottom lip.

"I bid you good rest." Marin comes around the table and kisses Bianca on the top of the head.

That's it? No singing together, no stories like with Mamma?

Bianca goes through a door with Lucia La Rotonda.

I follow Agnola through another door, and spend the rest of the night trying to will myself to sleep, as the woman beside me snores softly. The little dog lies on her chest and gives off tiny squeaks as he twitches in his sleep. Beyond those noises, I hear nothing. It's so dark in the room, I see no outlines.

This is the *serenissima*—the most serene. My eyes are dry; I blink and blink. I am not serene.

But when have I ever been?

CHAPTER 11

Advice

Agnola always speaks in a quiet voice. I have been here a month and have never heard her raise it. Our eyes meet often throughout the day, as we find ourselves side by side in a task. But we have talked little.

This morning I open my eyes in our wide bed when she asks in her warm, gentle way, "Are you awake?"

"Yes." I roll on my side without touching her.

Agnola is staring up at the ceiling through the gray air before dawn. As usual, Ribolin sleeps on her ample chest, which exaggerates the rise and fall of her breathing under the linen sheet. "It's going to be a busy day, Dolce. Meeting these people . . . Let me prepare you."

My cheeks heat up. "I am prepared for anything."

She turns her head toward me. "Thank you for saying that. I know you guard your privacy. But without help, the rules of Venezia will elude you, and the nobility will trample you in the end."

Marin fears this too. I have seen the way he frowns, then

tries to smile when we talk of my being introduced into society. "Why would you care?"

Ribolin stretches, all four legs stiff, and grunts. Agnola gets out of bed and sets the dog in the basket on the floor beside the open window that faces the rear courtyard. Then, hand over hand on the rope, she lowers the basket down to the courtyard. She secures the end of the rope under a slab of marble and comes back to sit on the edge of our bed. "Dolce, listen well. There's value in understanding what you mean to others. And I hate it that you don't see it yourself. You deserve to.

"First, you comfort Bianca. You comfort Marin, too. He was bereft after five deaths in a row. Our parents, in a boating accident. Then our older sister, Moderata, in childbirth, like his wife, Veronica. Marin and Veronica's son survived but one day."

"How awful."

She sighs. "And third, you remove my fear of being reduced to nothing. There you have it." She rises and uses the chamber pot in the corner, while I look the other way.

"What do you mean, reduced to nothing?"

"It's what would happen if Marin married anyone from the nobility. My life will be far better if he marries you."

"Marries me?" I sit up in shock.

"Marin hasn't let himself understand it yet. That's how he is. But I can see what's happening to him. And I'm glad he wants you. You don't look down on me—the maiden aunt, spared life in a convent only because her brother had mercy and claimed her to look after his child." She shakes her head. "Marin saved me because we've always been close. We see things the same way, even if I realize it before he does. He's been glad to have me help with Bianca. But others don't understand that." Agnola opens the doors of the large wooden wardrobe, selects a dress, and spreads it over the top of the painted chest at the foot of the bed. She opens a drawer in the bottom of the wardrobe and takes out underclothes. She stops and smiles at me. "I like how you think, Dolce. Get out of bed. We can talk as we dress. I need to explain what the morning will be like."

I'm not ready to dress. I run my hands down my torso and suddenly feel self-conscious. There was never a chance before that how I looked might matter to a man. But now . . . I allow all the vague hopes I had not let myself acknowledge to flood me. Marin is good. Marin is wonderful! Is it possible he'd marry me? He'd have to be mad.

High-pitched yips snap me back to the moment. They come from the courtyard. Agnola pulls up the rope and carefully wipes off Ribolin's muddy paws with a towel. Then the pup goes flying around the room, jumping on and off every bit of furniture. I anticipate a headache and perch on the edge of the bed so that if it blinds me, I won't fall. But it doesn't come. And I realize I haven't had a headache, or any sudden weakness, in days. My hands—I hold my palms before my face and spread the fingers—they're steady. The pink is still there, but my hands don't shake. I'm healthy. *Oh, Lord, please keep me healthy. Please make me worthy of Marin.*

Agnola talks as she arranges her hair. Her eyes follow herself in the silver mirror.

"You're so rich," I say. "Yet you look in a silver mirror instead of a glass one."

Agnola gives a little laugh as she pats her hair into place. "Glass mirrors the size of this one cost as much as a room's worth of furniture."

I'm astonished. I've made mirrors larger than the silver one.

Lord, that means the glassblowers got rich while they paid us hardly anything. I have the terrible sensation that it's easy to get cheated in the larger world.

I'm so lucky to have been found by this family and no other.

Agnola rouges her cheeks and lips. She darkens her brows with a pencil. I watch, fascinated, as she makes me repeat greetings after her, in exactly her way of speaking. We've been practicing for weeks. Agnola tells me to let her answer everyone's questions. She tells me to pay attention, and if I have to speak, I must try to mimic the way the other women talk. Their speech is refined. Mine is not. But I'll be all right, she says, because I'm a good mimic. She tells me I must allow the servants to serve me, not to help them as she and I do at home. I must laugh when she laughs, listen closely when she listens closely. I must smile at everyone, and she makes me practice that special smile: never big—not a grin, just a thin, small smile, as if I know something others don't. She says they'll be judging me. "You'll do well." She stands and puts her hands around my upper arms. "And if you don't know what to say, just stay silent."

I'm less nervous than she is, I can see that. "Whatever happens today can't be harder than what I'm used to. If they make me feel left out, I'll just think about my mamma. She used to say I was . . . things that gave me confidence."

"Surely you can find confidence in other sources, too."

"You're right. I can think about the fact that I am the master of mirrors, the best there is. In fact, I'm going to make you a mirror."

"Mirrors." Agnola's brow furrows. "Bianca said that you told her you make mirrors."

"I do. And—"

Agnola puts a finger on my lips. "Don't. Don't tell me anything more about what you used to do with mirrors. And don't speak of making mirrors to anyone else, either. Noblewomen don't do that kind of work, though we help in so many ways at home. Don't mention it, ever. Or you'll ruin everything for us right at the start."

"But how do I explain my pink fingers?"

"You don't." Agnola goes back to the drawer and comes out with two pairs of gloves. I've never seen white gloves before. "We'll keep them on all day," she says, "even inside. Maybe we'll start a new fashion." She smiles conspiratorially. "With you, who knows what can happen?"

I have been slowly dressing all this while. I hope I look the way Agnola wants me to.

We go out and stand in the grand hall, the *pian nobile*—the noble floor, where everything important happens and Marin and Agnola receive guests. Marin's room is across the hall from Agnola's. I've never even peeked in. Agnola and I walk the hall from rear to front. On the left, we pass Bianca's room; on the right, the sewing room. The facade of the palace is on the Canal Grande. It has five large windows on this floor and on the floor above. The windows are doors that open at the middle and lead to the balcony. The three middle ones offer light into this wonderful hall, while one end window lights Marin's map room, which is becoming a library, and the other end window lights the music room where Agnola sings and Bianca has just started taking harp lessons. The servants live on the floor above, and there are rooms for additional children and bachelor uncles, if this house should ever hold any of those. The canal cuts through the narrow entrance underneath the *pian nobile,* where we entered the evening I arrived. There's a stone foundation on both sides and at the rear. The rear holds the kitchen, and beyond it a gate that leads to the courtyard. The sides of the docking area are lined with storage rooms.

On Torcello we had the run of ruins that were just as grand as this palace once upon a time, some grander. The furnishings in this home are stupendous, but life here is impoverished, really. To eat a fig, Lucia La Rotonda has to run and buy them at a market. You can't just search the tree for the one that's bursting with such sweetness the ants are mad for it, and jam it all juicy into your mouth. Girls and women of the merchant and noble classes stay at home or visit other girls and women in their homes, always attended by servants. They never run or explore or swim or drop into the grasses exhausted and eat a fig.

So they can't scare me, these ladies of Venezia, no matter how much Agnola warns me.

In the music room, Bianca stands at the window munching a sweet biscuit. She sees me and smiles. I rush to her and we hug.

"You should share my bed," says Bianca. "Aunt Agnola doesn't need you like I do." She says this every morning.

Agnola enters behind me and runs a caressing hand around Bianca's ear. "You know your father says no."

"But I don't know why. He won't answer me."

Agnola shrugs. "Maybe you're old enough to figure it out for yourself."

I blink. "I can't figure it out, and I'm fifteen."

"Exactly. You're fifteen, Dolce. Do you want to be seen as a child, who shares a room with a man's daughter? Or do you want to be seen as a woman, who shares a room with his sister? How do you think Marin wants to see you?"

Bianca squeezes my hand, but keeps her eyes on Agnola. "You should have said that sooner, Aunt Agnola."

"We're eating at the Ghisi palace this morning." Agnola folds her hands across her belly. "Dolce's finally going to meet a few people."

"What's to become of me?"

"Antonin is taking you to the Contarinis'. You can play there."

"But who will take care of me there? Isn't the mamma going to the Ghisi palace to meet Princess Dolce?"

"No. And I already told you, please stop calling her princess."

"She is a princess."

"Not outside this palace, she isn't. If you keep it up, Bianca, you're going to slip and call her princess in front of people and then everyone will have questions that make her look like a liar—they won't understand. So stop it. Don't ever call her princess."

"Sorry. I'm sorry. I won't do it again. But why isn't the Contarini mamma going today? She goes to every party."

"Your father is one of the most eligible bachelors of Venezia. And Signora Contarini has a passel of daughters, the oldest of which is only a year younger than Dolce. She might block Dolce's acceptance here. No one wants extra rivals."

"Rivals?"

"For your papà. He's a catch, don't you think?"

"Oh." Bianca stands tall. She clasps her hands in front of her chest and looks me up and down. "You're better than the Contarini girls, on the outside and on the inside. Papà knows that."

"We have to leave," says Agnola. "Practice the harp until Antonin comes back for you."

"I'm too young for these lessons. That's what Signora Contarini says."

"That's because she's judging by her own daughters. You're smarter."

Bianca protrudes her lips in thought for a moment.

"Find what pleases your ear." Agnola ushers me out of the room and down to the dock, where Antonin waits with our gondola.

We climb in and the boat rocks. I sit quickly, thinking that there might be more to this game than I realized. I clutch at Agnola's skirt. "What if I'm judged poorly?"

Agnola's face goes soft and sweet. She links arms with me. "Well . . . it will matter to Marin, and to you. Because if he marries you and they decide to exclude you, Bianca will be left out. No more playing with the Contarini girls, that's for sure. But Marin can provide a heavy dowry for her someday. She will definitely marry. Still, but that won't make up for the years of loneliness as she grows."

"Years of loneliness as she grows," I say. I shiver and stare at Agnola.

She nods. She names each splendid palace along the canal and tells me about the families within, pausing often so I can repeat their names. *Lord, let me learn quickly.*

CHAPTER 12

Garden Party

Agnola has walked me around, introducing me to every group of women and girls. They ask the same questions and I give the same answers.

"Where are you visiting from?"

"Not far."

"How do you know the Cornaro family?"

I smile slyly. "Better all the time."

"But how did you come to know them in the first place?"

"We met on the island of the brothers—San Francesco del Deserto."

"What were you doing there?"

"Retreats don't lend themselves to conversation."

"But, come now, tell us a little about yourself, won't you? What's your family name?"

We had no family names on Torcello. That's what startled Marin when he introduced me to his household: he realized in that moment that he didn't know my family name. Agnola has prepared me for this question, of course. "Speaking of the dead saddens me." Which is true. This question makes Mamma linger in the back of my mind. I miss her more as time passes. How I wish she could know that a man might marry me.

Questions keep coming, and my answers remain evasive. Before long, the girls and women turn to asking each other questions, as though I'm not there. I can't blame them. They talk mostly of what they know about other Venetian families that have no one at this party. Mamma would have called it nothing but gossip. Druda often tried to draw her into talking about the others, but Mamma said our island was too small for that sort of nonsense.

Venezia is huge, and gossip appears to be a favorite pastime.

I am standing silent in a small group of women, wondering where Agnola has gone off to, when someone brings up the name Francesca. Suddenly, nearby groups come to join ours and listen.

"Do you mean the merchant's daughter?"

"What other Francesca is on everyone's lips?"

"That's exactly it—on everyone's lips—you're so clever."

They laugh.

"How do you know a merchant's daughter?" I ask.

They all look at me, startled.

"Well, we certainly don't go into shops," says one.

"But our brothers do."

They laugh again.

"Oh, don't look so baffled. Francesca is a loose one. They say she gives kisses."

"And more."

"My brother Sizzo says she's so beautiful that she'll wind up on the arm of a noble."

"Or on some other limb."

The women laugh. It feels like some sort of ritual.

"We should have a yellow gown made and sent to her as a gift."

"How kind," I say in surprise.

They laugh.

"Silly, yellow is the mark of the courtesan."

I just look at them.

"Of the prostitute," one whispers. "By law, women who sell themselves have to wear yellow."

"Just like Jews. It marks them."

I know about Jews. "Gesù was a Jew before he started his own religion."

"That was a long time ago. Jews are different now," says one girl.

The girl beside her looks askance. "Really, Martina, watch how you talk. My father says Jews bring good business to Venezia and we should all be grateful for them."

"Grateful doesn't mean we have to like them."

A smiling girl comes up. *"Baicoli!"* And everyone follows her out to the table, where piles of oval cookies are surrounded by bowls of fruit floating in water.

I take a fig in each hand and go back inside to sit by myself on a chest-bench.

The smiling girl sits down beside me. She takes a big bite of pear, and juice runs down her chin. She must be around eight or nine. Her hair is curled and pinned in place with pearls. "Don't you like *baicoli*?"

"I do. But right now I prefer figs," I say. "Don't you like *baicoli*?"

"I do. But right now I prefer a pear!" She laughs.

"Everyone here laughs a lot."

"You don't."

I laugh. "You have pear juice all over your dress."

"And figs are staining your gloves."

I laugh again. "I wish Bianca had come along. Do you know her?"

"Of course. But little girls weren't invited."

"Aren't you little?"

"Yes." She sits up tall. "But I'm Patrizia Ghisi. This is my palace."

I lean back against the wall and let Patrizia talk, opening my eyes to this new world.

CHAPTER 13

Books

Three days later, Signora Contarini follows me up the stairs from the docking area and into the grand hall. Her two youngest daughters trail behind, with Agnola bringing up the rear. Bianca stands at the top of the stairs and hops from foot to foot in anticipation, calling out happily.

I press my lips together. I don't have gloves on! I clutch both sides of my skirt and curl my pink fingers into the cloth.

My morning at the Ghisi palace didn't go as well as Agnola had hoped, but she says it will be a gradual process. She says my language is improving rapidly, so I can speak more at the next outing, and everyone will come to accept me. But doubt fills me. I might never understand their ways. And now, here's Signora Contarini—with a determined look. Yesterday we got the message that she'd be leaving her two youngest with us today.

The girls run ahead into Bianca's room.

"I'll return in the late afternoon," says Signora Contarini. Her eyes inspect me.

I tighten my fingers in my skirts.

"You better hurry after them, to make sure they don't get in trouble," she says to me, jerking her chin toward Bianca's door.

Agnola grabs me at the waist from behind, where the signora cannot see. "That's my task, of course." She bows her head formally to the signora. "Excuse me, please, Signora Laura. I look forward to spending more time with you soon." She bows her head to me now, something she hasn't done since our first meeting. "Excuse me, my lady. I wish you an enjoyable conversation." And she leaves.

What a fine performance. I take a breath and turn to the signora. "It is a pleasure to finally meet you."

She lifts that pointed chin again. "I know you only as Dolce. What is your family name?"

"Speaking of the dead saddens me."

"Come now, surely you have some living family."

I lift my eyebrows and shake my head.

Her hand goes to her mouth.

"You must be in a hurry," I say. "Shall I walk you downstairs?"

"I can afford a moment to talk. A conversation, like Agnola said."

I hate it that she calls her Agnola, instead of Signorina Agnola, while Agnola must address her as Signora Laura. A married woman has status, while a spinster does not. I try to look apologetic. "But I cannot afford even a moment, I'm afraid."

She blanches.

I didn't mean to be rude. "I beg your pardon. It's just that I mustn't disappoint the signore. He's counting on me."

"For what?"

For what indeed? Marin is in his library this morning. But I have no idea what he does in there. He says it's dirty and dusty. "To work with the books. His library, you know."

She pulls back her shoulders as if affronted. "Do you read?"

I laugh in spite of myself. What an enigma I must be to her. "I have to go help him."

"I'll go with you. I'm happy to give him a little greeting." She does a poor job of hiding her suspicion. Or maybe she's not trying. Maybe she's calling my bluff.

We walk to the library. What now? I give a quick, firm rap, then open the door. Marin stands at a table, a cloth in one hand, a large book open in front of him. A lock of hair dangles over his brow. My cheeks heat. He looks at me in surprise, then catches sight of Signora Contarini, flashes me a look I can't interpret, and comes around the table, smiling widely. "Good morning, Signora. You're looking lovely and well." He bows, the cloth clasped in both hands now.

"Good morning, Signore." Her smile seems genuine. But it falls as she gazes past him. "Look how many books you've gathered in the past couple of years."

"I've been working hard," says Marin with pride.

"You're dismantling the map room."

"Hardly. I'm just making accommodations so my new home can serve me best."

"Why don't you convert the sewing room into a library instead?"

"My sister loves sewing. That's her realm."

Signora Contarini shakes her head. "I know this home well. Your shelves for these massive books are covering paintings of constellations and planets. Why, you don't even have a wooden celestial globe!"

"It's true." Marin stands taller. "Fortunately, I can visit your home if I need to consult a map of the skies."

The signora seems to realize she may have overstepped, for

she gives a small smile. "I was hoping to steal your mysterious visitor for a few moments to get to know her a bit. A visitor shouldn't be all work and no play."

Marin looks at me. I look meaningfully at the book on the table, then beg him with my eyes. He looks back at Signora Contarini. "If she dislikes her task so much, I will excuse her from her promise to aid me." There's a touch of annoyance in his voice.

"I don't dislike it at all," I practically yelp. I turn to the signora. "Another time, please? Let me see you to the stairs."

The signora's eyes cloud. Her whole face falls. "That's quite all right. I know my way. These palaces are in my blood." She walks out, leaving the door ajar. Her shoes click on the polished floor, then clop on the rougher stairs.

"Forgive me for interrupting you," I say to Marin. "And thank you."

"It was no problem."

My hands go to my hair nervously. I quickly lower them. I don't want to be this way around him. I want him to see me as I am. That thought makes me pause. How greedy I am: here I have a chance to marry, perhaps, and I want more. . . . I want to be loved truly. "You sounded annoyed."

Marin gives a rueful little laugh. "I was. First, all that nonsense about me ruining this place. Then she called you a visitor. Twice. You are, of course. It was unreasonable for me to react like that." He hands me a clean cloth. "Come stand beside me. Let's turn our little play into the truth. I'll work on the top of the page, you work on the bottom. Wipe carefully everywhere. The point is to remove moisture and anything that carries moisture—any bit of mold. The smallest amount can cause a page to crumble. And dirt—a speck of dust is an enemy."

I take the cloth and press down.

His hand instantly catches mine and lifts it. "Gently. This is an old book. Fragile."

My hand tingles at his touch. I avoid his eyes, but nod and start over, patting softly. We finish the page and Marin teaches me to blow across the surface to remove anything the cloth missed. It's important to make a tight circle of my lips so the air is cool and dry, rather than hot and wet. Then we turn the page, holding top and bottom corners and moving it evenly.

We work in silence. A second page. A third.

"Thank you," I say.

He nods.

"I wasn't intending to interrupt you, but I panicked."

"You're afraid of her?"

"She might hate me. Agnola's afraid of that, too."

"She has no reason to dislike you, Dolce. No one does. You're unusual, that's all. They'll get used to you."

"You're wrong. People had plans, and I upset them."

"How?"

"Maybe her oldest daughter is meant for you."

Marin puts down his cloth and stares at me. "You always surprise me. You've been here a month, so I should be used to your directness by now."

"I'm blunt. Agnola is trying to teach me to—"

"No. Don't change. Not with me, at least. I'm grateful for your ways." He takes a deep breath. "The Contarini daughter cannot be thinking of me. I cannot say what she looks like. Or even recall her name."

"Agnola told me that girls here are betrothed to men they don't know. Family alliances."

Marin smiles. "I know. This is my world. But no one is betrothed to me."

"She might want to be, though. Any girl could wind up married to someone . . . decrepit and smelly, as Bianca would say. Or mean."

Marin folds his arms across his chest. "Are you saying I'm not mean, decrepit, or smelly?" His eyes tease. I smile, and he says, "There's more to a person than what you see in the here and now."

"I know. Agnola told me how you've suffered . . . losing your wife and son. It made me feel . . . that mere breathing hurt."

Marin's whole self tightens. He steps closer.

"The signora wants to get rid of me because I'm in her way," I say. "I can understand that. She doesn't hate me because of what she sees, but what she fears."

Marin steps closer still. His breath stirs my hair. "Who has ever hated you because of what they saw?"

"Nearly everyone. My ugliness shocked them."

"Ugliness?" He shakes his head. "Would you please explain?"

I knew it would come to this. "Will you swear not to send me back home?"

"Is there a reason I would?"

"No. I have no one there. No family at all."

"Then I swear."

"I lived on Torcello, in a community of dwarfs. My mother was a dwarf. I was forbidden to know about the world outside Torcello. They told me I was a monster. I had no friends but Mamma. Bianca was the first person I met after leaving the island."

"My God! Dolce . . ." Marin is silent. Then, "What that must have been like—growing up like that—then meeting us. You must have felt . . . like the world didn't make sense. A thousand questions crowd my head."

"Don't ask them. Please. Please don't treat me like . . . a curiosity."

"I won't." His chest heaves. "No one can look at you and not see your beauty. You don't even paint your face, yet you're the fairest."

"I don't care about that. I mean, I'm glad you like to look upon me. Very glad. I'm glad my mother did, too. But . . . how we look doesn't matter."

"Unless others have made it matter." Marin's arm circles behind me and his hand presses on the table. I stand in that circle. No part of him touches me, but I smell his skin, I feel the warmth that emanates from him. "If you were my bride," he says, so close my hair moves, "I can think of the perfect wedding gift. A mirror, of crystal. Then your own eyes can tell you how beautiful you are."

A mirror. It's as though he senses the whole of me, as though he understands and recognizes me, though I haven't said a word to him about mirrors. Somehow he knows I could look in one now, I could look and not cry. "I never knew someone might love me as a husband. I never thought . . ." My voice comes out as a broken whisper. His neck pulses just a breath away from my lips. "All I want to do is make up for the sad things that have happened to you, all of them, your whole life, all the things I don't know and maybe won't ever know."

"Good." His voice is hoarse.

"But you have to understand, Marin. I have never even thought about a man before. Do you see? It makes sense that I should feel this way about you. It's different for you, though. You are surrounded by women who can love you, who can dream about being your wife."

"I care for you. Does it matter why?"

I step back so that I can see his face fully. "Living here with you like this . . . I begin to see that it can't continue. We both know that."

"I . . . lead a cautious life. I collect books, for God's sake, what could be more careful? The Senate accepts my library work as fulfilling my responsibility toward the Republic. I told myself my only goal is to make sure Bianca grows up well, so that she can make the decisions that are right for her.

"And now . . . you appear. Dangerous."

"Dangerous?"

"You threaten the peace I have worked so hard to protect. You are strong, Dolce. I've listened to you repeating after Agnola. Sometimes you sound so much like her, if I close my eyes, I think you're my sister. You can live here and learn how this society works and the offers of marriage will flood in. You can marry whomever you want. I'll provide a dowry for you. Our old family palace was huge. It was meant to house my parents and bachelor brothers, of whom I have none, and passels of children, of which I have only Bianca. When I sold it, I wound up rich. I have more money than anyone needs.

"That's the right thing to do. To provide you a dowry. To help you along in life. Then set you free."

"I wouldn't be free, Marin. I'd be lost."

"Does that mean you want to marry me?"

My skin goes gooseflesh. "Yes. Oh, yes."

"Then I am to do the wrong thing?" he says tentatively. "We are to do this together?"

"Would it make you happy?"

Marin nods.

"I've never had the chance to make anyone happy, anyone other than Mamma. But you have to tell me something first."

"Ask."

"Do you want more children?"

"If children come, I would be happy. If they don't, they don't. We have Bianca and each other."

The world has flipped again. Before I was afraid of having a child like me, for fear the others would drown my baby in the lagoon. Now everything has changed. A child might not be like me. "What if I had a dwarf child? My mother had me."

"Children come to us or not, Dolce. On their own terms. A child is a gift. I know how to be grateful. Ingrates are the worst sort of people, don't you think?"

He understands the world the way Mamma did. He understands me. *Lord in heaven, he understands me.*

CHAPTER 14

The Gift

When Ribolin got sick, Agnola sent for an animal healer, who arrived with a satchel of medicines. Among his many vials was one that glistened. Quicksilver! A plan hatched instantly; I begged him to sell it to me.

Marin didn't even ask why I wanted the money. It was a pittance to him. He showed me a bowl in his room where he keeps the thin coins called *denari* and he said I could take whatever I wanted whenever I wanted. I stood in the doorway as he pointed the bowl out, of course. I wouldn't enter his room.

I went into that room the next day, though, when he was out. And I gave Lucia La Rotonda a coin for her small, round tin mirror. It reflects only dimly, no matter how much you polish it, and it distorts. These are the mirrors of the *popolo*, the ordinary people. Lucia La Rotonda's delight told me I'd overpaid. But when I offered Antonin a handful of coins to buy a piece of round, clear glass for me, no larger than my palm, he said, "Signorina, you'll need the same number in silver ducats if you insist on clear glass."

So I asked Marin. He went to the bank and came home with a heavy pouch. He didn't ask what I wanted the ducats for. He had sworn he would never question me over money. He said the worse disputes in Venezia are always over money. I don't really understand money, but if people fight over it, I think it's best he knows what I do with it. So I told him that I was making a present for someone. And that I hoped it would matter to us in the long run.

This is the only way I can think of to appease Signora Contarini.

And thus began my secret task. I wandered the house, looking for a place I could disappear to. On Torcello I was alone more than I wanted. Here, there's always someone about.

This palazzo offers few hiding places. Every room is used, on and off, all day, and servants come and go. I don't want anyone to happen upon me or touch the quicksilver. No one gets sick from handling glass or tin, that's clear. So it has to be the quicksilver that made Venerio and me shake and turned our fingers and toes pink and our heads into throbbing gourds. I won't allow anyone else to get sick from mirror making.

I found my spot: a storage room where garlic and onions hang from the rafters, above wine casks stacked on top of one another. Behind them is my workshop.

Lucia La Rotonda's old tin mirror was larger than the round glass piece that Antonin bought for me. Perfect. I set the glass in the very center of the tin mirror. As a table, I used a block of marble. A base from a broken pot served as a weight. My mirror is ready. But I haven't gone down to fetch it yet.

I sit in the music room and try to block out the sound of Bianca plucking at the harp. She likes me to be here while she practices, but my headaches came back with a vengeance the night after I poured the quicksilver on the new mirror. Darkness shimmers at the edges of my vision, it presses on me from both sides. But I know that will go away again. And the mirror will be worth it.

I am stitching a little velvet purse as I pretend to listen. One side of the purse has a circular hole in the middle, exactly the size of the glass piece. I will slip the mirror inside the purse, and the larger tin setting will fit snugly while the glass mirror center shows through that hole. The ribbon that closes the top of the purse will allow it to be hung from a waist sash. The velvet is pale yellow like sunshine. If yellow becomes something even Signora Contarini wears, then yellow will no longer be the mark of the Jew and the prostitute. It worries me a little that I have indulged myself in this small rebellion. After all, I don't know any Jews or prostitutes, but I do it for Mamma and for all outcasts. I could make dozens of purses this size from the piece of velvet I bought when the cloth merchant came by with samples. I feel giddy. Perhaps dangerous, as Marin said.

"Stitching isn't your forte." It's Agnola. Like Marin, her speech is speckled with words I don't know, often foreign.

I can guess what she means, though. "My mother never taught me. Her fingers weren't nimble."

"Let me help. Let's go in the sewing room."

She takes the little purse and we sit side by side in soothing silence. "Let's just do a simple loop around this opening," she says, and finishes it off beautifully. "I can embroider rosettes with leafy vines running between. What do you think?"

"It's fine as is. You are a wizard."

"And you are a puzzle. What on earth is the use of a purse with a large hole in one side?"

"I'm making a gift. It's a secret, but only because you've told me I'm not allowed to do it or speak of it."

There go her brows into those deep furrows I know well by

now. "It could be dangerous to keep secrets from me, Dolce. I can't help you if you need help."

"I'll tell you if you won't scold."

"I might scold, Dolce. But if you're doing something I've told you you're not allowed to do, you really don't care much whether or not I scold you, do you?"

"You reason like Bianca."

"We're all one family."

I snatch the purse from her and try to smile—if only the pounding in my head would let up, I could enjoy this moment. "Stay here. Inside this room." I close her into the sewing room and go downstairs as quickly as I can without jostling my head too much. It seems no one is about, but you never can be sure. I leave the storeroom door ajar to let in light, crawl behind the wine casks, and uncover my small mirror. I polish it with a soft, clean cloth and slip the mirror into the purse. It fits well. Then I pull a garlic head from a hanging braid of them. I carry the garlic conspicuously in my left palm. Everyone knows I feed little Ribolin garlic to ease his worms. I race up the stairs and put the garlic on top of the chest at the foot of our bed. Then I return to the sewing room.

"Tell me what you think." I hold out the purse.

Agnola's mouth falls open. She reaches for the mirror with care, and looks at herself a long time. "This is the finest quality, isn't it?"

"I told you I was a master."

Her head jerks up. "You made it?"

I nod.

She shakes her head slowly. "Does Marin know?"

"I haven't told him."

"Don't."

"I must. I don't want secrets between us. Besides, I want him to see what I can do. It took me years to perfect this method."

She presses her lips together and shrugs. Then she looks again at the little mirror in the purse and sighs loudly. "Will you hang it from your waist?"

"It's not for me."

Her face opens. "For me?"

"No. Oh, I'm so sorry, Agnola. Of course it should be for you. I'll make another."

"No, no, don't be silly. The glass alone must have cost a fortune."

"Nothing compared with the price of a mirror. I should have made this one for you. I'll make another fast. I need this one for today; the Contarini mamma is coming."

"You made it for Signora Laura?"

"It's a peace offering."

Agnola puts the purse on my lap and looks at me, awestruck. "You're a genius."

I smile despite my throbbing head. "You think it will work?"

"You've won the whole war, Dolce."

In the afternoon, Antonin announces that Signora Contarini has arrived. But she waits below in her gondola with her daughters, ready to whisk Bianca off to an afternoon garden party at the palace of the Mocenigo family. I am not invited. Agnola is, but she has declined, out of loyalty to me.

I need to get the signora alone so we can talk. I take Bianca by the hand and we go downstairs to the gondola.

Signora Contarini has the good grace to look a little flustered at my appearance. "Good day. Climb in carefully, Bianca."

"Please, Signora," I say. "Please, could you come upstairs just a moment?"

"The afternoon is already half gone."

"It will take just a moment. I have something for you."

"For me?"

"A little something."

"Well, surely you can bring it down to me."

I fight off tears. "It will be quick."

She holds out her hand and Antonin rushes to help her onto the dock. She follows me without a word. In the sewing room, I hand her the purse.

She stares at it. "What is this?"

"A mirror."

"Well, I can see that. A very fine mirror. The finest I've ever seen."

"Then you like it?"

"It's magnificent."

"Let me tie it at your waist."

She takes a step back. "What do you mean? You can't possibly mean this is mine."

"It's my gift to you."

"Such an extravagance! And why?"

"Because . . . I need us to be friends."

She stiffens. "You are the most extraordinary girl. Do you think a friendship can be bought?"

I look at her. "No. But I hope this will show you how fervently I want us to be friends. All my life . . . I never fit anywhere. Except here. I don't know how I was so fortunate to wind up with this family. I mean no harm. I didn't choose to upset anyone's plans. It just happened."

Signora Contarini holds the mirror to her face, then looks at me. She licks her reddened lips and her eyes seem sad.

"I don't want anyone in pain. Not on my account," I say. My eyes burn.

"My daughter would prefer an unfettered husband anyway, I think." She speaks slowly. "A man in his twenties, with no history, no children from a prior marriage, no memory of a first wife to live up to."

My fingers massage my forehead.

Signora Contarini gazes into the mirror. "It is a miracle of a gift. I shouldn't accept it."

"Please accept it. For my sake, and Bianca's."

She looks at me with troubled eyes. "You're . . . a rather simple girl. Straightforward. I should have been kind to you from the start."

"Do me this kindness now, please. Accept the mirror."

"There are many other, far less costly things you could have given me. Don't tell me I've entirely misjudged and you sit on an outrageous fortune."

"This is costly for me." My head wants to explode. "Very."

"Why a mirror?"

"I thought you would appreciate it."

"I do." She stares into it. "Absolutely colorless. Accurate. Maybe more . . . Some of the priests call transparent mirrors evil."

"Why?"

"It's only once we reach heaven that we see things clearly. San Paolo said that. In a mirror like this, we can see our own death, waiting for us. We can count the increasing number of lines on our faces. Just by telling us the truth, crystal mirrors can leave us bitter. Greedy for more."

"Transparent becomes murky," I say through the shadows that threaten my own eyes right now.

"You put it well."

"Mirrors also show beauty," I whisper.

"Appealing to vanity is never a good thing."

"Appealing to beauty is a different thing."

She looks ruefully at the mirror. "Who are you really for, little mirror?"

"You. No one else."

She swallows a small laugh. "Everyone else will want one."

I drop my hand and hold on to the back of a chair. I'll keel over if I don't hold tight.

She smiles. "Thank you, Dolce. This mirror is working the magic you wanted. Somehow I think we understand each other. . . . I look forward to knowing you better. Please call me Signora Laura. Why don't you and Agnola come with us to the garden party?"

"I'm afraid I'm not feeling so well."

"Nonsense. Don't you worry about a thing. The Mocenigo family will welcome you. I wouldn't allow it to be otherwise." She ties the purse to her waist and turns it so the mirror looks out. She smiles at me as she pats her skirts smooth. "You look lovely just as you are. No need to dress up. Let me go find Agnola." She tilts her head a moment, lingering. Her face looks different, soft. "I believe I can repay you for this mirror."

I shake my head slowly. "Friendship is all I want."

She touches my arm. "I will be a good friend."

She leaves me in the sewing room.

I will go to the party, but hold on to Agnola's arm all afternoon. I can sit quietly while the women chatter. This will mean that Bianca is included in Venetian society. She'll be invited to everything. She won't grow up lonely. I shut my eyes and will the pain away.

CHAPTER 15

Strategies

Sunlight sparkles off the Canal Grande, and I can enjoy this beautiful day, for I have no headache, no cough, and no itchiness, and my vision is clear. I listen to Bianca playing dress-up in the music room behind me. She traipses around in old costumes from masked balls, then goes up and down the grand hall, stopping to talk with imaginary people. I laugh.

An exceptionally long gondola rounds the bend. I recognize the iron on the front: Contarini.

I hurry down the stairs to the docking area. Signora Laura climbs out with the help of her servant Manfredo. We kiss each other on the cheeks and she darts past me up the stairs. I haven't seen her since the garden party a week ago.

Antonin intercepts her. "Shall I announce your presence, Signora?" He bows low.

"I'll surprise him. Is he in the map room?"

Agnola comes up beside Antonin. She smiles. "Marin loves his new library."

"That's obvious. He might be a lunatic." Signora Laura sweeps past Agnola into the library.

Agnola and I watch from the doorway. Antonin pretends to be busy adjusting a painting, but he stays within earshot too.

Marin wipes dust off his nose and smiles limply. "Signora, what a pleasant surprise."

"I've come to take Dolce away." She turns to me. "Gather your belongings."

I stare at her, then look at Marin. His eyes question me, but I know nothing. A frozen lump forms in my chest. I shake my head vehemently. I'm so stupid; I thought I had won her over.

"I don't understand," Marin says.

"She is of marriageable age. Fifteen is on the young side, but it's acceptable. Letting her stay in this house threatens her reputation."

"She shares a room with me," says Agnola.

"Which is fine if she's your younger sister or Bianca's older one." She turns back to Marin. "Dolce will live with us until a suitable marriage can be arranged."

"I intend to marry her," says Marin. He looks at me.

He said it. And in front of others. I can be his bride! I rush toward him, but Signora Laura catches my arm. "That's all good and well. The tradition, then, is for you to negotiate with her father."

"My father is dead," I say. "You know that."

"Which is why Messer Contarini will negotiate on your behalf." She turns to Marin again. "He'll meet with you in the cathedral of San Marco and—"

"Negotiate?" says Marin. "Dolce has nothing. I presume Messer Contarini does not have an extra 1,750 ducats lying around to furnish a dowry."

"Of course he doesn't. But he will speak for Dolce's well-being."

"I will care well for her. You know that."

"All right, then. I suppose you're right. In a few months, come by our palace and you can seal the agreement. You can touch her hand or give her a ring, and you'll be wed."

"A few months? Don't be absurd! If you take her today, I'll come tomorrow morning."

Signora Laura tsks. "You're acting like a boy, not a widower with a child. What's the rush? I come to take her away and you can't bear it?"

"Exactly. I'll come tomorrow."

Signora Laura sighs. "All right, all right. We can set a transfer date for changing homes. Perhaps in spring."

"Spring!" shouts Marin.

"Eight months is proper," says Signora Laura.

"It will be day after tomorrow," says Marin.

"Impossible," says Signora Laura. "That's a Wednesday. No one transfers homes on a Wednesday. It is a day of abstinence. Wednesday and Friday. Surely you intend to observe abstinence rules."

Marin's face goes red.

"Please," I say. "Will someone explain?"

"Really, Dolce. Sometimes you behave as though you've been living under the sea. Transfer—like in every marriage. Marin will come with his gondola and bring you and all your belongings to this house to live."

"My belongings are already here."

"We're taking them to my home now. This is how it's done, Dolce. Hush. Everything must be done correctly. You will be transferred here on . . ." She pauses.

"Thursday," says Marin.

"Sunday." Signora Laura brings her hands together in a loud clap. "No one works on Sunday. That guarantees the greatest audience for the transfer. I will lend Dolce an old chest for her possessions. A giant one so her audience can see she is a person of substance."

"We don't need an audience," says Marin. "And keep your old chest. All we want is each other." He looks at me. "Am I right, Dolce?"

His face is as open as a flower. I want to breathe him in.

"Don't answer him," says Signora Laura. "Talk to him through me. And believe me, you want an audience. You must be recognized in Venetian society as a proper wife for Marin. Proper, do you understand? For Bianca's sake. You want everyone to see you. We'll have to rush on getting a new gown. You can borrow some of my jewelry."

"I will buy her jewelry," says Marin. "And she will choose it. She will decide what it means to be proper."

"Then . . ."

"Signora Laura, please stop," I say. "Am I to be loaded into Marin's gondola like a sack of fruit?"

She smiles. "Not at all. Like spices. Pepper and cloves and cinnamon and ginger—exotic spices from India and the far islands and China. Everything wonderful from anywhere else comes through Venezia. You need to be recognized as something different from us, but just as good. Better, perhaps.

"Listen, Dolce. As Marin knows, there's been talk lately about changing the rules of who is a member of the nobility. Right now it's entirely patrilineal. Through the father. But they might change it so that the mother's origin matters too. It may take a year or more before they vote, but I'm betting they will pass a new law. What will become of your children if Venetian society doesn't recognize you as noble?"

"I have no idea."

"You don't want to find out."

"None of us do." Agnola comes into the room. "Now, here's my plan. Lucia La Rotonda makes a wonderful dish of roasted chicken with cheese, sugar, and cinnamon. We can have a feast on Sunday and invite everyone. The aroma of cinnamon will fill our palace. Everyone will accept Dolce as noble. We will start planning right now. Thank you a thousand times, Signora. And now you must excuse me." She races away.

"I'll help Dolce pack." Signora Laura takes me by the elbow.

I look over my shoulder at Marin. Our eyes meet. It's going to happen. We're going to marry.

"Thank you, Signora," he calls.

Signora Laura ushers me into the room I share with Agnola.

Bianca sits in the middle of our bed, her legs folded under her. "Don't go."

I should have known she'd be eavesdropping. I hug her. "I must."

"Then I'm coming with you."

"Don't be silly," says Signora Laura. "Dolce will be back on Sunday. And she's got a busy week in between."

Bianca's eyes are on me. "I'm talking to Dolce. I'm coming with you."

"There's no need to be rude to me, Bianca," says Signora Laura. "I know you want to be part of things. You'll act like a little hostess at the feast on Sunday."

"Take me with you." Bianca stares at me, solemn. "You're my mamma now. I need you."

I want her to come with me. But Signora Laura . . . "I'm coming back," I say softly. "In less than a week."

A tear makes its way down Bianca's cheek. "Promise me."

"I promise."

"Will you have children with Papà?"

"I hope so."

She clasps her hands together. "Will you still love me if you do?"

"Yes." I climb onto the bed and pull her onto my lap. "Yes, Bianca. I will always love you."

"Promise me."

"I promise."

Bianca turns her face to Signora Laura. "Will Dolce be recognized as noble?"

"I hope so."

"You only hope?"

"I can't know for sure. I will do my best to help. Dolce found a way to make me accept her. She'll find a way to make other families accept her."

"How?" Bianca pulls on the sleeve of my bodice. "How did you make Signora Contarini accept you?"

I put my mouth to her ear. "I made her a mirror," I whisper.

Bianca pulls my head down and whispers into my ear, "Then make mirrors for everyone."

"If I have to," I whisper, "I will." I fall backward onto the bed and look up at the plaster molding—grapevines with clusters of bursting fruit—on the ceiling. I love feeling clearheaded, seeing without pain. I don't want the mirror malady to come back. It's so much worse than it used to be. I don't want to go murky.

But those children, my unborn innocents, must be nobility. I don't understand why, but Marin accepts it. And I cannot bring harm to Bianca. Never.

CHAPTER 16

Spin

I jump from the bed and stare down at the tiny girl who looks steadily at me. "Who are you?"

Signora Laura stands behind the girl, and laughs. "We call her Zitta, because she says almost nothing. She's from Africa and speaks some strange language. She's my wedding gift to you."

"Gift?" I jerk my head up toward Signora Laura. "Are you insane?"

"You gave me a gift that was far more costly."

"You can't give me a person!" I clutch my forearms.

"Of course I can. Messer Contarini bought her for you at a slave market in Ferrara. He had to fend off Isabella d'Este, who desperately wanted Zitta. You've heard of her. Everyone else's slaves come from Eastern Europe and Central Asia. No one has slaves from Africa except Isabella. She collects them like art. But your slave is better—not just a black African but also a dwarf."

"No."

"You don't know what a dwarf is, do you? She's special. She

won't grow but a little taller. Really. And once she learns to speak Veneziano, you'll laugh. There's nothing funnier than seeing dwarfs gesticulating with their short arms. You'll love having her around."

"No! Not in our home. No!"

"Dolce! I know Marin doesn't have slaves, but Zitta is a gift. He can't refuse you that."

"It has nothing to do with Marin. I refuse."

"Don't be foolish, Dolce. We all must act loyal to our husbands, I understand that, but an African dwarf . . . nothing will bring you more attention in the transfer today. She can stand at the prow. The whole city is talking about it. Everyone wants to see her."

"The whole city? How could you do this without asking me?"

"I'm supposed to ask your permission to give you a fabulous gift? You ingrate! This is my strategy. I'm thinking of you! And Bianca!"

I drop to my knees in front of the girl. She must be ten or eleven. I take her hand gently. Her eyes try to mask emotions. Fear for sure. Hatred. "I wish I could talk with you. I wish we could understand each other. Please listen to the tears in my voice. Please look at my face and know what I'm feeling. I wish I could apologize for all that's been done to you. I'm sorry."

"Get up!" Signora Laura says sharply.

I stay on my knees. Zitta still stares at me. She pulls her hand from mine and hides it behind her waist.

"I am not a monster," I say.

"Get up right now, Dolce!"

"Please, Signora, if you want to give me a wedding gift, have this girl brought back to her home, to her family, where she belongs."

"Back to Africa? They're savages there. It's an unholy life."

"Who are you to judge?"

"I'm a Catholic! Aren't you?"

My poor mamma would grieve to know the doubt within me now. "Signora," I say, "I beg you. It's her life. It's where she belongs."

"I misjudged you. I thought you were simply a country bumpkin, but you might be as much a lunatic as Marin. Maybe more so."

The image of Marin bent over one of his books in concentration overwhelms me. I miss him. I miss all of them. "Can I go to him now, to my wonderful lunatic? Please?"

"I'll send in Raffaella to dress you."

"You know very well that I'll dress myself as she stands by."

"You exasperate me, Dolce."

"Did you expect a trained dog?"

"I certainly didn't expect one that would bite my hand."

I glare at Signora Laura, then smile at Zitta and stand. "I'll be ready in minutes."

Signora Laura leaves. Zitta looks from her to me.

"Go," I say. I stroke her shoulder, her hair. "Go, and good luck." I turn my back on her and dress myself. My heart bashes against my ribs. Maybe I'm making a mistake. Maybe I should bring this girl to Marin's palace and he can find a boat going to Africa to put her on. That's what I'll do. I spin back around. Zitta is gone.

I burst from the room to find Raffaella waiting. "Please, Signorina, come down the stairs. Your husband's gondola waits for you."

"Is the signora downstairs?"

"She's on the balcony with her daughters. They'll wave good-bye to you from there."

"And the girl?"

"The dwarf? The signora said you didn't want her. She's already gone."

"Where?"

"I wouldn't know, Signorina." Raffaella clears her throat. "Your husband awaits you."

I go down the stairs ready to weep. And there is Marin. Good, solid Marin. He takes my hand. I lean into his chest, and his arms come around me instantly. Yes. This is what I need.

"Are you all right, wife?"

"I don't know. I missed you. I was so happy that Sunday morning finally came. And then Signora Laura tried to give me a gift."

"And?"

"It was a slave girl. From Africa. I refused to take her."

"Good. We don't own slaves in our palace. You did the right thing."

"She's a dwarf."

"Oh." He cradles my cheek in the hollow of his throat. "Oh, Dolce."

"Maybe I should take her. We can send her back home, to her people."

"All right."

"Only she's already gone somewhere else."

"I will give Messer Contarini the fee for her passage home. Don't worry."

"Maybe they've taken her someplace awful. What if—"

"It won't be awful, or not awful in the Contarini eyes. Dwarfs are prized. We are husband and wife today, Dolce, at last. Let's go home. I can pursue this later. The girl will not be abused."

"She's already been abused. She's been stolen from her home."

"But she will be well treated. Besides, I couldn't bring her

with us now. Everyone would think I was supporting a practice my whole family finds loathsome. Agnola would be mortified. My sister, Teresa, is coming out of the convent just for this
wedding—I told you. What a way to meet each other. Let me
handle it. Later."

And so we ride in the gondola with Antonin standing behind
us, pushing and pulling on that single oar, and Signora Laura's
huge old chest in front of us, empty but for my shift, my underclothes, and my one other dress. *Slip, slip, slip* through the quiet
waters. But there's noise from the sides. Nearly every balcony
from the Contarini palace to Marin's is crowded with people
waving colored handkerchiefs and shouting good wishes.

It feels unreal. These people have no idea who I am. And I
doubt they have any real sense of who Marin is.

I look back and see that a flotilla has formed. Each gondola
behind us holds a family that is coming to our feast. So many.
"Marin, look. Look. Can we really feed them all?"

"This is your wedding ride, and you're spending it worrying
about feeding our guests?"

"I can't help it."

"Lucia La Rotonda and Agnola have helpers. The palace has
been busy all week. And the festivities over the next three days:
parties at friends' homes; the doge, the leader of all Venezia, is
offering a feast in our honor; and—"

"Three days!"

"Many go on for a week. But today and tonight, especially
tonight, I will not think about all that. I have only one thought."
He takes my hand and laces his fingers between mine. His hand
is hot and firm. It is real.

As soon as we arrive, Marin brings me to a slight woman
with lips too thin for a kiss, but eyes that are just like Agnola's.

My heart responds. Before Marin can speak, I embrace her. "Teresa."

She embraces me. Perhaps it is the way of nuns, or perhaps it is just her. She whispers warmly, "Welcome to the world."

I pull my head back. Has she somehow seen inside me?

We're interrupted by a group of men who whisk Marin off without apology. An instant later Teresa is absorbed by a group of women. She moves from me to them without a backward glance, asking questions, catching up, hungry for details. I find myself at the edge, excluded.

But Mamma would tell me that's the wrong way to think— I'm free to look around and take it all in. Our palace is decked out splendidly with flowers on every surface and colorful silks draped on the walls; guests mill about drinking wine; musicians play in the grand hall and in the courtyard; children and tiny dogs race around.

I wander slowly among the small clutches of women everywhere. When I approach, they hush.

Finally, I retreat to a corner. Agnola sidles up beside me, her hair pink as rhubarb, happy.

"Dear sister," I say, for we are now truly sisters, "do you think I'll ever be accepted?"

"Has someone been nasty?" Agnola's eyes glitter. "And on your wedding day."

"Perhaps if I give mirrors to the most important ladies of Venezia?"

"That will just cause jealousy among those without mirrors."

"Maybe I'll give to the ones most set against me."

"The others will figure out the pattern and then they'll all be mean to you. No, Dolce. You'll win them with your personality."

"My personality wasn't enough to hold on to your sister, Teresa, for even two minutes."

Agnola looks around and spots Teresa. She nods. "Can you blame her? She grew up going to parties with the women here. Their lives go on while she's stuck in the convent." She smiles. "This is your wedding day. Think about Marin. Come." She takes me by the hand and we weave through the crowds to Marin. Agnola twines my arm in his.

Marin lays his hand upon mine. I'm safe. After that, every time we part, I find him staring at me across the crowds with a ferocious thirst. Everything within me responds in kind.

We talk and eat and dance as in a dream. Finally we retreat to Marin's room . . . our room. I don't know if the guests have left. It doesn't matter; we are alone, husband and wife.

And now, at the worst moment possible, a headache comes. I rub in a circle between my eyes.

Marin takes my hand away and presses his fingers in exactly the right spot and rubs and rubs. He doesn't speak. I lean into Marin's touch for dear life. We fall onto the bed, fully clothed, his fingers never leaving that spot, and I realize how weary the day has left me.

With his other hand he wipes away my tears. "It's all right, Dolce. We have a lifetime ahead. Close your eyes. It will pass."

"I never told you I have headaches," I whisper.

"Shhh. Sleep now."

He pulls me toward him and my gown is crushed like a cushion between us, and his fingers keep going round and round. I close my burning eyes and yield to the pain.

When I wake, it's not yet dawn. Marin sleeps openmouthed. I untangle myself from him. He rolls onto his back and his eyes open.

We explore each other all through the glowing morning, far into the day, and then he falls back asleep.

This is my husband, here in my arms. This is his smell, his

warmth, his taste. I dig the fingers of one hand into his hair and leave them there. This is Marin. My Marin.

Every time he tells me I am beautiful, I don't want it to matter, but it does. It helps me. He bought me that mirror he said he would—his wedding gift to me. It leans against the wall in this room. This morning he had me look in it. He made me believe I am good to look upon; I am beautiful.

And I am strong. I know I can fight my way. He is a thousand times more fragile than I will ever be. He has loved and lost—death robbed him. He hesitates to hope.

But with me, he is ardent. Overcome. Out of control. I do that to him. I make Marin happy. I do that to someone. We are not alone, each in a private darkness. Marin and I are together. I change him. I make him happy.

I wake him again with a kiss.

Part III

BARREN

CHAPTER 17

Fire

The stickiness on my thighs wakes me. I rise from the bed.

Marin catches my hand. "Stay."

I look down at his innocent face. "Don't roll over. The sheet may be wet. I'll tell Lucia La Rotonda to scrub well."

He sits up. "Again?" He pulls me toward him.

I yank my hand away.

"Where are you going?"

"Shhh. Go back to sleep."

I leave and hurry down the stairs. He won't follow me. Men leave women alone when they are menstruating. Besides, we've had this conversation over and over for three years. I can't bear it. Better to distract myself . . . and I have just the chore to do it.

Blood rolls down the insides of my legs. I have the same sensation down the center of my back. That's not my monthly pains. That's anticipation of what's to come. I'll get sick from making mirrors. I always do. I'll feel like creatures are crawling all over me.

But that's tomorrow. Or the day after. It will last a week, at most two. It seems to be lengthening out, that mirror malady, taking longer to recover from.

In any case, right now I'm strong. It's been three months since I last came down to my little workshop.

I heave open the heavy storeroom door, let it fall shut, feel my way past the wine casks. My fingers press along the edge where floor meets wall to find the tinderbox. I wrest off the top and spread the linen char cloth on the floor. Now the flints. *Smack.* A spark catches the char cloth, just like that.

So many things happen just like that. But they don't happen to me. Marin and I have been married three and a half years. Where, oh, where is our babe? I cover my face with my hands.

And my thigh burns. This damnable anticipation of pain. Ai!

Good Lord, my shift is afire! I flatten myself on the floor and rock side to side till the flame is out. My leg hurts. It's what I deserve, though. It feels right to sear like this. I clench my teeth against the pain.

In all the rocking about, I extinguished not just my shift but the char cloth, too. I start over. *Smack.* An instant flame. I lift the char cloth by a dry corner and stand. The candle sits in an iron sconce on the wall. Our servant Carlo secured it there for me years ago. Carlo does anything I ask without question. I like that.

The candle lets off a gentle glow. I slap the char cloth against the wall to kill the fire. Then I crush the cloth back into the tinderbox, with the flints, and push it to the edge of the room. I set up everything and make my mirror.

I have made many mirrors since I came to Venezia. Signora Laura was well worth it. Bianca is close with her daughters. Agnola and I are invited to all the ladies' parties at her palace. She kept her word, though she never forgave me for not accepting the gift of Zitta.

Zitta was undoubtedly sold at a high price. But not to anyone inside the Republic, or I'd have heard. No, she's gone.

The second mirror I made was for my beloved Agnola. She wanted a tiny mirror, like Signora Laura's, to hang at her waist and walk around with wealth sparkling off her, hushing others who might want to make unkind remarks about her size and shape. They can say things not quite out of earshot, so that you know they're gossiping, but you can't scold them.

I don't have friends among the ladies of Venezia. I have only family: Agnola, Bianca, Marin. Some noblewomen are kind to me, though, like Franca.

I feel tired when I think of Zitta. I did exactly the wrong thing. But I've been doing the right thing since. I can't do anything about the dwarfs who are servants; they live their lives as they choose. But I know of every dwarf slave in Venezia. I am buying their freedom with mirrors. I've made many. The noble ladies of Venezia now curry my favor, yearn to be the next to receive my special gift.

No law has yet been passed saying a child belongs to the nobility only if both father and mother are of noble families. But it's coming. If I'm lucky, our babe will arrive before then. If not, the ladies with my mirrors will convince their husbands that I am noble. I count on that.

I give mirrors only to those noblewomen who have dwarf slaves. I offer a mirror in return for two things: the freedom of their dwarf and their utter silence about our conversation. The silence was not my idea. It came from my conversation with Agnola on my wedding day—when she said that if I gave mirrors to those who treated me the worst, others would figure it out, that they'd be encouraged to treat me badly. If the recipients of my mirrors told people I was giving them to those who had dwarf slaves, others would buy dwarf slaves. So I worked out a plan: they free their dwarf, with enough of a stipend that the former slave can begin life anew somewhere, and if anyone asks why, they find an explanation that will neither expose me nor cast aspersions on dwarfs. Then, many months later, at an event we agree upon together, I give them a mirror.

I cannot free Zitta, I cannot make up for whatever happened to my mamma in her youth, but I am doing the best I can. Sometimes I feel Mamma's spirit watching me. And she's proud of me. I'm her beautiful daughter, body and soul.

No one has yet seen a pattern in my gift giving. Not even Agnola.

I don't meet the dwarfs. I don't want to. Seeing Zitta shook me to the core. She didn't trust me. Why should any dwarf trust any tall person in this town? My past is past.

I finish making the little mirror and set the broken base of the planter pot on top of it. This one is for Iole Venier. Her dwarf left more than a half year ago.

I wipe my hands on my ruined shift and blow out the candle.

I limp into the kitchen.

Lucia La Rotonda takes me in with a gasp and rushes to help me up the stairs and into Agnola's room. Soon I'm submerged in water.

I love this tub. I squat with my arms over the sides and rest my head against the high back and fall into a half sleep.

Agnola and Bianca sit on the bed nearby and talk of their plans for the day. Sewing. Music. Watching the world from the balcony. It's tiring, this life of doing nothing. It exhausts all the women of Venezia.

Maybe I wouldn't even have the energy for a baby if it came.

Besides, Bianca is sturdy. At age eleven, she still practically skips from room to room. I'm used to this invincible girl who enters into conversation with the wit of an adult. What would I do with a newborn, a tiny mystery?

I rise and dry off carefully, wrap white cloth around the blistered burn, and dress. "Shall we invade Lucia La Rotonda's realm today?"

Agnola and Bianca have been discreetly ignoring me. Now Agnola tilts her head. "She does make rather tiresome meals during Lent."

"Franca gave me a nice recipe," I say. "What do you think?"

Bianca jumps to her feet.

And so we march down to the kitchen and give Lucia La Rotonda an unexpected holiday. I send Carlo to buy *merluzzo* and oysters.

"Oysters?" Agnola perks up.

"Enough for four guests," I say. I send Antonin to the Crispo palace to invite Franca and her husband, and our friends at the Giustiniani palace as well.

Agnola, Bianca, and I stand side by side and chop onions and parsley, beat eggs, grate ginger, soak raisins, then strain the soggy pulp. The golden sauce that will go over the baked fish will be cooked at the last minute so the aroma will remind everyone of the word Signora Laura persists in using for me: *exotic*. Ha! Exotic? I'm a peasant from Torcello. But only Marin knows.

Agnola and Bianca make the oyster cake, working so sweetly together, like Mamma and I used to do. We finish and go upstairs. I look at myself in my wedding mirror. I look like Mamma's daughter, that girl Marin married. But maturity has ripened me. In this mirror I can see what he sees. As the day progresses, I pass by the mirror again and again, glance sideways, look over my shoulder to catch my departing image, sneak up on the unsuspecting crystal. Every time, I am still me.

Marin is nestled within his library. Since spring has come, he's begun traveling again. Every year he travels intermittently, from the start of spring till the end of autumn, collecting books. I hope he's happy.

I'm standing on the balcony, waiting to catch a glimpse of our guests when I hear Marin come up behind me. He kisses the back of my neck. I smile and turn to face him, my burned leg pressing against his by accident. I yelp and pull away.

"What happened?"

I touch his cheek. "Do you want a child?"

"I have a child."

"I've heard the men tell you that they feel sorry for you, that our luck will turn. But it never does."

"We have each other. We have Bianca. I'd say the good Lord is treating us as well as anyone might dare hope."

Our eyes meet. His are wary.

I take his hand and kiss it.

"I missed you all day today," he says.

"But surely you were in the library learning something wonderful."

He smiles. "I was, in fact. I read about surgeries on eyes by Galen, that physician of ancient times. He removed cataracts with a long needle." Marin talks on and on.

I nod when I should. I try to follow what he says. He is a smart man, he absorbs knowledge easily.

This day began badly. But I changed it; I made it good, and I'm behaving well. *Please, don't let me make it end badly.* When Marin is finally done with his description, I turn and look out over the Canal Grande.

CHAPTER 18

The Lord

The next afternoon, Bianca is at the Contarini palace; Marin, in his library. Agnola and I are in the gondola, going to the Crispo palace, to see Franca. I listen to the regular dip, then the drip of water, then the dip, as Antonin circles the oar in the curve of the wood pedestal that holds it—the *forcula*. The sound usually mesmerizes me, like some sort of wordless song. Now, though, it adds to my restlessness.

The wind is sharp and the water of the canal rocks us hard. My hand gets splashed. Cold. Spring seems to have turned her back for one more glance at winter. I want to slap her. Hard. Sometimes I long for the old days on Torcello, to be alone, for the chance to scream without anyone hearing.

Screams fill my head.

Soon we are inside Franca's palace. I realize she and Agnola are talking, and we're sitting on a bench on their balcony, despite the chill. How we got up here, what everyone has been saying, I can't recall. One moment I was in the gondola, the next moment I am here. I must wake up.

"Franca," I say softly.

She looks at me. "So you are alive." She smiles and her fingers play along the delicate chains of gold at her neck. Her eyes are attentive. "You were quiet at supper last night, too. What have you been thinking about, Dolce?"

"I'm bleeding."

Franca purses her lips. "I'm sorry."

"I hate this."

"Agnola?" Franca's voice is light. "We're going to talk frankly of . . . married matters. Would you rather go inside?"

Agnola stiffens, but she maintains a smile. "Not at all. I'm interested."

All the little humiliations she suffers. I'd like to smack Franca, though Franca is by far the kindest of the lot. I must control myself.

Franca looks inquiringly at me.

"Go ahead." I keep my voice soft. "Speak frankly."

"We're lucky," says Franca. "You and I are very lucky. Our marriages have been consummated."

I nod.

"It's a blessing. Some men . . . cannot . . ." She glances sideways at Agnola, who blinks at her. Franca turns back to me. "I hear that Fiorenza has called in a healer for her husband, Marco."

"What can a healer do?" asks Agnola.

"Marco had to urinate through the wedding ring he gave Fiorenza."

"That's absurd," says Agnola.

"Now he's sleeping with the blade of a plow under his mattress."

"Ridiculous," says Agnola.

"What would you know about it?"

Agnola clamps her mouth shut.

I will myself to stay quiet. Franca is a friend.

Franca's cheeks color. "Signorina Agnola, I shouldn't have snapped at you," she says. "Probably you're right. Nothing has changed. Fiorenza wants the marriage declared invalid."

Agnola folds her hands in her lap. "She'd have been better off to stay unmarried."

"No." Franca shakes her head. "It's best to take a chance on marriage."

"You say that because your husband is kind to you. But wedding nights can be . . . Vittoria . . . well, her father said he'd slit her throat if she didn't marry Giovanni. He needed the family bond, for some plan he has. He needed it more than he loved Vittoria. By the second week of marriage she had sewn her nightgown together so Giovanni couldn't get at her." Agnola shakes her head. "I'm better off unmarried."

"No you're not," says Franca. "You'll never have children."

"Will you?"

Franca's bottom lip quivers.

"I'm sorry." Agnola touches Franca's shoulder. "It was unkind of me to say that. I don't know what came over me. Sometimes I'm thoughtless. I'm so sorry."

"You were right to say it, Agnola," I say calmly. "You are never thoughtless. You are clearheaded. Franca and I may never have children. And you almost assuredly will not." I rub my own head, which now pounds, and lean toward both of them. "We have so little control over our lives."

Franca pulls on her fingers. "If I don't produce a child, Sergio may find a courtesan and set up a second household."

"Has he said that?" asks Agnola, a look of horror on her face.

"He doesn't have to. It's what happens. Men need sons."

The idea of Marin in another woman's bed . . . I hug myself. "Marin says he doesn't care."

"He does," says Franca. "He must."

"I don't think he cares." Agnola takes my hand, holds it warm between hers. My pink fingers stand out in stark contrast against her white ones. I must have taken off my gloves when we came inside. I can't fathom why. "I don't think he cares at all," says Agnola, a little louder.

"Why wouldn't he?" says Franca.

"He has Bianca already. No one needs more than one child."

"Bianca's a girl."

"So what?"

"If a man has only one child, he wants it to be a boy. The Lord may decide to give only one child, but if He does, He should be fair and bestow a son."

"Listen to yourself," says Agnola. "If you were your parents' only child, would you feel sorry for them?"

"Of course I would. And I feel sorry for Marin, as sorry as I do for Sergio."

"Marin is happy with Bianca," says Agnola.

"Every other man in this city wants a son, an heir. Marin would trade Bianca for a boy any day. If he says different, he lies."

"My brother doesn't lie." Agnola squeezes my fingers. "Besides, he looks on childbirth with open eyes. His first wife died. Lots of women die. He doesn't want to lose Dolce. She means more to him than anything. I'll bet he feels relief each month."

"Sex when you don't want children to result . . . that's a sin. As bad as what homosexuals do. Those special police—the

Signori di Notte—they punish men for that." Franca presses her fists together. "Decapitation. Then they burn the body. Besides, it's disloyal to the Republic not to want to have children. It's everyone's duty."

"Every married person's duty, you mean," says Agnola.

"Stop," I say. I cough and cough, stumble inside, collapse in the hall in a heap of coughs. Finally they cease.

Someone pats my forehead with a wet cloth. It's Costantina, Franca's servant. My head and shoulders now rest in Agnola's lap. She has joined me on the floor.

Franca bends over me. "You're ill."

Such attention from women. "So what happens to us?"

"Us?" Franca looks alarmed. "I'm not ill."

"If it's a married woman's duty to have children, what happens to us?"

Franca looks stricken. Why is it people are shocked when you say what's on everyone's mind? "Without children, I am nothing," says Franca.

Ah, that's why—it gives them license to say the worst. I wish I could suck back my words. "That's not true. You will find a way to keep Sergio's interest."

"You can say that because you're beautiful. But even a beauty like you worries. Look at your pink fingers."

"What?"

"You dyed them. To be special, of course. You do odd things, say odd things, and I know you do it so that Marin will think he can never predict what you'll do. You maintain the mystique we all have before marriage, but almost none of us have after."

I hold my hands up to the light. "My pink fingers are part of my illness."

"Really?"

I put my hands together as if in prayer and nod.

"I'm sorry. I had no idea, Dolce."

"We better get going." Agnola strokes my cheek. "I want to put you to bed. Lucia La Rotonda can make you a nice broth."

Broth won't put a child inside me. Maybe nothing will. Maybe Franca and I are both doomed.

Once at our palace, Agnola accompanies me to my room.

Marin is stretched out on the bed. His look speaks of the exhaustion I feel.

Agnola clutches my hand a moment, then lets go. "Excuse me." She leaves and closes the door behind her.

Marin swings his legs over the side of the bed and sits. He looks at his knees. "You made a mirror again, didn't you?"

I take a step backward and steady myself against the closed door.

"The answer shows all over you. Why?" He rubs his chin. "We agreed that you wouldn't, Dolce. It makes you sick."

"Someone needs a mirror."

He scratches his chin. "Who?"

I look away.

"Whoever it is, after this you'll find someone else to give a mirror to. Some other potential enemy. You want those women to be beholden to you for the extravagance of a mirror."

He doesn't know the true design of my gift giving any more than anyone else does. If he did, he'd say that a much cheaper way to do things is to buy the slaves' freedom outright. But then it's Marin's money that's doing the job. I need to have a part. "You said you didn't care how much I spend."

"I don't. I have no heir, and Bianca's sons will inherit from their father. You can spend all you want."

"No heir . . ."

"It's a fact, Dolce, not a complaint. Money's not the point. You're trying to stupefy everyone."

"Stupefy? The mirrors I make are tiny."

"They're still costly. That awe that you manage to create—it's become a fetish." He drops his hand from his chin. "Making mirrors is a plague. It sickens you, body and soul."

"Only for a little while," I whisper.

"It seems like a long while. Last night you turned from me."

I have to fight to keep my hand from going to my throbbing forehead. "A woman is allowed to refuse her husband at these times of the month."

"Dolce, your head will ache. Your eyes will blur. You will have flashes of ill humor. I can't bear it."

"Franca says every man wants a son."

"I am not every man, Dolce."

"Franca says the Lord may decide to give only one child, but if He does, He should be fair and give a son."

"Franca may be an idiot."

"You really don't care if you have a son?"

"No."

"But you said Bianca will have sons. You didn't say daughters."

"Because I was talking about money. Inheritance passes to the oldest son."

"Maybe you don't know yourself, Marin. Maybe you want a son so bad, your teeth crack. Sometimes at night I listen to you grind them." *Maybe you'll kill me if I don't produce a son.*

Marin's mouth opens but nothing comes out. Good Lord, he looks as though I actually said the words in my head. He gets to his feet, opens his wardrobe, and spreads clothes out on the bed.

He folds them precisely, edge to edge. He moves in some unreal place and time. Floating.

He drops a comb. It hits the floor with a *thunk*. This is real.

A little cry bursts from me. "Where to this time?" I ask.

"There's always a next place." He looks up at me. "Like you with your mirrors."

"Don't go."

He smooths a jacket and tucks it into the small wooden chest he uses for traveling. He picks up the comb and runs his thumb along the teeth.

"Please, Marin."

He shakes his head, slow and heavy. "Do you realize how much your words wound me?"

"My headaches . . . I can't stop my mouth."

"I don't ask that you stop your mouth. I want you to tell me your thoughts. I just want the awful ones to end."

I stagger to the bed and sit beside his growing mound of folded clothes. "I'll try. I will. I promise."

He reaches for a shirt.

I put my hand on the pile. "You should stay."

"We need time apart."

"I hate it when you're gone. There's nothing to do."

"Do what other women do."

"That's the same as telling me to do nothing. Women of my position . . . I've never walked the alleys even closest to our palace."

"The alleys you so long to walk reek with garbage and sewage, until the street cleaners come along each day. There are beggars. Pickpockets. The wheels on carts make a tremendous racket in stone alleys. Hawkers follow you. You would hate it."

"I'd love to see it all, to hear it and smell it and, oh, to taste the food. I get tired of our fancy food."

"Listen to yourself, Dolce. You chose to enter this life." His eyes shine—tears. "Do you regret your choice?"

"No! No, I do not."

"I hope that's true, Dolce. While I'm gone, make no mirrors. Get well. Greet me when I come home. I want my wife back, my beautiful, sweet, plain-talking wife."

CHAPTER 19

Windows

"Glass," I repeat as I walk across the front of the grand hall. "I want glass in every window." I stop and look back at Antonin.

His mouth twists. "I can get workers to start tomorrow on the facade that faces the Canal Grande."

"Front and rear."

"But, Signora"—he spreads his hands—"glass costs. . . . Everyone else still has oiled paper on the rear windows."

"Do you have to fight me, Antonin?"

"Of course not, Signora. I just wonder if we should wait until . . ."

"Until Marin comes home? He left yesterday. There's no telling how long he'll be gone. And there's no reason to wait."

"Can I help?" Agnola comes out of the sewing room with Bianca.

I knew I was speaking too loudly. "Oiled paper on the windows is ugly," I say. "Don't you agree?"

Agnola looks from me to Antonin. Her eyes plead for him to explain.

"I agree," says Bianca.

I look right at Agnola. "Not many palaces on the Canal Grande still have oiled paper."

Agnola nods slowly. "That's true."

"So," I say, "glass, all around."

"No one sees the rear," says Antonin to Agnola.

"No one sees the rear," says Agnola to me.

From somewhere deep inside me comes a flame. I cannot see, I cannot talk. I put up a hand in the halt gesture until vision returns. Then I run down the stairs to the kitchen.

Lucia La Rotonda looks at me in surprise.

I scan the counter. There's the knife. My fingers close around the hilt so that the blade points down. I race back up the stairs.

Agnola and Antonin and Bianca look at the knife, dumbfounded. Why can't they understand what I have to do?

I jab at the oiled paper on a long window. The knife's tip bounces off the tough surface, but I'm pressing so hard that my hand keeps going forward, slipping along the hilt onto the blade. It cuts deep into my hand between thumb and fingers. Blood spurts. I transfer the knife to my other hand and jab at the paper. It cracks into sharp, stiff fragments that fall to the floor. I jab at the next window, and the next.

The room is filled with screams.

Someone has grabbed me from behind. Someone else tugs on my wrist with both hands.

"Stop, Mamma." Bianca's eyes are huge.

What have I done?

I uncurl my fingers and let Bianca take the knife away. I go limp.

Agnola puts her hand on my forehead and presses me against her. "It's all right, Dolce. It's going to be all right."

We sit weakly on the big chest-bench. Agnola sniffles as she wraps my hand in the white linen that Lucia La Rotonda holds out. Each loop reddens before she can wind the next in place. Finally, the cloth stays white. Agnola holds my bandaged hand, still crying.

They need words. *Please, come to me, words.* "Glass lets us see out," I say.

"Yes, it does." Agnola nods at me.

I nod back. "Sometimes I feel smothered. Do you under-stand?"

Agnola keeps nodding.

"For women locked away inside, glass is the only access to the world."

"We have balconies," says Bianca. She sits on the floor with her arms wrapped around my legs. Her chin rests on my knees.

"Only when the weather is good. Why should we be prisoners of the weather?"

"Why should we be prisoners of anything?" says Bianca.

"Exactly. I miss the outdoors."

"But you didn't have to grab a knife," says Bianca quietly. "You didn't have to keep stabbing the windows when you cut your hand."

"I wanted people to know . . . how much glass matters."

"You scared us." Bianca bites her bottom lip.

"Maybe for a moment . . . I wasn't thinking straight."

No one speaks.

"I want glass windows," I say.

"You shall have them, Signora," says Antonin. His face is ghastly pale.

Lucia La Rotonda looks horrified.

They must think I've gone mad. Have I? The bodice of my

dress is blood-spattered, but my hand doesn't hurt. I'm not sure I'm here in this body.

Bianca looks at me with a need sharper than any blade. Agnola cries.

Still, I press on. It has to be done right. "I want crystalline glass on the facade side. The whitest kind, made with kali."

"Kali?" says Antonin, in a mollifying voice. "Signora, I don't recognize the word."

"It's an herb from Egypt. It bleaches the glass. It makes it perfectly clear. It makes it the best."

"You will have the best glass," says Antonin. "With kali."

"I want glass in the rear, too. But you can choose what kind."

Antonin pulls his head back. "It's not my position to choose, Signora."

I look at him hard. But he's sincere. I've tormented all of them. I am awash with shame. "For the rear, blue-green glass," I say. "It costs far less."

"Of course, Signora."

"This whole floor will light up. Imagine it." I look from Agnola to Bianca. "Sun sparkling everywhere. You want that, too, don't you?"

Bianca nods.

"Ah! Let's replace this big, old dark furniture with glass! We can be the crystalline palace. Glass table, glass chest-bench."

"But then everyone will see our linens," says Agnola.

"We can put flowers inside the chest," says Bianca. "Bring the outside in to us."

"Perfect. You, Bianca, you can choose them from the flower monger each morning." I lift my chin to Antonin. "Have the glass chest-bench built first."

"Of course, Signora."

I look at Lucia La Rotonda, and hear my mamma's voice in my head. "For the evening meal tonight, I'd like liver and lungs, please."

"As you wish, Signora."

"Serve dried apples for dessert," says Bianca.

"Yes, little Signorina."

I gently move Bianca off to the side and stand. "My apologies to you all. It will not happen again. And now I'm going to lie down."

"Can I sleep with you?" asks Bianca. "I need you, Mamma."

She's not afraid of me. Good Lord, she's afraid for me, but not of me. How lucky I am. I nod. Then I nod to Agnola. The three of us go into my room and lie with me in the middle. Bianca twines her arm around mine and interlaces her fingers with mine. She is the first to fall asleep; her breathing tells me.

Agnola presses against me, shoulder to hip. Her breathing also is regular, but there's an alertness to it.

"I don't entirely know what happened to me," I whisper.

"Nor do I," Agnola whispers back.

"It's as though something else was in charge."

"Don't say that to anyone, Dolce. Rumor will spread that you're possessed."

"Maybe I am."

"I pray not, Dolce. People lose their temper. Sometimes with justification. You are right that transparent glass will expand our world. Maybe it was simply a tantrum born of frustration. Something understandable. Let us both pray that's what happened."

"I don't know if I am any good at praying. The Lord seems to give whatever He has in mind."

Agnola kisses my cheek. "Women can live without having babies, Dolce."

"Can men?"

"Marin has Bianca."

Agnola finally falls asleep, but I can't.

I didn't lose my temper today. I lost myself.

Part IV

MAMMA

CHAPTER 20

Women

I walk the long grand hall feeling weightless, singing to myself. I like this time of year, when the mornings and evenings are cool but the middle of the day yields to the sun. Everything feels good this morning; everything pats my cheeks lovingly. Today will warm like ripe fruit. I'm headed for the music room, where Bianca plays the harp most mornings. She plays like an angel, like the angel she is, a princess angel. I remember Mamma saying harps sound like angels singing. My smile lifts my whole self so much I have the sense I could fly.

I wipe sleep from my eyes and touch my teeth. They feel the slightest bit odd, but maybe that's because I just rubbed them clean. They are pearls now. I run my hands down my arms. My skin is smooth cream. My loose hair curls teasingly around my cheeks. I am happy. I walk with confidence. Marin is not here to see me, but I pretend he watches me. I pretend I am basking in his admiration.

It took the first six years of marriage for us to reach a method of living together, but for the past year we have managed very well. He gathers his books; I don't try to stop him from traveling or from squirreling away in the library when he comes home with new books; he doesn't ask how I pass the time. When we are together, we are simply together—man and wife. We have much to rejoice in.

Crying comes from the music room. Faintly—the door is closed. I slip in.

But it is not Bianca in tears. It is Agnola who kneels on the floor in her fine dress with her back to me. Her shoulders scoop forward. Sobs rack her. I was twelve years old when I witnessed Mella's grief, but the image still cuts me. I kneel beside Agnola.

She pets the body of Ribolin on the marble floor in front of her. The little dog is contorted and stiff. He must have died in pain, hours ago. Tears spring to my eyes.

I kiss Agnola's cheek. "He lived a good, long life."

She shakes her head.

"The fur around his muzzle is gray. Look." I am whispering. "Look, Agnolina, little Agnola. And on the top of his head. And his chest. Gray. See the lumps and bumps on his eyelids? There are so many. He lived a long life, Agnola. Very long. And you treated him better than any mistress anywhere. He slept on pillows. He ate from bowls. It was a very good life."

She turns to me like a child. "He was mine," she says between sobs. "All mine."

Animals are like that. Children, too. We think of them as ours.

Without Bianca, I'd be a shell. Hollow. I don't know what I'd do. But even with her, I feel the lack. I know I have to be grateful for her . . . and I am, I truly am. Still, I remember Franca's words that day years ago: the Lord should have made Bianca a boy. The Lord has been unfair to Marin. And to Agnola; here is a woman who deserves everything and has nothing.

I hug her tight and kiss the top of her head so she can feel it through her thick hair dyed silly pink. "I understand." I rock her. "You can pick a spot in the courtyard. We'll dig a hole. You and me."

"And Bianca."

"We'll dig a hole and Ribolin can rest there forever. You can visit him every day." *You can talk to him like I talk to myself.*

Did I say that or just think it?

Agnola pulls away from me and stands. There are so many things about her that please the soul. She tries to see the best in everyone. She tries so hard. And she loves Bianca, which matters more than anything.

She takes a bit of cloth from inside her sleeve and wipes at her eyes. I stand and tuck a lock of hair behind her ear. "Can I fix your hair?"

Her head tilts just the slightest. "Thank you." She walks out the door into the grand hall and heads toward her room.

I catch her by the arm. "Let's use the mirror here in the hall."

"But I love my own mirrors."

"They are beautiful, your silver mirrors. And you keep them polished. But glass is more revealing."

"Which is what I don't need."

"You have your charms, Agnola."

"Only you see them."

I shake my head. "Give me a chance to bring them out. Just this once."

Agnola looks mournfully at me, but nods.

And so I set her on a stool in front of Mirror, Marin's wedding gift to me. I pull off the white silk that blinds Mirror, and I allow myself to take one deep, quenching look. This is how Marin sees me. . . . Mirror tells that truth. And, *thank you, Lord,* I am beautiful to him. Marin said it not long ago, on our seventh wedding anniversary, and Mirror repeats it now. I love to hear it inside my head. But I keep Mirror covered so I won't look in it all the time.

I comb Agnola's hair and take my time with every little knot. My hands shake, of course. But her hair welcomes me, tremors and all.

"Why are you combing Aunt Agnola's hair so gently?" Bianca walks past us, already dressed. "You have to dig down to the very bottom to bring out the shine." She opens a set of doors inward and steps out onto the little balcony. A burst of chilly air comes in. Bianca turns and leans back against the stone railing. At fourteen she's a promise of loveliness to come. She has rouged her lips blood red. She has no need to tighten the middle of her bodice, for her waist is honey dripping from a spoon. Soon it will be hard to hold off suitors.

"You better put on a hat," calls Agnola.

"I don't care what others think," says Bianca. "Papà chose a woman who had never owned a hat before. And hats really don't cover anything anyway—everyone can see whether your hair is remarkable or not. Why else would Mamma be fiddling with your hair now, anyway? Hats are a trifle. A stupid convention."

"I'm thinking of your skin, not your hair. It'll color if you're not careful. Autumn sun is still strong."

"Besides," I call, "conventions are precisely that, and not all men are as forgiving as your papà." Marin is the very definition of forgiving. *Amen to that.*

"Your skin was colored by the sun when Papà fell in love with you," Bianca mutters. But she comes inside anyway, rubbing her cheeks.

Despite her words, I know she prides herself on her white, white skin. I know keeping it white is her way of paying homage to the mamma I have replaced, the one she remembers less with each day, the one who named her after snow. I'm glad she still misses her mamma. We should all miss our dead mammas, or we lose our past. In my youth, it was only Mamma who kept me from being hopeless.

Agnola gives a little shiver. "Close the doors, would you?"

Bianca closes the doors. She comes to stand beside us and looks at our reflections in Mirror. She touches Agnola's sleeve. "You've been crying."

Agnola's lips tremble.

"Little Ribolin has died," I say. "Call Antonin, please."

"Oh." Bianca picks up Agnola's hand, kisses it, and holds it to her cheek. "I'm so sorry, Aunt Agnola. He was a good pup."

The pressure between my eyes mounts again. I must hurry as best I can and finish Agnola's hair. "Antonin needs to wrap Ribolin in cloth and carry him to the courtyard for us. A good cloth. That wool I picked out last week. Antonin knows where it is."

Bianca stares at me. "That cloth came from Firenze, at a high price," she whispers. I give her a withering look. She nods in chagrin. "A very good pup," she says to Agnola.

Agnola's crying gets louder.

I flash my eyes at Bianca and silently mouth, *Antonin.* The girl leaves at a run.

I divide Agnola's hair into six locks. I twist them and loop them and fix them into swirls with pearl-tipped pins. So long as my hands move slowly, they are competent. Life in Venezia has taught me well when it comes to styling hair. I can give this gift to Agnola, insignificant as it is.

Agnola watches in Mirror. She will never turn heads, but she looks fine. Her eyes show she knows it. We exchange smiles in Mirror, though hers is still watery. The naked gratitude there catches me off guard. Perhaps this is not such a small gift.

At times like this I feel almost ordinary, almost like everyone else. I press my forehead. *Go away, pain.*

CHAPTER 21

Burial

I lay down the shovel and rest on the lip of one of the enormous urns, my breath short. I used to think that the way the Mocenigo family boasts about their garden was pure silliness. How could it have taken me so long to realize a garden in Venezia is special? It's a labor of love. When I see the Mocenigo mamma and girls, I will praise their garden lavishly. Let us each be proud of something. After all, none of them is anywhere near as fair as me. Marin tells me that because he thinks I need to hear it. But Mirror tells me that, too—Mirror tells me what Marin most believes.

Agnola took up the shovel after I dropped it, and now she stumbles over and rests beside me.

We watch Bianca dig. The girl is hardworking, and strong, for the hole grows deeper. I was once that strong.

All the while Antonin scratches his head and paces. I should have called on Carlo for assistance; he's the one who does this sort of physical labor. But Antonin's name popped into my mouth. Too bad. He feels pressure from Marin to watch out for me while Marin travels. "Don't worry, Antonin. Messer Marin will not fault you. We will tell him we insisted on digging it ourselves. He knows how strongly we can insist."

Antonin bows with a nervous smile. But I haven't said anything crazy. Have I? His eyes shouldn't twitch like that.

We place the wrapped body of Ribolin in the grave, the three of us, working together. He looks tucked away for the night. The eternal night.

"He was a good companion," says Agnola. She looks at me meaningfully.

"And a quiet, peaceful thinker," I say. I look at Bianca.

"And he didn't stink like some dogs do," says Bianca.

"Silent prayer now," commands Agnola.

I pray for . . . what? Dogs have no soul. That's what the church teaches. So I pray for Marin, for his safety and good health, for his cheer and success. And most of all, for his swift return. He's traveling in the north country, beyond the mountains, where they speak German on the streets. Marin can manage some German, and once he arrives at a monastery, he'll be fine, because everyone there speaks Latin.

A library is important; a library is a cornerstone of civilization. This is his duty to self and to the Republic.

That's what he says, at least.

He travels more than most husbands, and for longer periods. And when he's home, he asks Bianca to help him in the library more than he asks me.

So I know I am losing him.

I shake my head hard. I will not torture myself with that fear.

Bianca puts her arms around me. "Are you all right?"

"Yes."

"Antonin," she says, "would you cover him up now?"

"Of course," Antonin replies.

And so Ribolin disappears. Antonin levels the earth; then he and Bianca go inside. Agnola and I stay.

"Shall we sing?" I ask at last.

Agnola smiles and begins. We sing the songs she has taught me. When I first came, I tried to teach her a song of Mamma's. She told me that song was beneath my station in life now.

When we finish, we sit in silence.

We stay there for who knows how long, when a vision appears before me. Is it me, in my youth? I hallucinate these days. I blink.

It is Bianca. Of course. I knew that. "Aunt Agnola, you have a visitor."

"I do?" Agnola tries to look past her, but Bianca moves to block her view.

"I wouldn't let him step out of the gondola yet, because . . ." Bianca looks me up and down.

What? Oh, I'm still in my shift! "I'll get dressed immediately. Then I'll greet your guest, Agnola."

"Aunt Agnola can greet him herself. Let me help you dress, Mamma."

"I don't need help. But what I would love is to hear that harp. Please. And go tell Lucia La Rotonda to prepare liver and lungs."

"You and your liver and lungs."

"They help, Bianca. They can fix anything. They can soothe Agnola's broken heart. My mamma—"

"Taught you. I know, I know. Liver and lungs are to you what apples are to me." Bianca goes off to find Lucia La Rotonda.

I go up the rear staircase, pick out my clothes, and spread them on the bed. A visitor. Marin likes us to look fine when visitors come. I put on the pearls he bought me in Murano seven years ago. They are still my favorite gift from him. Well, besides Mirror, of course.

I think about bringing down jewelry for Agnola. But the visitor has undoubtedly entered already. I should have suggested jewelry in the first place. I should have made everyone delay until I had ornamented Agnola properly, with rings and bracelets.

Finally I hear the harp. Good. Bianca is at the other end of the palace.

She cannot see what I do.

What I do is stand at the rear window and look down into the courtyard. The many small, uneven squares of blue-green glass distort my view, and the lead that binds the glass together cuts that view into so many pieces.

But I can still see enough. The man in the courtyard with Agnola is a dwarf. My hand goes to my throat, though the burst of emotion that hits me every time I see a dwarf in a passing gondola is much less powerful now. I no longer expect to happen upon Venerio or Francesco or a grown-up version of Bini or Tonso or Tommaso. None of them ever come to Venezia; they go only to Murano. And how could they recognize me after all these years, especially with me high in a balcony and them on the canal?

I think of Zitta. So far as I know, there are no more dwarf slaves in Venezia, but I have one mirror ready, just in case. I make two at the same time so that I don't have to touch the quicksilver so often. It soothes me to know one remains.

Up here, I can hear nothing from the courtyard through the glass, of course. What would they have to talk about so energetically?

The man's hands fly through the air expressively and in such a familiar way that I choke up. How I still miss Mamma. Did that man grow up among tall people or small people? Does he find us strange and funny? Are we monsters?

But he'd never show his feelings, of course. In the land of monsters, you pay homage.

Agnola listens without condescension. A rush of love for her makes me sit a moment on the bed. I rest there till my blood calms again. Agnola was raised with Marin; her mind is as open and free as his and Bianca's.

Slowly, I dress. Then I walk along the hall to the music room. Between that door and the facade windows is the long glass chest-bench. Hortensia are scattered inside it—big balls of blue flowers. Bianca picked the perfect color.

I close my eyes and listen to my angel.

CHAPTER 22

New Dog

Agnola and Bianca and I sit on a bench in the court-yard.

"Are they late?" asks Agnola. "I better check that the food is ready."

"Relax," says Bianca, getting to her feet. "Lucia La Rotonda prepares too much and then feasts on the leftovers. We all know that. Besides, this is not a meal, just a light refreshment. But I will check on her all the same." She wags a finger in Agnola's face. "Solely to soothe you, my dear, but foolish, aunt."

"I am not a fool." Agnola straightens her shoulders and watches Bianca leave.

Agnola has been twitting about all day. She's waiting to meet her new dog, which will be like her new child. "He will love you," I say.

She clasps my hands.

The noise of the gondola thumping against the loading dock makes Agnola stiffen. She twists a ring round and round her finger. Today she is decked in jewelry.

The gate opens.

"Your guest," announces Antonin.

Agnola stands. "Show him in."

In comes Pietro, and in his arms is a small brown-and-white dog. Pietro bows.

Agnola curtsies low.

It's as though they are at a ball, doing the *révérence* before a dance. Agnola introduces us. Pietro bows. I curtsy appropriately. Before I straighten, though, he's already setting the dog on the ground.

"What's his name?" asks Agnola.

"He comes to *'cane,'* as any well-trained dog should. But I left the choice of name to you."

The dog follows his nose around the courtyard. His tail wags fast, which is really quite attractive because of the long fur that puffs like feathers. His dainty pointed nose sniffs at new delights.

"Thank you. I might get to know him a bit before I settle on a name."

"Names carry weight."

"They can reveal character. Like my sister-in-law. Dolce is as sweet as her name."

"And you, Agnola, you are the angel of your name."

I'm shocked that this servant would refer to Agnola without the title of signora or at least signorina. But it's true; I live with two angels, a pink one and a white one. I have an image of wings fluttering above me.

Agnola's cheeks flush. "By bringing me this fine dog," she says low and steady, "you live up to your name, as my rock."

Goodness—her rock? "He's not fuzzy," I say.

They both look at me as though I've rudely interrupted, which is true, I suppose. I point at the dog.

"He's a spaniel," Pietro says.

"How old is he?"

"One year."

"Isn't that a little old?"

"You are used to living with a mature dog. The introduction of a small puppy into this home would be disruptive."

Agnola nods. "Pietro trains dogs for all the best ladies."

"Ah." Why didn't she tell me this? We've had weeks to discuss it. Did she purposely keep silent about Pietro?

Bianca has been standing at the foot of the stairs and watching. "Pietro is famous these days. That's why I asked him to come. I went straight to the Contarini palace after . . . I mean, once we knew we needed another dog."

A memory stirs. Someone told me Laura Contarini had a dwarf servant. A man of wages—not a slave.

"My friends train the dogs: hunting dogs, guard dogs, work dogs," says Pietro. "I make the selection of which lapdogs would suit each particular owner in Venezia.

"Hence, my choice for your most charming sister-in-law and this most elegant household. This dog is completely house-broken. He will trot down the stairs on his own and out to the courtyard. If a door is closed, he'll sit by it and whine until someone opens it for him. He won't jump up on you. If he wants your attention, he'll settle at your feet, or"—he looks at Agnola and gives a little laugh—"sometimes even right on your feet. Spaniels are good foot warmers.

"He won't bark, not this dog. He won't run underfoot, so there's no danger of tripping over him. He won't growl during a meal. He will sit, come, walk at your heels, run on command. If you throw something, he'll race after it and bring it back. But if you want him to fetch a shoe, for example, you'll have to train him to know a special word for that pair of shoes."

"Do you like him, Aunt Agnola?" says Bianca.

Agnola squats and calls, "Cane." He comes and sits in front of her, alert and quite charming. Agnola touches the side of his muzzle. The dog offers a paw. "Oh, you dear little thing." She holds his paw. Then she scoops him up and sits on the bench. "You and your friends have done a fine job training him, Pietro."

Pietro's answer is a bow. Then he stands straight and beams.

Lucia La Rotonda comes outside with a tray that holds a jug of watered-down wine, glasses, and a high pile of biscuits made with raisins and pine nuts.

"Thank you," I say to her. "I'm so grateful you made these now, even though it's not Carnevale season. My favorite sweets."

"Mine, too," says Bianca. "I love your *zaleti*." She smiles slyly at Lucia La Rotonda. "Because of your secret ingredient."

Secret ingredient? And I don't know it. I feel as though I've just lost something. "I love these sweets most because of the yellow color. It reminds me of Gato Zalo, a dear wildcat friend I had when I was a child."

"A wildcat?" Pietro looks at me with renewed interest. "Some of our dogs would tree a wildcat just as quickly as they'd tree a bear, though most hunting dogs are used for boars."

Lucia La Rotonda sets the tray on a high table. She goes to pour the wine, but Agnola hands the dog to Pietro and hurries over. "This occasion calls for something a little finer than daily wine."

Lucia La Rotonda gives a small questioning smile.

"Prosecco," says Agnola.

Lucia La Rotonda bows her head. "I'll ask Carlo to fill a jug from the cask."

"Excellent." Agnola turns to Pietro with a bright smile. "Natural effervescence."

"Just talking with you makes me effervescent," says Pietro.

I step back, agape.

But Agnola simply takes two *zaleti* and sits on the bench. "Would it be bad for the dog if I gave him a *zaleto*?"

"Nothing you do for him will ever be bad for him. But if you begin by feeding him sweets, he may quickly expect sweets. Is that what you want?"

Agnola shakes her head, which is odd since she fed sweets nonstop to Ribolin.

"Come, Bianca," I say. I hold out my hand to her. "Let's let Pietro show Agnola some of the tricks the dog knows. I want to talk with you."

Bianca looks at me blank-faced. "We're supposed to go to a gathering at the Barbaro home. We promised to pick up the Mocenigo mamma and daughters. Did you forget?"

A sudden shyness overtakes me. "I don't feel up to it."

Bianca's face changes instantly. "Are you ill again, Mamma? Should I—"

"I'll stay home with Dolce," says Agnola quickly. "You go, Bianca. Convey our regrets."

"They'll be upset." Bianca's eyes search mine. I try to radiate reassurance. "But I guess it can't be helped." She touches her lips. "I'll go get ready. See you tonight." She kisses Agnola, then me. "Feel better," she whispers in my ear. "Promise me." And she's gone.

I turn to Agnola and kiss her cheek. "I'm going to rest now." I smile politely at Pietro. "Thank you for bringing us this charming dog. Your training skills are to be commended."

He bows. "The pleasure is mine."

I go up the stairs. It feels eerily familiar. I get the awful sense I will be going up the stairs alone many times in the future, leaving behind Agnola and Pietro. The very idea would probably be unthinkable to anyone in Venezia but me.

Good.

Good for them.

I strip off my fancy dress and lie in my shift on the bed. The room darkens. Rain's coming. What a pity. Where can Agnola and Pietro go where Antonin and Carlo and Lucia La Rotonda will not interrupt them?

I put on my dress and rush downstairs. The courtyard is empty. I go through the gate into the docking area. Agnola and Pietro stand on the dock, talking. The dog is in her arms.

"Please," I say, "please come upstairs. Use the music room. Use the library. Please teach my sister-in-law how to control her new dog. Don't leave before you've done a thorough job. We count on you."

Pietro looks astonished. "Of course. Whatever you wish, Signora."

Agnola rushes up the front stairs. Pietro goes to follow her.

"Pietro," I say quietly.

He stops. "Yes, Signora?"

"I'm surprised I've never run into you at the Contarini palace."

"I make a point of leaving when I know you are coming."

"But why?"

"Signora Contarini led me to believe you wouldn't be pleased to see me."

"Signora Contarini is mistaken."

"That's good to know."

"You better hurry now."

Pietro bows and rushes up the stairs.

I stand at the bottom for a moment. Already Agnola's laughter comes from the music room. I've outwitted the rain. Good. Nature isn't always right.

CHAPTER 23

Constipation

"Constipation came back?" The physician shakes his head. "Perhaps we should try some other method." He opens his satchel.

"You were so successful with the old medicine. I tell everyone how brilliant you are."

"I appreciate your confidence in me. But quicksilver isn't easily obtained in the quantities that you use it. If I give so much to you . . ."

"My husband is returning soon." I push up a sleeve and rub my wrist. Bits of dried skin come off. I quickly pull down the sleeve. "I haven't been able to sleep. I need to be well rested, I need to be ready for my husband. He's been gone for so long."

The physician's face changes. I knew it would. Men band together about such things. He puts the flaxseed elixir back in his satchel and takes out an iron flask.

I trade him for my empty flask. "Thank you a thousand times."

"Only this last time."

"Don't be hard-hearted."

"To the contrary. Your fingers are pinker than ever. Your eyes twitch. Your skin peels. I'm afraid the quicksilver has made you worse rather than better. This is the last time."

I watch him leave from the blue-green windows at the rear of the main hall. He exits through the courtyard gate, out into the narrow alley that I glimpse for only a moment, until the gate slams shut.

Marin comes home tomorrow. The messenger promised he'd be here by the evening meal. He'll be here in time for all the festivities of the *mosto*—the fresh wines of autumn. Everyone will wear their finest. And I'll give away another tiny mirror, to Signora Dandolo. She bought a dwarf slave at the start of summer. I lost no time; the slave was gone within the week.

Last night, when I padded silently down to my workshop to fetch the last of my mirrors, I found my iron flask knocked on its side, empty. I had to search around for the plug. Perhaps the smell of the drying apples and figs drew a clumsy rat.

That can't happen again. So I hide the new, full flask under the bed. With luck and care, I shouldn't ever need another.

I settle onto the bed for a rest and rub the back of my neck. The headache that has been lurking behind my eyes now creeps through my skull. I breathe slowly to try to fend it off, but it doesn't help. I rub my forehead in a circle, I pound on it with my fist.

Now worries come. Worries often accompany my headaches.

I still have tin mirrors, but no glass. If another noble buys a dwarf slave, I'll have to talk Marin into buying glass for me again. In the end, he never denies me.

The women and girls of the Venetian nobility look dazzling at parties these days, all thanks to me. I am known as the most generous lady of Venezia. The rumor is that I have rich family elsewhere. The most I ever say is that my childhood is behind me; my family is here now. Marin is equally silent.

Silence can be so useful.

I yawn. I've done good work. I can rest now. Everything will be all right.

CHAPTER 24

Change

Marin comes up behind me, folds his arms around my waist, and rests his chin on my head. Our eyes meet in the mirror. "You don't have to look there to see how beautiful you are, Dolce. You can simply use my eyes. You are my delight, for now and ever."

We have passed the last three days making love every night and every morning. We glow; decked out sumptuously for the first night of the *mosto,* no one could make a more handsome couple.

"I missed you terribly, Marin. I always miss you when you travel. Women should be allowed to travel with their husbands."

"What's the point of railing against things we cannot change?"

"Bianca used to go with you."

"When she was small. And people told me I should leave her behind, even at seven. Besides, alone I can travel through places I'd never want to expose you to."

"Why go to such places anyway?"

"You saw the magnificent books I brought home. The new

printed books are taking over everywhere, displacing the old texts."

"As you said, learning isn't only for the rich anymore."

"Indeed. But the older illuminated books made by scribes are works of art. It's my privilege to rescue them for posterity. The University of Padova has a growing collection. I could offer these. Or maybe . . . something very different. A public library. Not just archives of the state, but information about anything, anything that happens anywhere. The poet Francesco Petrarca donated his personal library to Venezia in 1362. Others have done the same. My contribution could make the Republic decide to actually acquire books of all kinds and open reading rooms for the general public. Then one day Bianca's sons can oversee the library."

I stare. Bianca's sons? Again he talks of her sons?

"Why so bewildered? The ancient Romans did it. They had dry rooms off the public baths, where men could look over scrolls at their leisure. Venezia could be the home to that kind of library. What do you think?"

"She's fourteen."

"What?"

"Bianca. You said her sons could oversee the library. She's only fourteen."

"An outstanding beauty already. And with a good head on her shoulders. She'll soon be the most sought-after young woman in Venezia. You must be looking forward to her children as much as I am."

I was thinking about her suitors myself not long ago. But it's different when Marin says it, and the way he says it. I feel robbed. Marin is supposed to notice my beauty, not Bianca's. He should still be hoping I will bear children, not looking ahead to Bianca's. "I cannot think."

He tucks my hand in the crook of his elbow and we walk down the wide central stairs, just the two of us. Bianca and Agnola went ahead earlier. The pouch that holds my gift mirror is hidden inside my cloak. It swings against my hip.

The gondola slides through our gates onto the wide waters. Night fog sits on the canal so thick, boats are little more than shadows until they are near enough for a collision. If it weren't for the bobbing lanterns, I might not even be sure they were there. Antonin cries out, *"Premi,"* and we pass a gondola going in the opposite direction, right side to right side, with the *slip, slip, slip* sounds of the water. Antonin cries out, *"Stali,"* and we pass, left side to left side, *slip, slip, slip.*

The palace of the Bernardo family looms above us in the foggy night. We go up the grand staircase and a servant takes our cloaks.

Marin looks quickly at the pouch that hangs from my waist. How can he begrudge me this indulgence when he's been gone so long?

People are noisy with laughter and talk. The wine has already taken effect. I see the lights and the gowns and the lavish foods, but my head is abuzz. Marin greets old friends right and left. I find a side room where people are sitting and chatting, and take a seat.

The women here talk of their children. They would look down on me, if not for my tiny mirrors.

Someone's speaking to me. A girl, three or four years older than Bianca.

I speak back. She kisses me three times. It confuses me. I'm used to only two kisses. She's delightful. She probably just wants a mirror someday, but she is charming anyway.

A woman comes in. Signora Grimani. She reminds me that they have a wonderful library, that they care about rare books just as much as Marin does. Her attempts are more obvious than the girl's. She goes on and on, letting her eyes dart toward my pouch now and then. I need help.

Bianca. Where is she?

But no. Not Bianca. Not after Marin said she was an outstanding beauty. I pinch myself; a mother shouldn't be jealous of a daughter. Still, I take the signora's arm and ask her to help me find Agnola.

No sooner am I hanging on my Agnola's arm than Signora Dandolo appears. We exchange kisses, and I hand her the tiny mirror. She produces a purse for it, one side open so the mirror can show through, the other side finely embroidered. She hangs the purse from her waist and turns the mirror-side outward.

"That's a beautiful blue purse," I say.

"Blue? It's yellow. Like the purse you gave to Signora Contarini."

I reach to flip the purse over, to show her the back is blue, but someone has already noticed the new mirror. Now everyone's exclaiming, and I am pushed out of the way. After all, they know only one mirror is handed out at a time.

I go back to Agnola, and the rest of the evening passes comfortably.

We ride home in the gondola, the four of us. The oar rubs with a smooth *shhhush* in the *forcula*. The water smells of fish and urine.

"Did you enjoy yourself, Dolce?" asks Marin. He stands near the prow, while we three women sit under the canopy. He comes to sit beside me on the bench. "Every time I caught sight of you, you were pensive. I hope you're not going into one of your shy periods again."

"Dolce was fine tonight," says Agnola. "We were together. She is loved by everyone for her kindness."

Marin rubs at the sides of his mouth. "Kindness? Or do you mean . . ." He reaches inside my cloak and feels the pouch that hangs there, empty now. "Dolce, did you give—"

"We can talk later, Marin. Please. It's very late. My head is on fire."

He is contrite; his arm circles my waist and he pulls me to him. "What about you, Bianca? How was your evening?"

Bianca laughs. "Unexpectedly exciting."

"I saw you talking with the young men," says Marin. "At one point you were the only girl in that corner."

She laughs again. "Don't worry, Papà. It was not in the least flirtatious."

"Really? 'Not in the least'?" he says, mimicking her.

"You can make fun of me all you like, but I'm not a child anymore, Papà. We talked of religion, politics, and philosophy."

"How can politics and philosophy interest you?" says Agnola.

"They're all one thing, Aunt Agnola. The church runs everything."

"We are a republic, Bianca," says Marin.

"Yet we cringe at any questioning by the pope, any suggestion of an inquisition."

"Cringe? Never act silly, Bianca."

"You taught me not to be afraid of change, Papà."

"And you should not be," says Marin.

"Situations change per force," says Bianca. "People learn new things. As our knowledge grows, our behavior must adapt."

Marin nods.

"So we cannot continue to swallow everything the church says without examination first."

"Be careful, Bianca. Our souls are at risk."

"We owe it to ourselves and to each other to live the best way we see fit."

"It's God we owe it to."

"Yes. God, as well. But the church may be standing between us and God. All of its luxury—the gold and silver—reeks of corruption and decadence."

"This is what you talked about?" Marin shakes with anger. "I hope those young men were smart enough to keep their voices down. The hypocrites, talking of decadence as they feast and are waited on." Marin jumps to his feet, and the gondola lurches. "We're almost home. And Dolce's right, it's very late. We'll continue this discussion tomorrow. It's an important one. But a private one, to remain within the family. Bianca, you are not to have these discussions with others, only with me. Agnola, Dolce, you are not to mention this to anyone else. We'll talk as a family. Talking openly about such subjects is dangerous. Do you understand?"

Something momentous has happened. Marin is concerned with threats to Bianca's soul. And to her reputation. To the reputation of the family.

Those concerns trump his worries about my mirror.

So why do I still feel as though I'm twisting in the wind?

CHAPTER 25

Rights

Marin folds a pair of breeches into his traveling bag and closes it.

I sit on the bed and watch him. "I don't want you to go."

"I thought we had a truce."

"A truce? Like in a war?"

"No, not a war. Just one of the many battles that happen in a marriage. You're not supposed to hinder me in whatever I do to build my library, Dolce. You know that."

I nod, for it's true. "This is different, though, Marin. I feel strange. I need you by me now."

"Winter is about to set in, Dolce. There are mountains to cross between here and Moscow. Many mountains. If I don't go now, I won't be able to travel till late spring."

"If you do go now, you won't be able to return till late spring."

"But I'll return with treasures."

"Six weeks ago, you said you'd stay home a long time."

"News came. Things changed."

"No. You're leaving because you're fed up with arguing with Bianca all the time. You're throwing your hands up. Like you used to do with me."

"That's not true. I've tried to tell you. Oh, Dolce, if you'd only let me explain." Marin sits beside me and takes my hands. "They are selling off some of the books that belonged to the last Byzantine emperor. Amazing works, in Hebrew, Arabic, Greek, Latin, Egyptian."

I shake my head. "Why would anyone sell them to strangers?"

"People want to make room for new possessions—printed books. Fools. These books are made by hand. Scholars from all over the world will rush to Moscow. But they won't brave a Russian winter. They'll wait till spring, and I'll already have bought the best works by then. See?"

"No."

"Because you don't want to."

"Because I'm afraid, Marin."

"Afraid of what? I'm a cautious traveler. Agnola will be beside you. And you have Carlo and Antonin and Lucia La Rotonda. Life will go on just as if I were here."

"It's not others I'm afraid of."

"What do you mean?"

"My dreams plague me."

"I've told you, Dolce, dreams are dreams."

"They've been worse lately. Unspeakable."

"Dreams aren't real no matter how vivid."

"Tell me . . ."

"Tell you what?"

"Look at me. What do you see? Can you see the illness within me?" I extend my hands. "Can you see the tremors?" I pick at the back of one hand. "Do you see how my skin flakes?"

"It's your own doing, Dolce. The physician—"

"Don't mention him!"

Marin stands. He rubs the sides of his mouth. "You're taking Bianca to the convent at San Zaccaria this week. Teresa will help her. You like Teresa."

I watch his lips move, trying to follow his words, concentrating my hardest. I hear nothing new. But there has to be something new in there. I search for the message.

"Go with Bianca."

"Of course."

"No, I mean stay there with her. She needs the seclusion, the sanctuary. She needs to think and reconnect with her faith. She needs the comfort of her aunt Teresa, who is completely absorbed in the work of the church."

"Completely absorbed? Do you even listen when Teresa talks? She misses high society."

"She only shows interest to be kind. Her work is the Lord's."

"Do you think that's how nuns are? Franca told me nearly half of all noble girls are forced into convents now."

"Nonsense."

"There are thirty-one convents, Marin. They can't all be full of the faithful."

"My sister is faithful. Bianca needs her help. But she needs you, too. You're her mother in every sense that matters. And you could use that opportunity yourself, Dolce."

I draw back. "No I couldn't."

"Listen to yourself. You talk about dreams plaguing you. You have hallucinations of talking mirrors."

"They're not hallucinations."

"Call them whatever you will, you're sick. You said it yourself. It's from those infernal mirrors you make."

"Truce, Marin. Remember?"

Marin presses his fist against his mouth for a moment. "Go with Bianca. Give the sisters a chance to help you—especially my Teresa. Give the Lord a chance to help you." He steps toward me.

I turn my head away.

"No kiss? We've never parted without a kiss."

"This is a mistake, Marin."

"Only if you make it one."

"I won't be able to help it. Voices come. . . . They terrify me. Do you know, the morning sun comes up the same color as the sky?"

"What on earth do you mean?"

"I can't distinguish blue from yellow. It just happened. Red and green are merging too. It makes it hard for me—colors play such a part in seeing beauty. Do you think it's retribution?"

"For what?"

"My bad thoughts. Do you think I should keep my color blindness secret?"

"I don't know what you're talking about." Marin hesitates, then shakes his head in frustration. "Go to the convent." He picks up his bag and walks out.

I don't listen at the top of the stairs. I don't rush to the front window to watch Antonin row him away to the mainland.

I walk slowly out of our room. I don't know why I glance at Mirror, but I do. And Mirror is uncovered. I didn't leave it like that. And Agnola loves her silver mirror. So it was Bianca who gazed at herself in my mirror. The feeling of being robbed makes me clench my teeth.

I study my image in Mirror. It is as though Marin stands at my shoulder and speaks. We are reflected in the mirror cheek to cheek. I focus on my reflection in the eyes of his reflection. His lips move. I try to hear them say I am beautiful, the fairest of them all.

That's what Mirror's voice always says; it mimics Marin's . . . because Marin knows the true me. Like Mamma did.

But it's silent now.

Well, Mirror's voice isn't real, Marin told me that. It's an illusion.

Marin has the real voice. Marin, the one who will be gone till spring. And when he finally returns, everything will have changed, bloomed, just enough to destroy me. I won't see beauty anymore, but he will. I'll hear his words; he'll say the fairest of them all is . . . Bianca.

I'm shaking.

Marin has left and no one here knows me. Not all of me.

Maybe even Marin doesn't know me. I can't tell him what I do with the mirrors, so he can't know me. He can't be proud of me. All he sees are my faults, which multiply every day. If he knew my dreams . . . the voices . . . And he wants me to give the Lord a chance? Doesn't he know I need it to go the other way around?

I put my hands on top of my head, and sink to my knees, and cry.

"What is it?" Bianca puts her arms around me and lowers her face to mine. "Tell me."

"Some troubles are unspeakable," I mutter.

"Not when you love someone. I love you."

"I know you do." I lean into her. If I let her know me truly, can she help me fend off the voices? She must. For both our sakes. I have to start at the beginning. "Mothers and daughters, we do things to stay together. Drastic things. We give up so much."

"Like what? What are you talking about?"

"I knew a mother who had a healthy, beautiful daughter. But the daughter didn't look like anyone else who lived near their home. Not even like her mother. She looked like people far away. Everyone around her considered her ugly. They gave up babies that looked like her." I sit back on my heels and face Bianca fully. I've wanted to tell her, but it never seemed like the right time. Relief loosens my tongue. "This mother, though, she loved her daughter fiercely; she wouldn't give her up. So the daughter grew up thinking she was hideous." I put my hands on Bianca's cheeks.

She gives a small smile and takes my hands in hers. "Why didn't the mother tell her about the others far away?"

"What?"

"The ones like her. Then the girl wouldn't have suffered."

"Of course she would have suffered, Bianca. Everyone said she was a monster."

"But she would have known she wasn't."

That is too simple—it's wrong, but I can't grasp how.

"You know what I think, Mamma?" Bianca says. "I think that mother was afraid her daughter would leave her. That's why she didn't tell her the truth. That mother wanted to stay with people like herself. She could have taken her daughter to the other people and the mother would have been the monster then, not the daughter. That's real love."

"Don't say that!"

"Why else would she have done it? She treated her daughter like her belonging . . . like a slave."

"Hush!" I pull my hands away and stand.

"What?" Bianca stands too. "Do you know this mother?"

"Leave me be, Bianca."

"But you were crying."

"I have a headache."

"Let me help."

"No one can help! Leave me!"

Bianca steps back, then goes into her room.

Agnola is bound to have been woken by all that, and I can't face her right now. I have to think. In peace. I hurry down the stairs. My white shift clouds out around me as I rush. At least I can still tell white.

I go into the storeroom, straight to my nest of cushions. Solitude.

What!

A candle sits in the sconce. Pietro's eyes meet mine. Agnola doesn't see me. I leave immediately.

I stand outside the storeroom in shock. Their naked bodies. Who would have known?

Thank heaven they're on the cushions. So long as they stay in the nest, there's no danger they'll touch any quicksilver residue from my last mirror. It disappears fast anyway. They're safe.

Safe. What I wouldn't give to feel safe.

I lean against the stone wall. Nothing is as it seems. Agnola and Pietro, that's good. It's Bianca's words that come back now and torment me. Her logic has to be flawed. But Bianca is so sensible.

Mamma didn't love me.

I can't breathe.

No! Bianca can't steal Mamma from me. She's about to steal my future—my place in Marin's eyes as the most beautiful— I won't let her steal my past, too.

And maybe I won't let her steal my future.

Energy surges through me. I lick my teeth. Clean them.

Marin is gone till spring.

Pietro is obligated to me now. That's the price of indiscretions.

And I am to go to the convent with Bianca.

Those three things must fit together to form a solution. If I just think hard enough, they will.

CHAPTER 26

Cold

I put my hand on Bianca's shoulder and shake her.

She comes awake with a start. "What is it, Mamma?"

"Quiet. We mustn't wake the sisters. I have an idea. Come with me."

She sits up and pushes the bedcovers aside. "Where?"

"Outside."

"Outside? Outside the convent?"

"Why not?"

"It's the middle of the night."

"If it were daytime, they'd stop us."

"We can leave any time we want, Mamma. We're not prisoners."

"Yes, but we can leave only to go back home. I don't want to go back home. I want to walk in the alleys."

"Walk in the alleys? Mamma, what a delightful idea! I've always wanted to walk in the alleys!"

"We won't be able to see the hustle and bustle of daytime, but we can at least see our city from somewhere other than a window or a gondola."

"I'll be dressed in a moment."

"Do you need to dress?"

"Of course, Mamma."

"I'm going in my shift."

"Don't be silly." Bianca struggles into her clothes. I sense her dark form more than see it. My hand reaches for her instinctively.

"What? Are you afraid? Don't be afraid, Mamma. This is a good idea. It's our city, too. It's our right. Put on your dress."

"No."

"I'll help you."

"No."

"It's cold out."

"You can walk with your arm around me, Bianca. Your cloak can spread across us both."

"You're being irrational."

"Don't call me that."

"Then behave. If someone stops us and you're in your shift, word will spread. You've been inside the convent, you've listened to the sisters at mealtimes. They are as much a part of the rumors as anyone. Aunt Teresa won't be able to protect us from gossip."

"If someone stops us, we'll be the target of gossip no matter what. Besides, this way we can say that I went out wandering in my shift and you came looking for me. Perhaps I was even walking in my sleep. People do that, you know, especially when they've run a high fever. You can say I was feverish before I went to bed. You woke and I was gone. It's no fault of yours."

"You sound like you've planned this."

"No, ideas are forming only as I talk, but they make sense, Bianca. This way, your reputation will be protected."

"I'm not sure I care about my reputation, Mamma."

"Your papà does."

"I'd feel like you were . . . less vulnerable if you had your dress on."

"Think about your father."

"I'm thinking about you, Mamma. The shutters are all closed. If we were to shout for help, no one would hear us."

"We won't shout for help because we won't need it. We're women, not men with a purse to steal. No one would gain anything from bothering us."

"Men can molest, though, Mamma."

"Do it my way, Bianca. Do it the way that will keep your reputation safe. For Papà's sake."

"In so many ways Papà is right. But in so many other ways, his mind is closed."

"You love him, Bianca. You agreed to come here, to spend time with the sisters, to pass your day in prayer and contemplation, all for his sake. So, please, for his sake, let's play this game."

She's silent. Then, "You have to put on shoes, though. Do that for me, Mamma. I need you to be safe."

"All right. But if I do that for you, you have to hold my hand."

"Why?"

"I want the comfort of your hand."

"Agreed." I hear her hands fall to her sides. "I suppose we needn't comb our hair." She gives a small laugh.

We go out, opening and closing doors as stealthily as thieves. The air is frigid. I shiver. Bianca was right; I'm grateful for these shoes. Poor, lost Bianca. Being right won't save her. Being right never saves anyone.

The night is clear, at least. Moonbeams illuminate the alley. Bianca's free hand touches the walls as we go. She peeks through iron gates. She whistles to a lone cat. I was right to ask her to hold my hand; being outside like this, just the two of us, sets me ajitter. I can hardly remember the girl who wandered Torcello on her own.

"Look, Mamma. Look at all the door knockers. When I traveled with Papà, when I was little, he'd lift me up so I could bang the door knocker wherever we stayed. He always said Venezia has the best door knockers of anywhere. But I never got to see them before now." She shakes her head and her hair brushes my cheek.

We walk straight as far as we can. When we come to a bridge, I halt. "They say it's easy to get lost. Let's go back and walk the alley all the way to the other end."

So we do. The other end comes out on the wide *fondamenta* that looks out over the deep basin of San Marco. Across the water is the island of San Giorgio Maggiore. I point. "A monastery in front of us, a convent behind us. As though the hands of the Lord gather us from both sides."

"It's more like they press upon us," says Bianca. "There has to be room for movement, for change. You agree with me, Mamma. I know you do. You just don't want to fight with Papà over one more thing."

"One more thing?"

"I know when you fight. I don't know what about. But I know every time. It shows."

I huddle against Bianca inside the cloak. Some things show, but not everything, thank the Lord.

"You're cold," she says. "Do you want to go back?"

"No. I want to keep moving."

So we walk in the other direction, cross a bridge, and take the first alley inland. My shoe slips in something squishy. The air is so cold, though, that smells are faint. I want to be looking around, like Bianca, and see everything; this is my chance, too. But I'm cold. And in the moment I feel ancient, like my blood hardly stirs.

"Your teeth are chattering. Let's go back." Bianca steers us.

We follow the alley back to the *fondamenta* along the wide-open water, cross the bridge, and arrive at the alley that leads to the convent. "Let's sit on the *fondamenta*," I say.

"Sit? You mean on the ground? It's filthy. And cold."

"You never used to be so fussy, Bianca. You were rough-and-tumble as a girl."

"That's because Papà used to take me places as if I were his son. But once you came to us, he stopped that. For seven years you've been my companion, not him. I'm not rough anymore."

"You talk about not liking rules, Bianca. Break your own rule. Sit on the ground."

"Why do you want to sit?"

"When I was a girl, I sat on a *fondamenta* all the time. I swung my legs and looked out over the lagoon."

"Aha! So you lived on the lagoon side. I wager it was on an island where we first met. Tell me more. You never tell me anything about your childhood."

"Sit with me."

We sit on the edge of the *fondamenta*. But the water is so high we can't hang our legs over. We have to fold them underneath ourselves.

"Have you ever heard of foot-fishing?"

Bianca shakes her head. "What is it?"

And so I describe that day with Giordano, long ago. How he stomped through the silt. How I gathered the crabs that appeared in his footprints and felt so proud of myself.

"Was Giordano your father?"

"I have no idea who my father was, but I pray to the good Lord it wasn't Giordano. In some ways he was friendly to me, and that was almost the cruelest thing."

"Cruel?"

"Did I say that? I didn't mean to voice that thought. I get confused."

"You told me you were a princess. Do you remember that?"

"I was a princess. I was, indeed. I lived on an island with my mother. Just the two of us. So that made her queen and me princess."

"A pretend princess."

"It was real to me. We'd cross the bridge in the morning and be surrounded by everyone else and suddenly we'd just be us again—Mamma and ugly me. But when we went home at night, I was a fair princess. The fairest of them all."

"You could never have been ugly, Mamma. You're beautiful."

"You don't understand beauty, Bianca. You're the one who is truly beautiful. I love you so much. Do you know you're the delight of your father's eye?"

"He used to say that when I was little. Did he tell you?"

"No. Thank you for telling me now. I don't know if I could have gone through with this otherwise."

"Through with what?"

"Here." I reach inside my shift and pull out the small pouch that hangs around my neck. My hands tremble as I try to open it.

"Let me help you." Bianca works at the little strings that hold the pouch closed. "What is this?"

"Something for you. Shake it into your hand."

Bianca shakes the pouch. A small tin mirror slides out into her palm. And a pill. "A tin mirror? Sometimes . . . I don't know. What is this pill, Mamma?"

"Chew it."

"Why?"

"I'll explain. Chew it."

She puts the pill in her mouth and chews. "It's bitter."

"Chew and swallow."

She swallows. "All right," she says with a hint of a slur already. "Explain."

"You'll sleep now. You'll sleep long enough to travel away."

"Travel?" She leans against me heavily.

"Look in the mirror. Can you see anything?"

"It's dark, Mamma. And who can see in tin?"

"The heavens conspired against us, Bianca. They made you steal my future, but then you stole my mamma. You stole everything."

"What are you saying? Are you crying? Your voice . . ." She slumps and her head lies in my lap. Her hand that holds the mirror hangs over the edge of the *fondamenta*. "I don't understand. Wha . . ." The mirror falls into the water.

I listen for the sound of the oar.

He's coming.

I don't hear it. I could still call for help.

He's coming, he's coming.

The voices are wrong. I could reverse everything before it happens.

Wait. Don't you dare move. He's coming.

And I hear it. Just in time.

See? Like Bianca said, she is the delight of Marin's eye. The timing is perfect, everything as we said it would be.

I nod.

Pietro throws me a rope. He takes off his gloves and sets them on the gunwale and brings his hands to his face, breathing on them.

He reaches for Bianca.

"Move aside," I say. "If you drag her, you might hurt her. I'll roll her. You can't lift her."

With one roll, Bianca falls into the boat. It rocks so hard, water splashes her head to toe. I hand Pietro her cloak. He spreads it over her.

"Make sure you do it on the mainland. Promise me. I don't want to take the chance of her body washing ashore somewhere. That would be too hard on Marin."

"Of course."

"And don't forget what I asked for."

"Innards," he says.

I can't see his face, but I hear his disgust. "Liver and lungs."

"Yes."

Remind him.

"Do as we agreed."

Be fierce!

"Don't even think of backing out of our deal. My word against yours; I'll ruin you. And I'll ruin Agnola. It doesn't matter that I love her, I'll still ruin her."

"I know."

"Go the fastest way."

He rows off into the night.

Liver and lungs can fix anything.

I squat and wrap my arms around my knees. I'm so cold. So very cold. My tears stick like ice on my cheeks.

I listen hard.

Silence.

I'm alone. Me here. Totally alone.

Everything is wrong. I've made the worst mistake ever. Unforgivable. Mamma would be appalled. Marin . . . Good Lord! I curl into myself and moan. *Lord, Lord, Lord.*

But the dream voices told me I'd feel this way. Grief confuses people. I just have to wait it out. They'll come back to me. They always do. They'll rock me.

Finally, day dawns over the island of San Giorgio Maggiore. The *marangona* in the piazza bell tower tolls, telling the workers to get moving. It's time. I can barely unfold, my joints have locked so hard into place. I manage to half jump, half fall into the water. Lord, it's cold! It stabs me from every side. And the tide has been going out, of course—the *fondamenta* is higher now, out of reach. I need stairs, water stairs. But I don't know where the closest ones are. All the ones I can think of are far away, on small canals.

It's so cold. I've never been this cold in my life.

I scream. My voice is but a raucous croak.

I swim to the closest bridge. It takes so long. Why is the water so deep here? I swim into the little canal, and there's a gondola tied up. Gondolas ride shallow in the water, but this one is empty, so it's higher. I can't reach the gunwale.

I'm so cold.

But it doesn't hurt anymore. I'm not afraid. Everything is quiet, peaceful, gray. The voices don't even fight me. This is what's right. Finally. From far away comes the sound of an organ. What a lovely way to die.

"Woman in the water!"

The gondola rocks hard beside me, and hands are pulling me up.

I mean to be giving thanks, but all that comes from my trembling lips is "Liver and lungs."

Part V

OTHERS

CHAPTER 27

Pietro

The small boat usually handles very well, even with a passenger, but it's hard to maneuver tonight. Pietro looks in all directions continually. No one should see him. No one should stop him. He knows the laws of the Republic very well. For assault or rape, one might be beaten, at the least, and, at the worst, branded. Jail, a steep fine. Being a servant, he'd get more jail time and less fine. But this would be considered attempted murder. He could be killed for this. And given that he's a dwarf and she's nobility, it could be a ritual execution, public mutilation. His hands chopped off and hung around his neck. He'd be marched through the streets to Piazza San Marco preceded by a herald proclaiming his guilt. He'd be hanged between the columns of justice. People would cheer.

Pietro has never harmed anyone in his life. If he were truly a murderer, he would have thrown her overboard immediately. But he isn't a wretched sort. He'd say that if anyone caught him. He'd say it was obvious that he wasn't a wretch, because he could have killed her easily.

Would it matter? Who would believe him? He isn't even sure Agnola would. After all, who could imagine what The Wicked One had forced him to do? No one. It was unthinkable. She was unthinkable.

Pietro jumps at every noise from the banks as he goes through the series of quiet canals. This is the quickest way to cut from one side of Venezia to the other, but it's still too long for comfort. Someone will catch him. His life is over. All because he loves Agnola. Blackmail is the worst of crimes; The Wicked One is the worst of criminals.

He eases the boat out into the lagoon now. The forest of the Isola della Certosa looms to his right. He rows harder. His arms and back and thighs strain with the work. His hands feel frozen to the oar. His gloves were lost in the water when The Wicked One rolled the girl into the boat. What a mistake to take them off. The wind whips off the water and steals the feeling from his cheeks.

Murano is asleep. The whole lagoon seems asleep. Pietro feels dead on his feet. But he's alive. He needs to keep rowing to stay alive.

The girl gives a little moan.

The Wicked One said the girl would be unconscious till morning. Looks like she is as much a dunce as she is a devil. At least the girl is coming to . . . at least she's not dead. Pietro dwells on that. If he can keep her from doing anything rash, this could still end well.

"Are you awake? Can you hear me?" How can he hope to get away with this? He does not seem a likely winner against The Wicked One.

Gull cries come from behind him. Dawn is breaking over the lagoon. The black-and-white ducks fall behind quickly. The mainland grows closer. Let his luck hold out—let him make it to the mainland unseen.

The girl groans. Her eyes open. She pushes herself up on an elbow. Her mouth falls open when she sees him. "Pietro," she says plaintively.

He can't pretend he doesn't know her. She's Bianca. She knows his name. Agnola loves her and Pietro loves Agnola. Hatred for The Wicked One makes his mouth go sour. This should never have happened.

"We're almost there," he says.

"Where's Mamma?"

"You shouldn't think of her as your mamma anymore. She isn't worthy of it."

Bianca's brow furrows. She cups one hand over the other and exhales on them. "Where are we going?"

Warming her hands like that, it's just what Pietro did back at the *fondamenta*. He feels an eerie sense of connection to her, as though this is fated. "I have friends. They'll take you in."

She shakes her head. Panic in her eyes. But she doesn't scream. Good.

"Take me in? I should go home."

"You can't go home. She has to believe you're dead."

"She?" The furrow in her brow deepens. "You mean Mamma? You want Mamma to believe I'm dead?"

"If she finds out you're alive, she'll take out her anger on Agno . . . on your aunt."

"What are you talking about?"

Pietro turns the boat northward, and they skim along the mainland shore. "She'll ruin me, too."

Bianca pulls on a lock of hair. She looks around, then back at him. She seems to be assessing him. "Will you make her think I'm dead?"

Her voice is steady, but she can't possibly be feeling steady. She's trying to be smart. Maybe she's planning an escape.

"Please answer. Will you make her think I'm dead?"

"Yes."

"How?"

"Does it matter?"

Bianca lets out a little cry of distress; it sounds as though she's all alone in the world.

Pietro winces. "Don't worry. I have no intention of harming you. I told you, my friends will take you in. You can live with them until your father returns in the spring. You just have to stay away as long as The Wicked One is in charge."

"The Wicked One," she says slowly. "You're confused."

Pietro rows harder.

"Mamma isn't well, you know."

"You're going to make excuses for her? She's rotten through and through."

Bianca pulls her cloak up to her chin. "Who are these friends?"

"You'll see. We're going ashore now." Pietro steers the little boat onto the beach. He sees no one on the shore as far as the eye can reach. Where is Alvise? Damn! Pietro lets out a sigh of dismay.

The boat gets stuck in the sand. The water is still up to Pietro's ankles. His boots will be ruined. But there's no dock anywhere safe. And the pine grove in front of them offers a hiding spot. Pietro jumps out. "Come on."

"No."

"You've been good so far. Stay good. This is the only way. Or the only way I could think of. The safest way for you."

"For me? I don't even know you."

"Yes you do. I brought Pizzico to—"

"I know who you are, but I know nothing about you! You could be a murderer."

"I'm saving your life. That's all you need to know. Get out of the boat. Now."

"My boots will be ruined."

"Mine already are."

"But you'll get new ones. All I have"—she holds her arms out to both sides and the cloak falls into her lap—"is what I'm wearing. I don't even have gloves. A noble girl without her gloves." She gives a little laugh that ends in a choked sob.

Let her talk. As long as she talks, she's not doing something stupid, like trying to run away.

Bianca's face goes unreadable. She straightens her shoulders. "If I'm in exile, as you seem to think, I've been impoverished overnight."

"You're alive. Think on that. Get out of the boat."

"Ferry me on your back."

"You weigh too much."

"Your back is strong."

"All right." Pietro stands beside the boat with his back to it.

"Ha!" Bianca grabs the knife from his waistband. "You have to do as I say now."

"No I don't. I can just walk away and leave you."

"And I can row back across the lagoon."

"You don't know how to manipulate the oar."

"I'll figure it out."

"Go on, then. Row to Venezia. Find your way through the streets to your home. Walk in the door. And wait for The Wicked One to find someone else to kill you. The next person might really do it. That's the likelihood. As horrible as it is, you're better off with me. That's how I see it."

Her eyes plead. "I don't . . . I can't . . . I won't believe you."

"What choice do you have?"

Tears roll down her cheeks.

Pietro holds out his hand for the knife. She gives it to him. He wishes she weren't so pathetic. He wishes the world would change back to how it was before. He turns around and offers his back.

Bianca climbs on. She's gigantic. He has nothing against big people as a group. He's in love with Agnola, after all. And no one should be judged by their size. But having a big person perched on his shoulders, now, that's an absurd image if ever there was one. He slogs through the water and sets her on firm mud. Then he goes back and pulls the boat up onto the mud. He turns the boat over and lifts it above his head and carries it through the shore grasses and into the woods.

Bianca follows.

Pietro puts the boat behind a tree. He checks that it can't be seen from the shore. Still . . . He pulls out his knife and hacks off low branches from a pine tree and covers the boat. Then he walks quickly. They can't stay on the shore, where they could be spotted by any passing boat.

He tramps through the underbrush. Within minutes the wet boots pinch his toes and rub at the top of his feet. If he walks too far, his feet will wind up all swollen; they'll be a mess for days. Where, where, where is Alvise? He agreed to meet Pietro on the shore. Maybe he confused the day. That's just like Alvise; he never gets anything straight.

Pietro puts a hand on his forehead. He's cold and tired and his feet hurt and behind him tramps a petrified girl. What could be worse than your mother wanting you dead? Pietro looks over his shoulder at Bianca.

She's just two steps behind him, her eyes steady, hands clasped under her chin, holding her cloak in place.

"I can't walk you the whole way," he says.

"What?"

"You can do it on your own. I'm sorry."

"I can't. You know I can't."

"It's not that far, and you're strong. You just walk straight ahead. And listen hard—at a certain point you'll hear a dog, then a few dogs. Just head toward the dogs."

"What if there's a bear?"

"They go to rivers, not the lagoon. Besides, they're more frightened of you than you are of them."

"I hear a dog."

"We're too far still. You can't hear one yet."

"I do." Bianca points. "Over there."

Pietro hears it now, too. Another dog as well. Maybe three. They're barking like mad. "They're chasing something. Come on." He runs toward the barking, crashing through the dry cane and scrub brush.

A boar races toward him. The dogs are at the beast's heels. Pietro draws his knife.

The boar is coming straight for him. He closes both fists around the hilt of the knife and spreads his legs so he can hold his stance. The boar charges, its snout chest-high. A dog nips the beast in the rear. The boar spins at the last minute to face the dog. Pietro stabs it in the haunches. The dogs go wild, all three of them. They're nipping and barking and the boar is turning in circles, slashing with his tusks. Pietro can't wield the knife again or he might stab a dog.

Alvise dashes onto the scene. "You're killing it! Are you crazy? Down!" he shouts at the dogs. "Down! Down! Down!"

The dogs back off, whining, muzzles bloody, nipping at each other now. Alvise mutters curses. He pulls out a knife and plunges it into the side of the boar's neck. The air is filled with squealing. Pietro jumps in and sinks his knife into the boar's neck too. Blood spurts in his face, on his chest, everywhere.

The boar shakes, then stops moving. The dogs keep yipping and nipping. Alvise has to swat them away. He points at Pietro. "You stabbed him in the rear. What on earth were you thinking? We can't kill boars, you idiot! And the dogs can't be allowed to jump on it once it's cornered."

"It wasn't cornered. It came at me."

"You should have run!"

"I can't run that fast. Neither can you." Pietro's shouting now.

"You may have made a big mess for me."

"I'm sorry, all right? I'm sorry." Pietro looks down at the boar. It dawns on him: this is an opportunity. It'll save him money he doesn't have. He jams his knife into the boar's chest cavity and rips it open. He carves and digs.

"What are you doing? If we're going to get in trouble for this boar, at least we're going to be the ones to eat it."

"I need the liver and lungs."

"What?"

"It's part of the deal. I have to give them to The Wicked One."

Alvise's face contorts. "Good God, she's crazy. Move over. I'm faster. Let me do it."

"No. You stay clean. I need your clothes. Anyway, I have to be careful with the organs. I need them whole." Pietro is almost grateful for the excuse; the hot innards warm his hands. He throws the entrails to the dogs, which jump onto them with snarls. Finally, he holds the liver in one hand and drapes the lungs over his other arm. He stands and looks around.

Bianca is gone.

"Damn!" Pietro shakes his head. "Where has the girl gone to?"

"I'll find her," says Alvise. He pulls his clothes off. "Hurry up."

"Take care of her."

"Hurry up, I'm freezing. If you don't want to return to Vene-zia looking like an assassin, strip now. You have ten seconds to take my clothes or I'm putting them back on."

Pietro sets the liver and lungs on a branch so the dogs can't get at them. He wipes his hands and face with pine needles as best he can. He and Alvise exchange clothes, down to the boots. "I'll bring you new boots next time I come," says Pietro.

"You better. Now get back to Venezia. Go on, clear out of here. And you owe me."

"Take care of her."

"We will."

"I mean it. She's not a bad sort. And her life has gone wrong."

"Get out of here. Really."

CHAPTER 28

Bianca

*H*orrible, horrible, horrible, horrible, horrible.
Don't see it. Don't see that mouth, those tusks.
See the trees.

That's what she must do.

Pine, cypress, oak, beech, an occasional ash, elm, hornbeam. Over there a poplar. Yes. She knows this. Papà taught her. This is a wild forest. It grew up naturally, all kinds of trees mixed together. She can hear Papà's voice in her head. So long as she hears his voice, she can keep running.

So many kinds of trees. She could be far from any village, far from any home. *Bad news. This is very bad news.*

But she mustn't think like that. That kind of thinking means defeat. Bianca cannot be defeated. Even wild forests have visitors.

And people—especially nobles—come to forests like this one to hunt birds, bears, boars. Nobles would know Papà. They might even know her.

But no one hunts in weather this cold.

Her dress is damp. How did it get damp? She shivers so hard that she fears she'll fall.

She sees the boar again, she can't keep the image out of her mind. But there won't be another one. Will there?

Bianca peers hard through the crisscross of leafless bushes and wintry branches as she runs. Pietro said bears were unlikely here. He said they'd be more afraid of her than she was of them. That's right. Papà explained that to her once when they saw a bear from the window of a monastery near Trento. He told her: Be calm around wild animals. Never run. But if you do run from a bear, go downhill. Bears are bottom-heavy, so they can't run downhill nearly as fast as they can run uphill. They tumble.

What if they tumble right past their prey and then jump up and attack going uphill?

And that hideous boar ran straight for Pietro. What kind of animal attacks a man like that? Maybe the boar killed him. Bianca was running so hard, brush cracking under her feet, blood rushing in her ears, that she couldn't be sure, but she thinks she heard a cry. A death cry.

And the boar was chased by dogs.

Bianca thinks, *Wolves.* She's never seen one. Their teeth . . .

No point in thinking like this. No!

She finally stops, leans against a beech, and rests her cheek on the smooth bark. She's grateful for the years she had as a child traveling with Papà. What little she knows about nature comes from those years. That knowledge had better help her now.

Everything had better help her. *Think hard.*

She should have run in the direction they had come from, toward the lagoon. She realizes that now. She could have walked along the shore and flagged down a passing boat. Instead, she ran away from the boar.

But that wasn't stupid. That kept Pietro between her and the boar. That was the sensible thing to do.

She tries to picture the whole scene again. The boar came from Pietro's left . . . didn't it? So that means she ran toward the right. So if she turns right again, she should wind up out on the lagoon. It's as good a plan as any.

Bianca turns right, or she thinks she does. It's hard to be sure which direction she came from. She was just trying to get away.

Well, she's going somewhere else. And somewhere else will be at least as good as here, because here is completely lost. She can't do worse. She walks quietly. Pietro might be dead. She'd be sorry if he was dead. He wasn't mean to her. He must be a demented soul to have taken her like that, but he didn't mistreat her. If he was dead, then God rest his soul. But if he was alive, he could be following her.

What about those dogs? She walks faster. There hadn't been a hunter with the dogs, but maybe he was far behind. If there was a hunter, he'd help her. That means she should head toward the dogs, not away. If there was a hunter.

Too many possibilities. She's chosen this direction. Straight. Find the lagoon. A hunter could be anywhere by now. The lagoon doesn't move. That makes her plan sensible.

She marches. She lost her cloak when she ran, and now that she's going slowly, the cold strangles her. She coughs. Then she stuffs a hand in her mouth. *Quiet.*

Nothing but trees. She can't smell the lagoon. She can't see it or hear it.

Her mind keeps going backward. She remembers a bull-baiting, ten months ago, at the feast of Santo Stefano. Men held on to the bull with ropes, and dogs barked at him and bit into his tail and thighs until he went crazy and reared up. Bianca had buried her head in Mamma's shoulder. The crowd cheered and screamed. When Bianca looked again, the bull was on his knees, lowing, bleeding.

An innocent beast. All beasts are innocent.

Bianca is innocent too. What has she ever done?

She's been walking a long time. Hunger gnaws at her. Exhaustion weighs her down. And the air itself is wet; it chills her even more. A tear rolls into her mouth. Could a person get lost in the woods forever?

She stops. She should have arrived at the lagoon hours ago. She looks around for a tree to climb to spot the water. The oaks go up too high before they branch. The beech are the same. Pines offer no strong branches; besides, the needles would poke her eyes out. She turns in circles. *Please. Let there be something. Please.*

There! The dark green leaves are unmistakable. The laurel is bigger than any she's ever seen before. The answer to her prayer. She should have prayed earlier.

Is there a trick to climbing? When Papà would take her on a forest walk, he'd teach her how to identify the trees, but he wouldn't let her climb them. Papà has his limitations. But Bianca will not be limited.

It's not hard, really; the worst of it is how the rough spots dig into her hands. Her skin must be brittle from the cold. In minutes, she's up as high as she can go; the branches got slender fast. And she's not that high, after all; her hopeful eyes played tricks on her. She clings to the trunk and looks in every direction, but the thick leaves don't provide a clear view. The branch cracks under her. She slips to the next one down, scraping her face on the trunk, then climbs to the ground. She puts a laurel leaf in her mouth and chomps on it; her hands curl into fists.

She saw it. Not the lagoon. A thatched roof. A house. She sets out for it.

The noise of dogs comes from ahead. The dogs that chased the boar? She stops and listens hard. Barks, bays, yips. Many kinds of dogs.

That's what Pietro said. He said to listen for the dogs and head that way. Oh! These are his friends who train dogs. Of course, of course. Well, they can't be awful then. They're businesspeople. Businesspeople can't be maniacs hidden away in a forest. They have to be reasonable. Bianca is nobility. There's something to be gained by treating her well. They could even get new customers if they treated her right.

She walks on. The house appears. No dogs. No people.

She's never seen a dwelling so low. The front door reaches only to her chin.

There's no knocker. Somehow that makes her feel sad. She calls out; no answer. The latch lifts easily. She ducks down and walks inside. The roof beams are high enough for her to stand. At one end of the single large room is a hearth with a table and stools. Seven of them. All small, as though made for children. The table is also low. Against a wall are seven beds. Short. At the foot of each is a chest. Bianca turns and studies the door.

Pietro's friends are dwarfs, like him.

The embers in the hearth still glow. Pietro promised her that these people would take care of her, so they won't mind if Bianca does what she needs to do. She's helped Carlo light fires all her life. She takes several sticks from the pile of kindling. Her arms shake. Her teeth chatter. But she gets a fire going till the flames lick high. She puts on two pine logs. They hiss and sizzle. The smell intoxicates her. She takes off her boots, pulls one of the stools close to the fire and sits on it, then rubs her icy feet. Won't Pietro's friends please come now?

Once Bianca has thawed out, she looks around. On a shelf she sees the heel of a loaf of bread, a flask of black wine, a basket of roasted chestnuts, and a bowl of truffles still coated in dirt. She's famished; they'll understand. Besides, Papà will pay them back handsomely. She pours wine into a mug. She heats the bread and chestnuts in an iron pan over the fire, then slides them into a bowl. Her teeth sink into the soft, sweet flesh of the chestnuts. She rips off a hunk of bread and dips it in the wine and chews. The wine runs across her tongue, around the sides. Who knew such coarse bread in such young wine in a cracked mug could be so delicious?

The wine has gone to her head. She should have mixed it with water, but she didn't see any. She falls back onto the bed closest to the fire. The bottom edge hits her calf midway.

She looks at the dark wooden beams above and her mind can no longer hold back the image of Mamma. Dolce. Pietro said he stole her because of Mamma. He said Mamma wanted her dead.

Mamma gave her a small mirror and a pill. Bianca remembers the bitter taste. Her tongue still tingles slightly. She remembers Mamma talking about the heavens. Then memory ends.

Mamma drugged her.

The mamma Bianca loves, the one she needs so very much, that mamma drugged her.

Bianca covers her face with her hands. She rolls onto her side and curves into the shape of the Canal Grande. She fits now. She's warm and cozy. The fire crackles and spits. That's what matters—that fire, this bed, her full belly. If she can just empty her mind, she can manage not to scream. She can't see with her hands covering her face, but she closes her eyes anyway.

CHAPTER 29

Pietro

It's midmorning by the time Pietro makes it back to the Contarini palace. He ties his boat up at the dock under the *pian nobile* and then lies on his stomach on the *fondamenta* and washes his face in the canal. He can't free himself of the feeling that he's spattered with blood. He rubs and rubs. He splashes his hair. He even rinses his mouth with the dirty water.

He stands and rushes into a storeroom. He grabs a piece of cloth from the pile that the servants use for cleaning, wraps the liver and lungs in it, and holds the cloth package at arm's distance. Rid himself of them—get it over with.

As he comes out of the storeroom, Signora Contarini is standing there. Her face curious, her little dog in her arms. What could he have expected? There are servants, spies.

"Come upstairs, please."

"Please excuse me, most dignified signora. An urgent task calls me away. I'll return quickly."

"I don't excuse you. Follow me."

The signora leads Pietro up the stairs. The Contarini women

are gathered at the top, eyes wide, faces eager. They all hold lapdogs. Pietro supplied them. The women jostle each other like hungry dogs themselves, vying for the first piece of flesh.

"You've been out all night," says Signora Contarini.

"You know I have business elsewhere." Pietro looks meaningfully across the dogs.

"Indeed, I do. We have always taken pride in your business endeavors. But tell me, Pietro, is it business that makes you leave in the middle of the night and return without a dog in your boat and in shabby clothes, all roughed up?" She shakes her head. "You look a fright. Speak plainly."

Speak? This business is unspeakable.

"What's in the package?" asks a girl. "Birba wants to know. She's practically jumping out of my arms."

Birba barks.

Now all the dogs bark.

An idiotic household. Pietro has never understood why the girls take delight in having trained their dogs to bark at the same time.

"I insist you open it," says the signora.

The women seem to move toward him just the smallest bit. They have a nose for gossip, all of them. It's as though they can smell it on him.

"It would be best to hold the dogs tightly," says Pietro. He goes to a side table, unties the string, and unfolds the cloth. He stands aside so the women can look.

"Liver . . . lungs . . . ? Have you been to the butcher's?"

"My friend killed a boar."

"And you must have helped him, by the looks of you."

Pietro nods.

"Where are you taking this?"

From nowhere comes the right answer: "It's a delicate matter."

The signora frowns. Had they been alone, she would have pursued it. But now, it would be undignified. Respect for delicate matters is a mark of nobility.

Pietro folds up the package, bows, and leaves. He runs now, turns into another alley, runs to the end, and turns again. If the signora sent anyone to follow, Pietro has surely lost him. But if that servant should ask shopkeepers or even shoppers which way a dwarf has gone, many voices will answer. Pietro is used to eyes following him.

He gets to a campo and runs down one alley, then back to the campo and down a different alley, then back to the campo and down a third alley, and this time he keeps going. It's the best he can do.

He runs straight to the iron gate, clanks the bell. He looks over his shoulder. No one has followed. He clanks again and again.

Antonin arrives at last.

"Please," says Pietro through the gate. "I've brought something for the mistress."

Antonin reaches through the bars.

"I need to give it to her myself," says Pietro. "Besides, it can't fit through the bars."

Antonin paces. He shakes his head. "Something has happened. The physician says it's not advisable to let her have visitors."

"Would you just ask her? Please. If she doesn't want to see me, I'll leave. But I am sure that she will want to see me."

"You don't understand," says Antonin. "It's a disaster."

"I do understand."

Antonin looks shocked. "How could you? No one . . ." Then his face changes. "So . . . you've already talked with someone."

The man thinks he's being a model of discretion. Pietro wonders if everyone in this palace knows about him and Agnola, if everyone everywhere knows. For a second Pietro hates Venezia. He nods solemnly.

Antonin opens the gate so Pietro can enter. "Please wait here." He goes up the stairs.

Pietro looks down at Alvise's boots. They are scuffed and dirty. Pietro needs to clean up properly as soon as he gets home, as soon as he puts this behind him.

This disaster. The girl disappeared.

Alvise will find her, though. He's found her already, he must have. Her cloak was lying in the brush. All he had to do was hold it to a dog's nose and they'd track her down.

Is that true?

Well, somehow Alvise will find the girl. Or all his friends together will find her. No dwarfs who make a living off their own business can be dunces. To the contrary, they are geniuses.

They must find her and treat her well. It must not be that Pietro did a terrible thing. It absolutely must not be. In fact, he has done a good thing. He saved Bianca's life. Anyone else probably would have just done what The Wicked One demanded.

"You may come up."

Pietro follows Antonin up the stairs. That's another thing he hates about Venezia, all the stairs. They're too high going up, too low going down. Pietro's sick of living in a world made for others.

He's shown into the music room and told to sit. He hates to sit in those high chairs, with his legs dangling. Big people tend to smile when they see him like that, as though he's cute, like a child. But Antonin waits, so Pietro finally takes a seat. Antonin closes the door behind him. Pietro can't hear what's happening outside.

Agnola comes in. She leaves the door open. She stands by the harp, one hand on it as though for support. Her face is ghastly, ravaged by sorrow.

Pietro jumps to his feet. He longs to hug her. He sets the package on the chair and turns to her.

Agnola lifts a hand to her mouth, then chews on her knuckle. "Something awful has happened."

Pietro doesn't want to lie. It's not in his nature, and he should never have to lie to the woman he loves. This is another reason to hate The Wicked One. The Wicked One has reduced him, diminished his humanity, soiled the dignity he has given up so much to attain. He stands silent and helpless in front of Agnola.

"Bianca is gone, and Dolce is nearly dead."

Pietro jerks to attention. "Nearly dead?"

"She jumped into the water. She tried to save Bianca."

"I don't understand."

"I know," says Agnola. "It doesn't make sense."

"Tell me what happened."

"They were asleep at the convent. Dolce woke. Bianca's bed was empty. She looked everywhere for her. Then she searched outside. Bianca was standing on the *fondamenta*. She looked back at Dolce and jumped in."

"Bianca jumped into the water?"

"Yes. Jumped. Dolce thinks Bianca did it on purpose. Dolce ran and jumped in after her. She knows how to swim. Bianca doesn't. Bianca had already disappeared, though. She was wearing all her clothes, dress and cloak and everything. She sank instantly. Even Dolce would have sunk if she'd been wearing all that weight. Thank the Lord she only had her shift on."

"How . . . how do you know all this? If the signora had been in the water, she couldn't have gotten out. She . . ."

"She made it to a side canal and someone pulled her out. She was half frozen. They brought her home. Raving."

"Stark raving mad."

Agnola tilts her head and tears well in her eyes. "I should be, too. We all should be. We'll never feel whole again. Bianca's lost."

"Bianca's not lost."

Agnola shakes her head slowly. "If she jumped, it's suicide. Her soul is condemned to hell."

"Bianca would never commit suicide."

Agnola looks at him with wide eyes. "Thank you for saying that. You can't know her very well, but what you say feels so right. Bianca never would have given up."

If only he could hold Agnola. He's tempted to shut the door, but she's already distraught. "The girl did not give up."

Agnola takes a deep breath. "I wish Dolce believed that. If she doesn't, we won't be able to bury the body in the family crypt. We can't even have a funeral."

"They found a body?"

"They're looking. It will show up."

"It will not show up. She's not dead, Agnola."

"Oh, Pietro, she has to be. If . . . no, there's no 'if' . . . the water is so cold, her clothes are so heavy, she can't swim. . . . She's gone." Agnola's voice cracks. She weeps.

Pietro takes the package off the chair and sets it on the floor. He guides Agnola by the elbow to the chair. She sits, slumped, heaving. He wraps his arms around her. The damn door is still open, but he has to hold her, she's in such pain. "Bianca is alive," he says very quietly. "Believe me."

"How? How can I believe that?"

"You'll see. They won't find a body. It will be as though she's disappeared. But she's alive. Don't tell anyone. Just know it in your heart."

Agnola nestles against his chest. "I can try."

"I'll help you."

Someone clears their throat right outside the door. Pietro moves away from Agnola and picks up the package. A moment later Antonin appears in the doorway. The man is kind. Pietro feels enormous gratitude. The Wicked One is an aberration in this decent household.

"The mistress will see you now. In the library."

The Wicked One sits in a chair with a blanket across her lap and legs. She's wearing a black dress, with white crepe at the collar and cuffs. Her face is ravaged like Agnola's. What a good actress.

The Wicked One holds her hands, palms up, in front of her chest. She stares at them. "Leave us, Antonin."

"The physician said—"

"Just for a little while. You can help me back to bed soon. Go. And shut the door."

Antonin leaves.

The Wicked One looks from her hands to Pietro. She seems bewildered. "What have you to say for yourself?"

This is not the question Pietro expected. And her manner is not at all what he expected. Pietro works to keep his face blank. He hands her the package.

"Liver and lungs?" she whispers.

He nods.

"I'll have Lucia La Rotonda boil them with salt."

Pietro's nostrils flare in revulsion. *She'll eat them?* He thought they were simply proof.

She hugs the package to her chest. "This will fix it all. Then life can go right."

Pietro stares at her.

"You weren't meant to be the fairest," she croons to the package. "And you certainly weren't meant to rob me of a loving mother. So now it's fixed." She looks up at Pietro. "Thank you." She seems earnest. And frail.

Bianca said her mother wasn't well; maybe she's right. Maybe The Wicked One has lost her senses. "This is the end of my obligation," says Pietro. "You will leave Agnola and me in peace."

The Wicked One looks at him; then her eyes slide away.

Pietro leaves.

CHAPTER 30

Alvise

"So you really don't know who she is?" Ricci shakes his head. "I don't even care who she is. What I care about is why is she in my bed?"

They are sitting around the table, all seven of them, each holding a candle that illuminates his face. Behind Alvise's back comes the crack of burning fat that drips from the quarter of boar roasting in the hearth. The wheel cage to the side of the hearth squeaks as the dog inside it runs, causing the spit to turn. Alvise set up the system and trained the dog. He's proud of his invention, but no one has praised him. They got worried when they saw the meat . . . and they should have. Pietro made a big mistake. Still, they're going to eat boar tonight and for weeks to come, so they should at least say something good about it. Instead, Ricci won't shut up about the girl. The others are looking at Alvise for the answer. And the girl keeps sleeping. Why does she keep sleeping?

Alvise sets his candle upright in one of the little bowls of sand in the middle of the table. "Let's be quiet till the girl wakes up."

"She can go in your bed, Alvise," says Ricci.

Alvise jumps to his feet, knocking his stool over.

"Whoa," says Bini. "No need to get in a tussle. She can sleep in my bed." He grins. "With me. She owes it to me after eating from my bowl."

They all laugh, except Tommaso. "She's closer to my age. She should sleep with me."

"No one's ever going to sleep with you, Tommaso," says Giordano.

They laugh.

Giordano and Bini like to tease Tommaso, and Tommaso cares about them too much to take offense. The three of them used to live on Torcello before the big people moved back there. They spent an entire year in hiding, moving from one deserted lagoon island to another until they met Alvise.

Alvise can see how the three from Torcello are different from the rest. The others were slaves before; they didn't know other people like them—they didn't have real friendships.

It's Alvise's job to hold them together. He's taught all the others how to train dogs. Giordano is the oldest, but he would be a recluse if you let him, like a bear in a cave. Under his gruffness, though, he's softhearted.

"Listen!" says Alvise. "We treat the girl with respect. Gently. Tommaso"—Alvise points at him, though he's only across the table—"you can show her around."

"Teach her not to drink out of my mug," says Baffi.

"Show her how to cook," says Giallino.

Alvise points at Giallino. "Good thinking. She can cook, and you and Baffi won't have to anymore. She can sweep the floor and fetch water and gather firewood. None of us has to do that anymore. We've got a servant!"

"A lazy servant," says Ricci. "She's not waking up."

The girl rolls over. "Someone's going to have to give up a bed for me." She sits up and swings her legs over the side. Seated like that, her knees come up to her chest. "My papà will reward you handsomely for your kindness."

They all stare.

Alvise gets a good look at her face. She's fetching. He wishes it weren't so. She'll make trouble, for sure.

"You've been pretending to sleep," says Giallino. "Eaves-dropping. You're deceitful."

"No," says Tommaso. "She's nice."

"She is not."

"I am nice. I'm very nice. I thank you for taking me in." The girl's voice wavers. "You'd do the same if you were in my spot." She looks at them defiantly. "So who will be a gentleman and give up his bed?"

"I will." Tommaso plants his candle in a bowl of sand and stands. He walks to a bed and pats it invitingly. "This is your new bed. And you can have my candle."

The girl takes the bowl with the candle. "Thank you."

Tommaso bows. "Tommaso at your service." He stands very straight. "I'm a gentleman."

"Yes," says the girl, "you are, Tommaso. You're the one who's supposed to show me around?"

"Wrong," says Alvise. "Giordano can show you around. We don't need any chumminess here."

"Or chumps," says Ricci. "It doesn't matter how straight you stand, Tommaso, or how nice you act, or how sweet you talk. The girl will always think you're ugly, stupid, and inferior."

"True," says Giallino. "You don't know how big people are. You never had to play the jester to nobles in Firenze and Vene-zia, trying to make them laugh even when you were sick."

"Or a slave to some rich rogue who kicked you for no reason," says Baffi.

"Or a pet," says Alvise. "In Pietro's last job, before his owner set him free and he found a paid job, he was a little girl's pet. Instead of a dog, she had a dwarf."

"Pietro?" says the girl quickly. "The Pietro I know?"

"The one who saved your life," says Alvise.

"Pietro was someone's pet?" The girl's lower lip quivers.

"Don't act so shocked," says Ricci. "I bet you've ordered dwarfs around. I bet you've laughed at them. And get the hell off my bed."

The girl moves quickly to the next bed. "I have never ordered a dwarf around. You don't know me, so don't make assumptions about me. And Pietro is a well-respected person in Venezia."

"He's a servant," says Alvise.

"He trains dogs," says the girl.

"We train the dogs," says Ricci. "He finds us the buyers."

"Whatever his part is," says the girl, "I do not consider him ugly or stupid or inferior."

"Well, aren't you an angel," says Ricci. "Maybe you belong in heaven. Maybe Pietro shouldn't have saved your life. How did he do it anyway?"

The girl looks down at the candle in her lap.

"How?" says Baffi.

The girl presses the back of a hand to her mouth.

"Tell us," says Bini.

The girl just looks at them.

"Someone wanted her killed," says Alvise. "Pietro whisked her away. Now that's a real gentleman."

"Who wants you dead?" asks Giallino in a quiet voice.

She doesn't answer. They all look at Alvise. But Alvise doesn't know. Pietro only called her The Wicked One. He looks at the girl.

"My mother," the girl says at last. She stands. "It's not my fault." Tears stream down her face. "I know how it sounds. You can believe I'm awful—what kind of daughter makes her mother want to kill her, after all—but I'm not awful. I'm nice. It's not my fault." She stamps a foot. "It's not, I swear it. And my papà wants me alive. He's the one who will pay you. But if you want me to, I'll leave."

"You'll just walk out into the forest at night?" says Bini. "Sure you will."

"It's night already?" asks the girl weakly.

"Your cloak is right over there on the hook," says Ricci. "Alvise fetched it for you when you were stupid enough to run off without it."

"Wait a minute," says Giordano. "Let's find out a little about her first."

"Are you a good cook?" asks Giallino.

The girl shakes her head. "I can make oyster cakes."

"Can you wash clothes, sweep the floor, keep house, and make candles?" asks Baffi.

The girl sits on the foot of the bed. She puts the bowl with the candle on the floor. She pushes her hair back behind her ears with both hands. "I know how to do things—I can play the harp." She shakes her head. "I didn't mean that. I mean, you don't have a harp, but if you could get one, I'd play it for you. It's not easy, and I'm good at it. You have no idea how calming it is for my papà to listen to the harp when he's got worries." She fingers the bedsheet. "If you have a needle, if you can get one, I can make point lace along the edges of your sheets. That's not easy, either. I'll trim them beautifully. And if you have books, I can clean them with a soft goatskin and turn the pages gently and often so they don't stick or grow brittle and fall out." She blinks.

"We're not going to trade our dogs for some fancy harp or a useless book," says Ricci. "Who reads, anyway?"

"And we like our sheets just as they are," says Baffi.

The girl knocks her fists on her head. "Of course not, no. But I'm smart. I know trees. Like someone said before, I can gather firewood. And I'll learn to cook. I'll learn to clean. How hard can it be?"

"Said like a rich girl with no respect for the work of servants," says Ricci.

"You're not being fair." She looks at them hard. "I bet that each one of you knows what it's like to be treated badly through no fault of your own. Don't do that to me. Give me a chance."

They're silent for a moment.

"So she's clever at making us feel guilty," says Ricci at last. "Is that what we want to live with?"

"She stays," says Alvise in a booming voice. "We are doing this for Pietro. And he's placing our dogs without taking a cut for as long as she lives here."

"You made a deal with him?" says Ricci. "You didn't talk it over with us."

"If she's done something disgraceful, the authorities will come looking for her," says Baffi. "You're putting us all in danger."

"She hasn't done anything disgraceful," says Alvise.

"If her mother's really determined, she'll be the one to come looking for her," says Giallino.

"Her mother believes she's dead," says Alvise.

"She'll come," says Giallino. "Mark my words."

"Pietro told her mother nothing," says Alvise. "She has no idea where we are. She has no idea we even exist. Besides, who could find a cabin in the woods that has no path leading to it?"

"I don't want to find out," says Ricci. "Let's get rid of the girl."

Giordano shakes his head. "We can't cast her out. It would be the same as if we'd killed her ourselves."

"And her father," says Tommaso. "She said he'll be grateful."

"Right," says Alvise. "The girl stays."

"But—" begins Giallino.

"She stays!" Alvise glares at all of them.

Giordano turns to the girl. "What's your name?"

The girl opens her mouth to speak.

"No!" says Alvise. "Not your real name. We're better off if we don't know your real name. What do you want us to call you?"

The girl closes her eyes for a moment. "Neve."

"Neve?" says Tommaso. "Snow? Who goes by such a name?"

"My mamma loved snow."

"Your murderous mother—you want to remember her?"

"The mamma I had until I was three. She died." The girl folds one hand over the other on her chest. "Thank you for letting me stay, no matter your reasons. You are Tommaso," she says to Tommaso, "but what do I call the rest of you?"

They go around the table. "Alvise." "Bini." "Baffi." "Giallino." "Ricci." "Giordano."

She nods as each says his name. "*Alvise* and *Giordano* and *Tommaso*, they're real names. But *Bini* . . . How did you come by that name, Bini?"

Bini shrugs.

"His mother used to belong to a family in Treviso that went by that name," says Giordano. "They bought her at a slave fair in Venezia. The eldest son in the family fathered Bini, which caused a crisis. Lots of noblemen father sons with a slave mother. And Venetian law is moving toward recognizing their freedom and their rights of inheritance. There was no way that family would allow its fortune to eventually fall into the hands of a dwarf. So they granted Bini's mother her freedom if she'd leave and never return, and she came to live with us."

"Here?" Neve perks up. "There's another woman here?"

"Not here. On Torcello, where we used to live—Bini and Tommaso and me. But she died immediately, of marsh fever."

"I'm the son of nobility?" says Bini. "Why didn't anyone ever tell me?"

"What? You want to claim your inheritance now?" says Alvise. "If you're stupid enough to try, they'll probably find a way to kill you."

"Maybe not. Maybe the old head of the family is dead by now. Maybe the son who's my father is in charge. Maybe he'd welcome me."

"And maybe our latrine has a seat made of gold," says Baffi.

"All those years of living on Torcello with only other dwarfs, they made you ignorant of how the world works," says Ricci. "No noble is going to recognize you as his son. You're an idiot to think otherwise."

"I'm not an idiot."

"Good. Then you know our latrine doesn't even have a seat."

"You three," says Neve, "Baffi and Ricci and Giallino—you have nicknames. *Baffi* for your mustache, *Ricci* for your curly hair, *Giallino* for your blond hair. What are your real names?"

"Those are our real names," says Ricci. "We were named by the big people we lived with. And we hold on to those names, to remind us that we can't get lazy, we can't forget who we are and what we went through. Not like Alvise." He shoots a look of disgust at Alvise. "We don't pretend it never happened."

"That's one way of doing things," says Alvise. "Another way is to put it behind you. To recognize who you are and stand firm in your own name. I'm not pretending anything. My mother called me Alvise. I have a right to that name, no matter what big people called me."

"You and Pietro," says Ricci. "Fools."

"I'll tell you what I want," says Giallino. He points at the hearth. "Let's eat that pig."

"Finally," says Alvise. "Finally someone's showing some appreciation. Let's eat."

"You can have my stool," Tommaso says to Neve. "I'll sit on the floor."

"Oooo. Suffer, suffer, suffer," says Ricci.

"You can build yourself a new stool," says Alvise. "I'll help you."

CHAPTER 31

Agnola

gnola looks at the wall. With a groan, she rolls over. Waking up is the hardest part of the day. She has to face it—Bianca.

She stands and reaches high to touch the tip of the green damask that stretches over the top of the canopy bed. The coverlet matches it. Agnola and Bianca have identical bedcovers in deep green, Bianca's favorite color.

Agnola dresses. Lucia La Rotonda has left a tray outside the door. Bread and raisins and chamomile brew. Agnola eats alone, sitting on the rush-bottom stool at the table. The food is without taste. She gives half of her bread to Pizzico.

The house is so quiet. Not even Pizzico makes a noise above the little *sht, sht* of his chewing. Agnola walks the dog down the rear stairs and waits while he does his business in the courtyard. Carlo comes out instantly and cleans it up. Antonin is nowhere to be seen, but Agnola is sure he's in the wings somewhere, waiting. Everyone is solicitous. Everyone misses Bianca. Christmas without Bianca was bleak. Every day without Bianca is bleak.

When Agnola goes back up the stairs, she sees Dolce standing in front of the long mirror at the front of the big hall. Agnola walks up behind her slowly. She looks at Dolce's face in the mirror, but their eyes don't meet. Dolce stares at herself. Her lips move.

"What does the mirror tell you today?" says Agnola gently.

"The same," says Dolce. She turns and faces Agnola. "Always the same."

Dolce hardly speaks these days except to that mirror. Agnola thinks sometimes of covering the mirror like in the past—and forcing Dolce to be part of the household again. "We need a change."

Dolce looks slightly alarmed. "Who needs a change?"

"The feast of Santo Stefano was a week ago today," says Agnola.

"Time passes." Dolce traces the edges of her lips with her fingertips, those pink, pink fingertips.

"We're already a week into Carnevale," Agnola says with forced enthusiasm. Carnevale is the last thing Agnola wants to participate in. But Dolce's hold on this world is weakening day by day. "Let's be part of it. I'll tell Franca we'll go to her party, after all."

"Franca? I don't care about Franca."

"Friends are important, Dolce."

"Anyway, we didn't have gowns made this year."

"We can use last year's. And I can buy us new masks. That's all we need, really."

"You don't care if others remember the gowns?" asks Dolce.

"Let's talk." Agnola touches Dolce on the arm as softly as she can. "Come. Let's sit in the music room."

"Not the music room. The library. The music room was Bianca's."

Agnola sucks in air sharply. The words hurt. But at the same time she's glad of them. This is a rare admission of the fact that Bianca is gone; perhaps it's a healthy sign. "It's true, sweet Dolce. The sight of the harp always brings tears to my eyes." She follows Dolce into the library. They sit near the table where Marin liked to stand hunched over his large, heavy books. He would spread open two or three on the table at once and move from one to the other like a bird hunting through bushes for berries. He was always eager, delighted. He used to smile so much. "Is there any word from Marin yet?"

"Nothing."

Agnola's head feels heavy. Her poor brother. He will come home with gifts for everyone, for a wife who's gone mad and a daughter who isn't here. He'll learn the news and . . . simply break. The whole household will begin the process of grieving all over again. She looks around. So many books. And still Marin wants more. What makes people like this, focused on only one thing? In some ways Marin is as bad as Dolce. But he has some perspective. When he finds out, none of these books will matter to him anymore. None of them holds the answers he'll need. He'll cry. He won't pretend that nothing has happened.

"You wanted to talk?" says Dolce.

The physician has urged Agnola to try to get Dolce to engage in conversation. "Do you know you hardly talk these days, except to that mirror. It's sad, Dolce."

"Most things are sad."

"It's odd, Dolce."

Dolce raises an eyebrow.

"An obsession, really. The physician says talking to the mirror allows you to block everything else out."

"What else is there?"

Agnola shrugs. "Carnevale, for one."

"Does anyone really care about Carnevale?"

"Of course they do." Agnola inspects her hands. "The students at the university, for instance."

"Oh?"

"You didn't listen when Pietro came yesterday?"

"He appreciates your company more than mine. I sit with you only to maintain the necessary propriety." Dolce yawns.

That's another thing Dolce does too much of: sleep. But they all do, even the servants. "That's thoughtful of you. Thank you. Well, let me tell you the news about the students in Padova."

"If you must."

"The university faculty decided that Carnevale was frivolous—a waste of time. It's not a liturgical necessity, after all. It's only tradition. So they declared that they would continue lectures all through the Carnevale season. No break. They said they'd be saving the students from folly. The students went wild."

"What does that mean? They barked and growled? Defecated on the floor?"

"They did the student equivalent. They smashed classroom benches. One tutor lectured on Aristotle—some philosopher in Greece long ago—and they beat him. Another dared to lecture on Galen—a great physician in Rome long ago. You've heard of him, I know you have, because Marin likes to talk about him. Remember? Anyway, they beat that tutor, too."

"Absurd," says Dolce.

"But understandable. Carnevale is a time of breaking rules. People need it. We can't be good all the time."

"That's the truth."

"Right. The university faculty can't be as smart as they think they are if they don't understand that much about human nature."

"I don't like human nature," says Dolce. "Not really."

"What a sad and terrible thing to say."

Dolce protrudes her lips in thought. "I guess you're right. But it's true. We'll do anything to satisfy our needs. We'll ruin the lives of the ones we love."

Agnola rushes to Dolce and kneels at her feet. She takes Dolce's hands in her own. "Don't think like that. Forgive Bianca. She didn't mean to ruin our lives. Whatever she did, however much it wounded us, that wasn't her intention."

Dolce blinks. Her face is all surprise. She does that a lot. She seems not to be in the same world that everyone else is. Agnola can't bear seeing Dolce so undone anymore. It's not possible that Bianca committed suicide. It's not! "Sweetest Dolce, let me help you." Pietro told Agnola not to repeat his words to anyone. But Dolce is suffering so. Agnola kisses Dolce's hand. "Bianca is not dead."

Dolce's face goes flat. "What?"

"She's alive."

Dolce grabs Agnola by both wrists so tight, Agnola can't hold in a yelp. "How do you know this?"

"I believe it. It helps me. When I can't think anymore, when my head is so heavy I can't hold it up, I remember those words. Bianca, our dear Bianca, she lives."

Dolce lets go of Agnola's wrists. "Oh." Her head falls back against the chair. "You can believe what you choose to believe."

"You can believe it, too. I can tell you that every day. I can whisper it in your ear whenever you need me to. We can sit in the music room and pretend we're listening to Bianca at the harp."

Dolce shakes her head.

"Why not? Please, Dolce. They never found her body."

"Of course not. She sank to the bottom because of her dress. That's what the authorities say."

"But they don't know. They can't know for sure. Bianca's alive."

Dolce shakes her head harder.

Agnola reaches up and holds Dolce's head still between her hands. "Listen to the words. They will help you. Really. They help me when Pietro says them."

"Pietro says them?"

Agnola nods.

"What does he say?" Dolce sits up again. She pushes Agnola's hands away. "What does he say exactly?"

"He says, 'Bianca is not dead.' He says, 'Trust me.' And I do. It helps."

Dolce looks at Agnola. "I need to speak with Pietro."

Agnola smiles. "Of course. I'll send for him."

"Send for him now. Hurry."

Agnola gets to her feet.

Dolce grabs her hand. "And tell Lucia La Rotonda that I need to see her. Immediately."

"That's a good idea. Let's have her make a fine dinner tonight. Let's grow fat before Lent comes." Agnola moves quickly down the stairs.

Antonin is dispatched in moments. And the cook is right where she's supposed to be. Lucia La Rotonda follows Agnola up the stairs, to the library.

"Yes, Signora?"

"Liver and lungs," says Dolce.

"Excuse me, Signora?"

Agnola goes to stand beside Dolce. She shakes her head in warning at Lucia La Rotonda. "She just needs a moment to think more clearly." She leans over Dolce. "You don't want liver and lungs, Dolce. . . . You want—"

"Hush!" Dolce points a finger at Lucia La Rotonda. "You boiled me liver and lungs two months ago. Do you remember?"

"Of course, Signora. With salt, just as you requested."

"Did you recognize the animal they came from?"

Lucia La Rotonda looks offended. "I have been the cook of this family for eighteen years, Signora. I recognize all meats."

"And what animal was it?"

"A pig, of course."

Dolce puts her hands in her hair. "Where did the pig come from?"

"Now that I think of it, it was probably a wild boar. The liver wasn't all caked with fat, like with domesticated animals."

"And where did the wild boar come from?"

"I'd say on the mainland, just the other side of the lagoon."

"You can tell that just from looking at the organs?"

"It's not advisable to transport fresh meat far, Signora, even in cold weather."

Dolce points a finger at Agnola now. "Tell Pietro to come immediately!"

"Antonin is already fetching him."

Dolce stands. "Get out of here, both of you!"

Lucia La Rotonda bows and runs.

Agnola's eyes burn. She walks into the hall and closes the library door behind her. She leans back against it. Her heart pounds. What's going on? The liver and lungs of a boar can't have anything to do with anything. But Dolce changed in an instant. She acted angry. Who is she enraged at? Agnola chews on her knuckles. Why, oh why, did she say that about Bianca being alive, especially when Pietro has always admonished her not to talk of it? What has she done?

CHAPTER 32

Agnola

gnola moves aside so Carlo can knock on the library door.

"Come in."

He opens the door. "You have a visitor, Signora."

Dolce shrieks.

Agnola rushes in. "Dolce! What happened?"

Dolce gives a hideous attempt at a smile and looks at Carlo. "Don't be alarmed, Carlo. I didn't mean to do that. I expected Antonin. Surprises . . . surprises irritate me."

Carlo bows, keeping his wide eyes on Dolce. "Please forgive me, Signora. Shall I show the guest in?"

"Pietro knows his way. And, Agnola, I told you, I don't want you with us."

Agnola's heart races. Everything is wrong about Dolce. "I'm staying."

"Get out!"

Agnola flinches.

"It's not Pietro, Signora," says Carlo in a loud whisper. "And this visitor would like to see both you and the signore's sister."

"I'm not taking visitors," says Dolce.

"This one insists. He says it cannot wait."

"All right. Show him in. But explain to him that I'm expecting someone else, so this has to be short."

"No, Carlo," says Agnola. "Please don't say that. Treat the gentleman with utmost respect. The signora is not feeling well. Let him know that. Say we implore him to be sensitive to the circumstances. A truncated visit will be much appreciated."

Carlo bows and leaves.

"You have to behave, Dolce." Agnola speaks with a steady voice, though her insides are all jumbled. "You have to behave no matter how irritated you are."

"I'm the signora of this household."

"And I'm the one who has lived all my life in Venezia. You scared the wits out of Carlo with that scream. You can make amends to him later. But you must not scare anyone else. No screaming. And you must not offend anyone else, including me. I love you, but you cannot abuse me. This is Marin's home. Act like Marin would want you to act."

"Marin wants me to be happy."

"And you should want him to be happy. This is his society, his friends, his world. Don't ruin it for him. Or for yourself. Someday you're going to want to be part of it all again."

"I miss her. Do you know that?"

"Of course I know that."

"But I shouldn't. Not me."

"Don't speak like that. It isn't fair to either of you."

Dolce exhales noisily. "You're suddenly stronger, Agnola."

"Am I? Perhaps my manner is deceptive, Dolce. I am not weak. I might be a bit shy—but I am not weak. I refuse to be weak."

"I wonder," says Dolce slowly, "I wonder if you could help me."

This has taken a more positive turn than Agnola could have dared to hope. "I would do anything to help you. Anything that does not harm Pietro. I hear them coming in the hall—Carlo and the visitor. We'll talk when they leave." Agnola moves to the side of Dolce's chair and folds her hands in front of her waist. She must be ready to deal with Dolce's behavior.

Carlo leads in a man dressed all in black. Not in the black gown of the priest, but that of magistrates and officials.

"You may leave, Carlo," says Dolce.

Carlo bows and leaves.

The man bows. "Let me introduce myself, dear ladies. I am—"

"Messer Sanudo," says Dolce. "We—my sister-in-law and I— have been entertained in your home on several occasions by your dear wife, Caterina."

Agnola is startled. She curtsies to Messer Sanudo, but keeps her eyes on Dolce. How can a person be so changeable?

"You come about a matter that cannot wait?"

"Indeed. A serious matter."

Agnola puts a hand on the back of Dolce's chair for support. Have they found Bianca's body? Is all hope finally lost? *Please, no. Please, please.*

"Please," says Dolce, as though voicing Agnola's prayer. "Please, have a seat."

"I prefer to stand." Messer Sanudo reaches into a pouch hanging from his waist and takes something out. He holds it in front of Dolce. "Do you recognize this?"

"Of course."

Agnola forces herself to look. A mirror. It's only a small mirror. It's not a necklace or an earring, nothing that belonged to

Bianca. Her legs feel weak from gratitude. She sinks into the chair beside Dolce's.

"I've been told you are in the habit of giving out mirrors just like this. Exactly like this. In fact, this is one."

"You've been told correctly."

"Indeed?" Messer Sanudo's face shows surprise. "So you don't even want to know who made the denunciation?"

Dolce looks bewildered. "Denunciation? For what?"

"It was Signora Grimani."

Dolce smiles. "I remember talking with her at the festival."

"She saw you give this mirror away. You were standing with your sister-in-law." He makes a small nod at Agnola. "I procured it from Signora Dandolo."

Color rises in Dolce's cheeks. "Then I'll have to give Signora Dandolo another one. I can't imagine why you took this from her."

"A rebellious spirit will do you no good, Signora."

"First you speak of a denunciation, now you call me rebellious. I'm sincerely confused. It is not against the law to give gifts."

"Where did you obtain these mirrors?"

"I don't see how that's any of your business."

"It is definitely the business of the Republic. The mirrors were not made on Murano. Not a single mirror manufacturer there claims them as his own."

"So?"

"So we have a problem. An enormous problem. These mirrors are made with the methods of the Murano mirror manufacturers—and those methods are secret. They are among the most guarded secrets of the Republic."

Dolce blinks. "Why?"

"Why? Are you sincere? Our mirrors are an important part of Venezia's wealth."

Dolce smiles and sits taller.

It's clear that Dolce doesn't understand the import of what Messer Sanudo is saying. Agnola wants to warn her, but who knows how she'd react?

"You must tell us where you bought them. Once we apprehend the thief, if it's clear that you didn't understand you were buying from a scoundrel, you will be exonerated."

Dolce shakes her head. "I don't buy them from anyone. I make the mirrors myself."

Messer Sanudo looks taken aback. Then he laughs. "Making mirrors is complex."

"More complex than you probably know," says Dolce. "Everything matters. The ratio of tin to quicksilver has to be just right. The pressure when the glass is placed on the tin and quicksilver has to be enough to affix it but not so much that the glass breaks. The whole thing cannot be handled too soon, or all is lost."

Messer Sanudo's face is stricken. "Who told you all this?"

Dolce puts her fingertips together and touches them to her lips. "Do you know that the people on Murano did not discover their secret method themselves?"

"What? Are you claiming that Murano got its secrets from elsewhere? Such a lie borders on treason."

"It's not a lie. The people on Torcello experimented for years— and the people on Murano paid them to do it." Dolce's smile is wide. "They came up with the present method around . . . let me see . . . over eight years ago now."

"Torcello?" Messer Sanudo's eyebrows lower. "Dear signora, eight years ago the island of Torcello had air so foul it literally reeked with death. The whole island was abandoned a couple of decades back because of marsh fever."

"Not entirely abandoned. People lived there all along. A small group of people. In fact, a small group of small people." Dolce laughs. "And they make mirrors."

"I am in charge of regulating our mirror industry, and I've never heard anything of the sort."

"Go ask them. Let them show you. They'll make mirrors with exactly this method."

"You can be sure I will. But what has this to do with you and these small mirrors?"

"That's where I learned the method. I invented it, in fact. Me. So, you see, Signore, I am among the great and valuable secrets of Venezia. And I am a source of delight, me in my little nest."

Messer Sanudo stares at Dolce. Then he turns to Agnola. "What do you know about this?"

Agnola has been dumbfounded throughout this exchange. She knows Dolce makes the mirrors, but she's never heard Dolce speak about Torcello. If there really is a group of people on Torcello making mirrors, and if they happen to make tiny mirrors like these, then wouldn't it be better that the authorities think Dolce bought the mirrors from Torcello rather than made them herself? It will ruin Dolce's reputation if it's known that she does that kind of labor. She's been making those mirrors only in order to build up a good reputation. It would be hideously unfair if it all went wrong now.

Agnola lifts her hands helplessly. "My brother is generous with his wife to the point of being indulgent. Look how precious these little mirrors are—so delicate and graceful. They look like the work of a professional artist—and Dolce had the money to pay a professional artist."

"I talked with every artist on Murano," Messer Sanudo says. "Our investigation requires the utmost thoroughness."

"Investigation?" Agnola thinks she may be sick. "We have

been through a terrible shock, Messer Sanudo. A personal tragedy."

"I am aware of that. And I am sorry for your loss. But these mirrors remain. And the signora's explanation is sheer non-sense."

"I am confident there is an explanation that can satisfy all of us, Signore," says Agnola. "Please understand, grief can make one lose hold on the daily truths, if only for the sake of survival. If you have nothing more to ask us right now . . ." She lets her voice trail off. The man must have at least a shred of decency; he must leave now.

"Have you quite finished with your conversation about me?" asks Dolce. "Amusing though it is, I'm tired of it. I suspect you are quite busy, Messer Sanudo. Or you should be. You should be hurrying to your boat and off to Torcello right now. It's time to right the wrong."

"Well, the fact that you understand it is a wrong is positive," says Messer Sanudo.

"Of course it's a wrong. The mirror makers on Murano should be ashamed of themselves for taking credit for the work of others. I'll bid you good day now, as I am expecting someone shortly."

Messer Sanudo doesn't bother with niceties. He bows and leaves.

Agnola stands. "I've been a bad friend to you. I should have stopped you from making those mirrors."

"If Marin couldn't stop me, what makes you think you could have?"

Agnola knows Dolce is right. A husband has more sway over a woman than a sister-in-law does. But she didn't try to stop Dolce. She liked seeing the other women vie for the mirrors.

It gave her a sense of power in a world where she is powerless. Shame coats Agnola. "What will we do now?"

"About the mirrors? Nothing."

That doesn't seem right. There must be something to do. It's an investigation—a formal thing. They must take action, if there's any action to take. "Where do you make the mirrors?"

"In one of the storerooms. I keep all my materials there. Except my flask of quicksilver. I've hidden that in my room because I like to open it every day. I stick my nose in—there's no smell, but just breathing the vapor makes a change inside me. It's dizzying, how exciting that can be. Quicksilver is like my own blood by now. One breath reminds me of who I am, what I must do. One breath reassures me all day long."

Agnola works hard to keep panic off her face. "Quicksilver? I had no idea. You know they say quicksilver can poison you. What if all your health problems are because of that quicksilver?"

Dolce smirks. "I don't eat it. I don't touch it. It can't hurt just to breathe it. Anyway, you agreed to help me. Here's what I need for Carnevale: a peddler's dress and a basket of bodice laces."

"No gown? Instead, a disguise of an ugly peddler's dress?"

Dolce grasps Agnola by the wrist. "I thought you sympathized with the *popolo*."

Agnola pulls away before Dolce's grasp can get too tight. "Sympathies aside, a noblewoman goes to the masked balls in the finest clothing possible. Only the mask disguises us, not a whole costume."

"Weren't you just saying how people need Carnevale because they need to break the rules? The rules of Carnevale itself should be held no more sacrosanct than any others."

It's true. How Dolce can reason so well when it's clear that she's half mad dizzies Agnola. "So, go ahead, ask Antonin to buy one. He can get it for practically nothing."

"No, I want you to do it. Don't say a word to Antonin or Carlo."

"All this secrecy, Dolce. It's not healthy. You must see that. Antonin and Carlo couldn't care less what you ask them to buy for you."

"Indulge me, like you said Marin does. Who can it harm, after all?"

"I can't go outside to buy things."

"Get Lucia La Rotonda to do it for you. Say you're helping your sister, Teresa, with a charity case."

"I won't lie to Lucia La Rotonda. Clear away this deceit you want to hide behind."

"You said you'd help me!"

"I will. I'll simply tell Lucia La Rotonda to do it. No lies."

"All right, have it your way. Make sure the basket is brimming with laces in beautiful colors. Some of them must be green."

Bianca's favorite color. Agnola feels tears form.

"And red."

"Red laces sold on the streets by a peddler woman? Only the nobility wears red, and nobility would never buy from a peddler," Agnola says gently. "It will be a poor disguise."

"Yellow, too. Bright yellow. And you check the colors—your eyes are sharp." Dolce rubs her hand along one sleeve. "Do you hear me?" She shakes her head and looks around, then her eyes settle on her hands. "And I want cheap gloves, too. And boots. And a cloak. I want the full outfit."

"All right."

"By this afternoon."

"Yes, by this afternoon. But now you must hear me." Agnola puts force into each word. "When Pietro arrives, I'm going to tell him to go away. Whatever it is you want of him, you have to stop. Leave him alone. He's nothing to you."

Dolce looks at Agnola. One side of her mouth goes up in a smile. "You're quite right. I don't need Pietro."

CHAPTER 33

Tommaso

Neve wipes the sleep from her eyes. She rubs with the back of her hands like a child. Darling. As darling as a puppy. She yawns wide, and stretches.

Her eyes open and meet Tommaso's. She sits up quickly and turns her back to him. "Go outside," she whispers. "Please."

Tommaso goes outside. He grabs the shovel and heads for the wrecked area. That's what he calls the place where the big tree fell in the storm the day before Christmas. It knocked off branches of other trees as it fell. Firewood lies on the ground for the taking. He laughs. He's no dummy, no matter what the others say. But today he's not picking up those branches. Yesterday he noticed that a little tree broke clear off when the big tree fell against it. So today Tommaso has come equipped. He has to hunt around quite a while in the predawn fog before he locates it. Right! There it is! He digs. That stump holds on to the earth with all its might. This is hard work, harder than he thought it would be. But Tommaso does it. He's strong. Now he bashes the stump against the trunk of another tree. He bashes it and bashes it until all the dirt shakes loose and the stump is as clean as it's going to get. He marches back toward the house, the stump in both arms, with the shovel balanced across the top.

Neve comes through the woods from the opposite direction, a bucket in each hand. They slosh as she walks. She's already visited the little stream off the Marzenego River where they get fresh water. She stands tall, like a mountain with the sun's first rays poking out from behind her. She's strong, too. They're alike in that. Young and strong. The others are old. Except Bini. But Neve doesn't like Bini. She never talks to him. She talks to Tommaso.

Tommaso rushes ahead so that he reaches the door before Neve does. He smiles as she looks at the stump in his arms. "It'll burn longer. You won't have to go out in the middle of the day for more firewood."

Neve nods. "Thank you, Tommaso."

She follows him inside and sets the buckets by the hearth while Tommaso blows at the embers way down low. Neve kneels beside him and flaps a cloth to fan them. They blow and flap and blow and flap. Gradually flames rise around the edges of the stump till it smolders and burns.

"We need a bellows," whispers Neve. "The one in my room at home is quite pretty: green velvet with walnut handles and a bronze nozzle. I never thought before how lovely such an ordinary thing is."

"A bellows isn't ordinary. It takes skill to make."

Neve presses her lips together. "Right. Nothing's ordinary when you have to make it yourself. But you all get money for the dogs. You could spend some of it on things that make life easier."

"Things that make *your* life easier," says Ricci from his bed.

"That's what you really mean." He throws off the covers, stomps across the room, and pees into the chamber pot in the corner.

Tommaso hates it that he does that right in front of Neve.

"The others use the latrine in the morning," says Neve.

"It's cold out in that latrine." Ricci scratches his belly. He reaches for his drawers draped over the back of his chair. "And then I'd miss the pleasure of knowing the fancy noble girl cleaned a pot I dirtied." He stretches. "Cleaning the chamber pot—that makes you good for something." He throws off his nightshirt—naked right there behind Neve—and pulls on his clothes.

It's all right, though. Neve doesn't look. She's modest. Just like she won't let Tommaso watch her dress. She's good.

Neve drags over the big pot. Tommaso helps her hang it from the hook above the fire.

"Thank you, Tommaso." Neve empties one whole bucket of water and half of another into the pot. She throws in a handful of wood ash from the tin pail beside the hearth, and a small branch of cypress needles from a pile beside that pail. "Pass your nightshirt to me, Ricci. Please. I'm doing the big laundry today."

"Again? Is it a new month already?"

"I'm your calendar," says Neve.

"That makes you good for two things," says Ricci.

Neve puts her hands on her hips. "I pick the lice out of everyone's hair."

"Three, then."

"I mend your shirts. . . ."

"Enough."

"I sweep the hearth. . . ."

"Enough, I said."

"I—"

"Enough!" Ricci throws his nightshirt into the big pot.

"The list is long," says Neve. Her cheeks are flushed and her eyes shine. "I earn my keep and you know it."

Ricci twists his mouth to one side. "You do work hard."

"Buying a bellows would be good for everyone, not just me. It would make fire building faster and easier and—"

"Think about it, Neve. You act so clever. Think! Imagine one of us walking into a town and holding out a coin to buy a bellows. You know what would happen?"

Neve looks confused. "No."

"Exactly. If a big man did it, he'd go home with a bellows. If one of us did it, dressed like we dress—obviously not anyone's servants but men living on our own—if we did it, who knows what would happen? We might get roped up like a bull on the way to a stabbing—roped up and sold. We'd be slaves again."

Neve gasps.

"I was never a slave," says Tommaso. "Bini and Giordano and me—we were never slaves."

"You hid for a year, living in an open fishing boat, or you'd have been caught like the others from Torcello. Whatever happened to them would have happened to you. So don't think you're better than us."

Neve's hand goes to her forehead. She massages the spot between her eyebrows with two fingers.

Tommaso watches her fingers. He loves it when she does that. She touches her lips now. "Not everyone is horrible, Ricci."

"She's right," says Tommaso. "Our landlord isn't horrible."

"His father wasn't, at least. But who knows what the son will be like now that the old man's dead?"

Tommaso bites his knuckles. "What? Are we going to be thrown out?"

"No. Don't worry about it. You're right, there are decent big people. But think about it, Tommaso and Neve, think. You want us to take chances on who is decent and who isn't?"

Neve looks at Tommaso. "Please bring me your nightshirt. And would you get mine, too? Please?"

Tommaso loves the way Neve always says "please." He pulls his nightshirt from under Bini's feet. Bini groans and rolls over. They sleep head to foot, Tommaso and Bini, in Bini's bed. Tommaso goes to his old bed, Neve's bed now, but he thinks of it as their shared bed. They're destined for each other. He takes her nightshirt and holds it to his face. He breathes deep. This is the best odor in the world.

"Stop slavering over that," says Ricci. "You're embarrassing Neve."

"Thank you for your concern, Ricci," says Neve, "but I don't need protection against Tommaso. He's kind to me." She takes the bread she baked yesterday from a shelf and sets it on bricks near the fire. "I could take money and go into the nearest town and buy bellows."

"And what do you think would happen to you?"

"People would talk." It's Bini. He sits with the bedcovers pulled up to his chin. "Word would get back to The Wicked One, and she'd come to kill you."

"Please don't call her The Wicked One, Bini."

"Why not? That's what Pietro calls her."

"I hate it when he says that. I've asked him not to. Please, Bini."

"Give me a kiss and I'll never say it again."

Ricci walks over and smacks Bini across the back of his head. He deserves it; still, Tommaso gives a little shiver.

"You seem to be protecting my honor a lot this morning, Ricci," says Neve. "Thank you. But I can stand up for myself."

"What? Are you going to tell me now that Bini is kind to you, too?"

Bini's still rubbing his head. He makes a face at Neve. Good. She can't like him if he makes ugly faces.

"Ricci, explain something to me," says Neve slowly. "If you can't buy anything with your money, what are you saving it for?"

"Why, to buy back one of us if we get enslaved, of course." He makes a disgusted face. "We can't count on being freed out of the blue again."

"You were freed?" says Neve very softly.

"Five of us were. Don't get any ideas that we ran off. We have the rights of free men."

"Five? If Tommaso and Bini and Giordano were never slaves, that leaves only four of you."

"Pietro, too. You knew that. Alvise told you. Pietro was a slave to the Zeno family, just like I was a slave to the Loredan family."

"I know those families," says Neve so softly. "Mamma gave the mothers of those families tiny mirrors. Do you know why you were freed?"

"Maybe a burst of conscience," says Ricci. "Though Venezia isn't known for conscience. Maybe random luck."

Neve frowns. With two fingers she massages between her eyebrows in a circle again.

"I love it when you do that," says Tommaso.

"Do what?" says Neve.

"Massage your head like that. That's what the first woman I loved used to do, long ago on Torcello. Do all big women do that?"

Neve drops her hand and shakes her head. "I'll cut up the bread and make a hot drink. Please wake everyone else, Tommaso. It's time to start the day."

"I'm not getting out of bed," comes a voice. It's Giallino. "I feel awful. Someone has to feed the dogs for me."

"I'll do it," says Neve.

"No she won't," says Ricci. "I will."

"Thank you, Ricci," says Neve.

"I'm not doing it as a favor to you. You can't be allowed to feed the dogs. You're like Giordano—softhearted. You'd talk to them all, even the hunting dogs, and maybe scratch them under the chin or behind the ears. You do that with the lapdogs. Don't deny it. But hunting dogs and guard dogs can't get any affection at all—none—except from their trainer or owner. Those are the rules. It's the only way they'll learn to do what they have to do. You can't be trusted with them."

"I know the rules, Ricci."

"Are you really telling me you wouldn't pet a hunting dog, even if he was a pup?"

Neve bites her bottom lip.

Ricci throws a hand at her in disgust. "Come on, Tommaso and Bini. Let's feed those dogs."

Tommaso gives Neve one last look. He likes that she's softhearted. He likes everything about her. He loves her.

CHAPTER 34

Biancaneve

"All you do is work." Bini sits in bed with his arms crossed. He's been watching Biancaneve all morning.

She looks at the clump of celery roots clutched in her hand. These four were among the larger ones in the bin; they should be enough for the soup. She rinses them in the water bucket. "If I don't work, you'll throw me out."

"No one's going to throw you out."

"Ricci will." Biancaneve peels the roots. She's learned to peel well, go way down, past the hairy parts; otherwise fibers stick in your teeth. She chops the root. If she had the right tool, she'd shred it. She's sure Lucia La Rotonda shreds celery roots, and they taste better that way. But chopping has to do.

"That's a pile of junk." Bini puts his hands behind his head and leans back against the wall behind his bed. "You know Ricci is as wrapped around your little finger as the rest of us."

"I know nothing of the sort." Biancaneve throws the diced-up roots into the big pot, the only big pot, which is now on its second task of the day. She used it for the laundry, which hangs from the rafters. Without these rafters, she'd be at a loss. The household is so poorly equipped. The fireplace doesn't even have andirons. A vision of the brass andirons in her room in Venezia flashes in her head.

"Oh, yeah? Why else do you think he defends your honor?"

Biancaneve laughs. "Maybe because you're always attacking it." She sighs. Bini probably isn't sick at all. He just wants to be alone with her. He's always trying to corner her. She takes down a long strip of dried boar meat and saws away at it, throwing all her weight into each push and pull of the knife.

"I never thought I'd say this, but I'm sick of boar stew," says Bini. "Dried meat can last forever. Don't you know how to make anything else?"

"I didn't even know how to make this until Baffi showed me. Sometimes I helped my aunt Agnola, for special dishes. But only sometimes." Biancaneve looks at her hands. They're raw and red, as red as Dolce's fingertips. She shudders. So far this morning she has fed the chickens, gathered the eggs, milked the goats, washed the nightshirts. She still has a pile of mending to do. She needs to sharpen this hateful knife. And Giallino told her to cut a couple of new bottle stoppers. That will keep her busy all day. And there will be more chores tomorrow. She hates them. And she needs them. They keep her from counting the minutes till spring, when Papà returns. She jabs the meat hard.

Bini gets out of bed. He's already fully dressed, thank heaven. He goes out the door. Good. He's going to use the latrine. She's already washed out the chamber pot.

The water boils. She throws in the chunks of meat and stirs. They need rice. If they had rice to put the stew over, it would be so much better. But the men don't grow rice, so they don't eat rice. The only thing they buy from others is flour. She pulls a garlic bulb off the braided strand that hangs on the wall and smashes the cloves. The sharp smell goes up her nose right to her brain. She sniffs and smiles.

Bini comes up behind her, clumping across the floor. His head is level with her waist. She turns around quickly. "You're not sick. Go help train the dogs." Her voice is sharp. She wishes she could step backward, but the fire is right there. It warms her almost too much.

His eyes hold hers fast. "You lie, Neve."

She shakes her head. "I haven't lied to you. I haven't lied to any of you."

"You say we shouldn't call her The Wicked One. But you know she's evil."

"I do not."

He smiles. He looks like he almost feels sorry for her. "How come you're hiding out here, then? If she's good, if she loves you like a mother should, you'd go back to Venezia."

Biancaneve lets out a little cry of despair. She didn't mean to.

"It's all right. I never had a mother's love, either. Mine died— which is bad, especially since I didn't have a father—but other people loved me. So maybe it wasn't as bad as having a mother who wants to kill you."

"Bini, people are not just wicked or good. They're complicated. Haven't you ever known anyone who sometimes was wonderful and sometimes fell apart?"

He looks at her. "There was this man on Torcello. Venerio. The mirror maker. He grew mean. Horrible. But sometimes he was nice, like he used to be."

The mirror maker? Biancaneve feels shaky inside. She can't hear any more of this. "What food do you know how to make, Bini?"

"Me?"

"Surely you watched Baffi and Giallino when they cooked—before I came. And you must have watched other cooks on Torcello. What do you know how to make?"

Bini looks away a moment. Then he grins. "Hazelnut sauce to put over roasted hedgehogs."

"Good."

"But don't think I'm going to cook. I'll show you the first time, then you have to do it."

"That sounds fair. In fact, I've had venison with hazelnut sauce. So once you teach me the sauce, we can have venison, too."

Bini gives a half smile. "Venison is rich people's food."

"What do you mean? You live in the woods. You can kill whatever you want."

"What gave you that idea? You can take down birds—partridges, skylarks, thrushes, pigeons, anything you want—but you can't kill big game. Especially not deer. You have to have permission if it's not on your land."

"Alvise hunted this boar."

"Not to kill it. We teach the dogs to hunt them down, but we don't kill them. The landlord lets us stay here in exchange for dogs now and then, so he can show off to his friends by giving them a fine hunter or a cute lapdog. But he forbids us to hunt." Bini scowls. "Did you think we cheated our landlord? That would be as bad as dirty squatters, paying no rent at all."

"I never thought about it," says Biancaneve.

"Well, we're not cheaters!" His face goes red-black. "We don't steal from anyone."

"I never thought you did." Biancaneve talks softly. "I truly never thought such a thing. Please know that. You are decent men; you prove it every day. So"—she tilts her head and talks even softer—"why did Alvise kill this boar?"

"He didn't. Well, he did. But Pietro wounded it mortally first. It was Pietro's mistake. He said the boar was going to kill him. But I think that's a bunch of garbage; I think he did it because he wanted those offal."

"What are you talking about?"

"Liver and lungs. He cut them out of the boar. That's why they were missing, Alvise told us. Pietro wanted the liver and lungs."

Biancaneve stumbles away from the fire, past Bini, and sits on the foot of Giordano's bed. Liver and lungs. Dolce says liver and lungs fix anything. She says her mamma told her that. Biancaneve's fingers snake into her hair.

"Are you all right, Neve?"

Biancaneve may never be all right again. "We have plenty of dried hazelnuts, Bini," she says with slow deliberation. "But no hedgehogs."

Bini grabs a sling. Biancaneve knew he would. "I'll get Alvise. We can hunt hedgehogs this afternoon."

"If you do, this boar stew can wait until tomorrow."

"We will. We've got the best dogs ever." Bini leaves.

Biancaneve feels unreasonably tired for so early in the day. This isn't really exhaustion, though; it's sadness. Her eyes are heavy.

Liver and lungs.

No, she can't think about that. It's a coincidence. It can't mean anything.

Heavens, she's tired. It's only early January. It's so long till spring.

She counts back in her head to the day they called Christmas. Oh. It's her birthday tomorrow. She'll be fifteen. She should be preparing for a party. She should have a new dress and all sorts of wonderful foods and sweets prepared. Venison? Sure. Anything she wants she should have. These men aren't allowed to hunt what lives all around them. Maybe they've never tasted venison. Maybe they've never had a roasted peacock. But Biancaneve has! And she should again! She throws herself backward on the bed.

The door creaks as it opens. The wind whooshes in.

Whoever it is better not scold her for lying down for a moment, because if he does, she just might scream at him, and if she starts screaming, she just might never stop.

"Sweet signorina, would you like to see my wares?" It's a woman's voice, croaky and broken.

Biancaneve turns her head toward the door. An old woman stands there, hunched over. Biancaneve's breath comes quick. It's easy to hunch over, pretend to be old. White wisps of hair stick out from under the woman's bonnet. Well, wigs are simple to find. The woman's coat is thick and coarse. Peasant clothes are easy to find. This could be Mamma—only nothing about her is familiar. The woman straightens a little and Biancaneve sees:

Her hands are gloved.

Biancaneve lunges for the fire poker. She stands facing the woman, poker in hand. "Take off your gloves."

"I'm so cold."

And it must be true. The woman's hands shake as she puts down her basket and pulls at the fingers of the gloves. She tugs and tugs, the way old people do when their joints are swollen and painful. But, really, she could be putting on a show—she could be a good actress. She's not making any progress on the gloves, after all.

Still, her eyes are rheumy. And it's not just her hands that shake; she shivers everywhere. She shivers so hard it seems she'll come apart, just fly to pieces. Her ribs show through the back of her dress as she turns this way and that, struggling with the gloves. She's shorter than Mamma. . . .

"It's the burns, you see," says the woman apologetically. "I made soap this week. I'm so clumsy."

For heaven's sake, Biancaneve should show a little human decency. "Don't worry about it. Keep the gloves on and come in, please," she says in a burst. "I'm sorry I spoke so brusquely. Shut the door behind you, would you? Come sit by the fire. Please."

"Thank you." The woman closes the door and moves to the table faster than Biancaneve would have thought she could. She must be half frozen. The woman puts her basket down, then sits on the stool closest to the fire.

Biancaneve stirs the fire with the poker. She wonders about that basket. But so long as she has the poker in her hand . . .

The woman pats her cheeks. There's something wrong with those cheeks. They look caked with some kind of gunk.

"You've got a lot of makeup on."

"Pigeon droppings."

Dolce would never put that on her face. Besides, Venetian women know how to use makeup that doesn't look cakey. Venetian women know all about how to fix their faces. They're experts. "It's thick," says Biancaneve.

"The only way to cover a multitude of sins."

Biancaneve grips the poker tighter. "What sins?"

"Scars from a pox in childhood. I try to make it easier for others to look upon me."

Biancaneve has heard about horrible skin conditions among the poor. "I didn't know peddlers came around here."

"I don't ordinarily come this way. I took a shortcut through the woods and seem to have gotten lost. The whole time I was terrified of boars. They say this is the best country for boar hunting."

"Probably they say right."

The old woman bobs her head. "And I haven't seen a single other cabin. If smoke hadn't curled up from your chimney, I wouldn't have seen your cabin, either."

"Would you like something to drink? I have—"

"Water. Hot water will do. I don't want to ask too much. Thank you."

Some people expect nothing of life. That's what Biancaneve needs to learn—to expect nothing—at least until spring. She moves the poker to her left hand, and with her right she puts a dipperful of water from the bucket into the small pot.

"The stools are low," says the old woman. "The beds are short." Her voice cracks, as though the sight of the beds makes her sad. Does she think they are for children?

Biancaneve nods. Her eyes fall on the covered basket again. "What do you have in there?"

"Good things," says the woman. "Beautiful things."

Biancaneve is overwhelmed with pity. What ugly things might this woman think of as beautiful? "May I look?"

"Please do."

Biancaneve pulls off the cloth. The basket is piled high with bodice laces. Silk, and in the best colors of Venezia. She fingers her own bodice lace. It's grimy and frayed at both ends.

The old woman reaches out a hand tentatively. She touches Biancaneve's hair. Biancaneve looks at her in surprise. The woman seems wistful. Almost longing.

"Take yours off," says the woman quietly. "Throw away that shabby old lace."

Biancaneve grips the poker tighter in one hand and pulls out the old lace with her other. Her hand flutters above the basket. "Which one? They're all so beautiful," she breathes.

"You can't ask me," says the woman. "I mix up colors."

"How funny, to sell such glorious things and not be able to appreciate them."

"Pick the color of the sun—warm and comforting, like you."

Biancaneve hesitates, but only a second. She puts the poker on the floor. The yellow is, in fact, more dazzling than even the green. She plucks a yellow lace from the basket and holds it to her cheek. It's soft and smooth and perfect. It's everything her life used to be. Then she puts it down. "I'm sorry." She steps back, to fight off temptation. "I wasn't thinking straight." This is so unfair. "I don't have anything to pay you with."

"Nothing?"

"Nothing. And tomorrow's my birthday! I can't have anything."

"Your birthday? Well then, let me give it to you as a present."

Biancaneve blinks in amazement. "These cost too much. I couldn't take such a present."

"Try it on, at least."

"I shouldn't."

"Doesn't everyone have the right to pretend, just for a moment, that they can afford something nice? One silk lace?"

Biancaneve picks up the lace again. She threads it through her bodice.

"Here. Let me help you tighten it." The old woman takes both ends and pulls. She pulls and pulls. She's so strong.

"That's too much. It hurts. I can hardly breathe."

"Neither can I," says the old woman, eyes miserable. "That's the problem, you see."

She pulls harder.

CHAPTER 35

Alvise

The smell of burning stew slaps Alvise in the face. He comes through the door with Bini at his heels. "Neve!" The girl lies on the floor, her face as pale as her name. Alvise drops the dead hedgehogs and rushes to her. He grabs her hands. Icy. He puts his cheek to her nose. Let there be a hint of breath, Good God, let it be. He slaps her cheeks. "Neve!"

"Is she dead?" Bini's voice cracks.

"I don't know." Alvise rubs her arms.

"What's that in her bodice?" Bini leans in from the side. "That lace, it's new. Someone's been here."

Alvise pulls out his knife and tries to slide it under the lace, but it's too tight. He forces a finger under one part and cuts straight. The lace pops open. He rips it the rest of the way.

"She was suffocated," says Bini.

"Don't say that. Get her closer to the fire." Alvise pushes on Neve's shoulders. "Pull her!"

They push and pull her as gently as they can. Then they stand over her and watch.

"You've messed her clothes." Bini points.

There's blood everywhere that Alvise's left hand touched. He sucks on his bleeding finger. Then he squeezes it tight in his right fist. "Get the stew off the hook before it catches fire."

"It'll take two of us."

Alvise grabs the bucket and throws what's left of the water onto the fire. It sputters and goes out.

"What'd you go and do that for?" Bini gapes at Alvise. "You know how hard it is to get a fire going again."

"What if the stew caught fire and it spread and we couldn't get Neve out of here in time?"

Giallino comes through the door. "What's all this smoke? And the fire's out."

"We had to," says Bini. His face colors, but he doesn't look at Alvise. "The stew was catching fire, and I couldn't lift it down myself, and Alvise cut his finger open so he couldn't help me and—you would have done the same thing."

"Why's Neve on the floor?" Giallino runs over.

The others come in the door now, shouting questions. Alvise keeps shaking his head.

"Shut up, everyone." Ricci claps his hands once, then shakes his clasped hands at them all. "Give Alvise a chance to speak."

"We came in and she was lying on the floor, cold as snow." Alvise jerks his chin toward the yellow silk lace in the middle of the floor. "Someone tried to suffocate her with that bodice lace."

"The Wicked One," says Giallino. "Yep, that's who."

"Neve's not stupid," says Baffi. "She'd never let The Wicked One in."

"How could she keep her out? She's a girl and The Wicked One is powerful." Giordano shakes his head. "We need to put a bolt across the door."

"I bet Neve let her in willingly," says Bini. "She always says we shouldn't call her The Wicked One. She refuses to believe her stepmother wants her dead."

"She won't refuse now," says Giallino. "If she lives. She's not moving."

"Ai!" Tommaso falls to his knees. "She has to live. I love her."

"We all love her, Tommaso." It's Ricci.

Alvise knew the girl had won their hearts, one by one. Every time she said "please," and meant it. Every time she sat on a stool and didn't complain about it being so low. Every time she didn't smile at them as though they were cute or funny—that sealed it. How you can love someone for what they don't do, for simply being a decent person . . . that's how it happened, though. Neve treats them like people. She works hard. She doesn't always do things right the first time, but she learns fast and does them right the second time. And her smile, it could make a man fall to his knees. Alvise doesn't even know if the girl likes any of them, but he knows all of them love her. He's grateful Ricci was the one to say it. He senses a change in the room. They're more united than they ever were before.

Good God, let this girl live.

Giordano gets his pillow and puts it under Neve's head. "Her color's returning. Don't you think so?"

"It's hard to tell, it's so dark." Giallino goes to the door. "I'll get dry firewood. Tommaso, help me. You're our best fire starter. You've got the patience."

Tommaso stares at Giallino. Alvise watches: the poor kid, he's not used to praise. Alvise has to find opportunities to praise all of them.

"It's the best thing you can do for her now," says Giallino. "We need to keep her warm."

Bini takes the blanket from his bed and lays it over Neve. He looks at Tommaso. "Our blanket's thicker than hers, right?"

Tommaso nods. He leaves with Giallino.

An hour later, the fire is roaring, the hedgehogs are roasting, the water buckets have been refilled, the burned stew has been fed to the dogs, the big pot has been scrubbed out by the riverside with pebbles, and the table has been set. Everyone worked, no one grumbled. Alvise calls them to the table.

"We shouldn't eat till Neve can join us," says Tommaso.

Alvise kneels over Neve. "Neve?" He puts his face closer. "Neve?" Did her eyelashes flutter? *Thank you, God in heaven. Thank you!*

Neve looks up at him. Her mouth opens, but she doesn't speak.

Alvise helps her sit up and get to her stool. Her hands press against her ribs. Her bodice hangs open, but she's fully covered by the smock underneath. Still, it feels wrong to leave her like that. Her old lace lies on the floor. Alvise grabs it and holds it out to her.

Neve pulls away, shaking her head. She blinks fast. She's panting now.

Alvise doesn't know what to do. "Well." He turns to the others. "What are we waiting for?"

Giallino serves the meat. Bini comes around with the sauce. They eat.

"Oh," murmurs Neve. She's the first to break the silence. "It's delicious."

"You almost died," says Tommaso.

Neve's lips part, then close, then part. "The hazelnut sauce is so good."

Bini nods. "Tommaso's right."

Neve sits up tall. Resolve masks her face. "Bini gave me ideas. Teach me recipes, all of you. We'll eat better from now on."

"Recipes?" says Ricci. He gives her a hard look. "We're waiting."

Neve's hand trembles. She puts down her knife. "It was an old peddler woman."

"The Wicked One," says Bini.

"I told you she'd come looking," says Giallino. "Yep, I told you."

Neve takes a deep breath. "Maybe." Her shoulders fall. She looks around at them. "You saved me." She's blinking fast.

"We're putting a bolt across the door tomorrow," says Giordano.

"And we'll take turns coming back to the cabin every so often all day long to check on you," says Baffi.

"If she comes this way again," says Ricci, "I'll kill her."

Neve puts her hand over her mouth. She shakes her head.

"Oh, yeah?" says Bini. "You want to die?"

"It's you or her," says Giordano. "That's the long and the short of it. And we won't let it be you."

Neve stares at Giordano. Tears well in her eyes. Alvise doesn't know what to do. Tears stream down her face now. "I didn't believe it. I couldn't. The last night we were together she said I was truly beautiful. She said she loved me so much. Why?" Her voice strangles on a sob. She looks around at them. Then she folds one fist inside the other and beats them rapidly against her chest right under her throat. "Recipes? Please?"

"I can gather porcini," says Tommaso quickly. "They're good with squirrel. I know a special place. And they're big ones—rust-colored and heavy as a goose egg." Tommaso leans forward. "On private property. But I can sneak them."

"Don't get in trouble just for mushrooms," says Neve quietly.

Baffi frowns. "Never call porcini 'just mushrooms.'"

"I saw other mushrooms at the base of an old fig tree," says

Ricci. "Tall and skinny and white, with little ball crowns at the top. They might be *chiodini*."

"*Chiodini* and chestnuts—they go perfect with pigeon," says Giordano. "And we've got plenty of chestnuts."

"It's a strange winter when porcini and *chiodini* are still popping up after the feast of Santo Stefano." Alvise smiles. He raises his glass. "To a strange winter, and a safe one."

They all drink.

"Who cut my lace?" asks Neve. Her hands are on her ribs again.

"I did," says Alvise.

"How did you guess it was too tight?"

"The ends were knotted. Otherwise, I could have pulled it out. But I had to cut it. You never knot the ends. You make a bow." As soon as the words are out of his mouth, Alvise realizes how revealing they are. He shouldn't know so much about Neve's bodice. He swallows in confusion.

"It was new," says Bini. "We saw the new yellow silk. That was it."

Neve looks hard at them. Then she smiles. "Thank heaven for that."

CHAPTER 36

Agnola

Agnola stands behind Dolce in the large hall. Dolce's looking in the mirror again. She was muttering to it just moments ago, but as Agnola approached she stopped. "What were you saying, Dolce?"

Dolce twirls around. Her speed surprises Agnola, for she sometimes moves across a room stopping at each piece of furniture as though to steady herself. Dolce just looks at her.

"I'd really like to know what you say to the mirror."

Dolce doesn't even shrug.

Agnola gives up. "Your skin looks strange. Did you do something to it?"

Dolce nods.

"It looks like you've been scrubbing at it. Hard. Why, your cheeks are practically raw. Do they hurt?"

Dolce touches her face. She's wearing gloves. Gloves, and she's still got her shift on. "Yes. I hurt everywhere."

"Let's go back to your room."

"How can that help? I hurt inside."

"Let's try." Agnola rings the bell on the wall and takes Dolce's arm.

Lucia La Rotonda comes up the stairs in an instant. Dolce and Agnola haven't even walked halfway down the hall yet. Everyone seems to be moving faster than Agnola expects them to. It makes her feel suddenly old. "We need a lovely, soothing lotion, please."

"Of course, Signorina," says Lucia La Rotonda. She turns toward the stairs.

Agnola hates it when people address her as "signorina." At her age, she deserves the title of "signora" just as a sign of respect. Still, she knows Lucia La Rotonda does it out of history—Agnola will probably always be "signorina" to her. "No, wait. I learned a new recipe."

Lucia La Rotonda turns back around. She folds her hands at her waist. "I have many good recipes."

"You'll be glad to learn this one," says Agnola, with what she hopes is grace. "I just learned about it at the Pisoni palace."

Lucia La Rotonda quivers just the slightest bit. She's as ambitious as anyone could be. Like a harp, touch her in the right place and she sings. Agnola feels slightly guilty playing her this way.

"Yes?" says Lucia La Rotonda.

"Boil equal parts rose water and lemon juice—"

"Excuse me, Signorina, but the lemon juice has gotten stronger, sitting so long since summer. Perhaps less lemon, then?"

"That sounds sensible. Certainly," says Agnola. "Once it has reached a boil, add crushed almonds. But they must be crushed very finely. Stir and boil till the whole mixture is milky and thick. It could take—"

"A quarter hour to a half hour," says Lucia La Rotonda.

"Of course. When it's smooth and cool, please bring it to us. With a sponge. And we could use your masterful hand with the bathing."

Lucia La Rotonda gives a satisfied smile and leaves.

"You are a model of patience, Agnola," says Dolce.

"Maybe that's my problem."

Dolce nods. She puts a hand on the glass chest-bench against the wall and lowers herself onto it. "Nothing is easy." She looks down.

The chest-bench is empty. Filling it was Bianca's job. Agnola makes a mental note to get flowers tomorrow. "Let's go to your room, Dolce. I'll help you out of your shift and into something pretty."

Dolce mumbles.

"What did you say?"

"Clothes can't make you beautiful."

"No, they can't." Agnola pats Dolce's arm, half lifts her, and guides her the rest of the way. Dolce seems more childlike every day. "But clothes can help in other ways. Maybe today you can wear something different. Something to lift your spirits. Clothing can remind you of the lovely things in life. It can remind you of who you are."

"Who am I?"

"Oh, Dolce!" Agnola's heart breaks. "Life goes on. For a while . . ." Her own voice catches. Then she gets hold of herself. "For a while we may forget why. Why we get up in the morning and dress and eat and talk and sleep. We can forget. I know, Dolce. I miss her, too. So very much. We've all come undone inside. But you, you are coming undone outside, too. And that makes it worse."

They go into Dolce's room.

Dolce walks to a rear window and lifts one corner of the red taffeta curtain. Sunshine frames her head and shoulders in a rosy haze. "I saw her."

Agnola doesn't know how to respond. So she keeps her mouth shut.

"I couldn't touch her. I wanted to. I wanted so much to feel her skin on mine. But I couldn't take off my gloves, you see."

Agnola's breath is stuck in her chest.

"She has nothing anymore. No luxuries. No silverware. No porcelain or brass or copper. No linen chest even. She's desolate." Dolce turns around. Tears fill her eyes.

"Dolce, dear Dolce." Agnola hugs Dolce, who stands rigid in her arms.

"All she has is her beautiful hair. It's still glorious. She's still beautiful. Insanely beautiful. But no one can see it. No one except . . ."

"Except . . . you?"

"The beds."

"Beds?"

"I believe Bianca is like me now. Like I was as a child. The odd one, the lonely one. Isn't that funny, Agnola? Bianca is back where I started." A sob catches in Dolce's throat. "I never wanted that. I hate it that she should feel that way. So lost."

Agnola runs her hands up and down Dolce's arms. "However Bianca is now, that's how she's supposed to be. That's how the good Lord wants it."

Dolce pulls back and her eyes light up. She looks sharp again. She does that. Dolce pulls off her shift.

"Your skin!" Agnola's hands go to her cheeks. But she drops them; she mustn't alarm Dolce. "You're peeling."

Dolce looks down at her chest. "I'm flaking away."

"You just need that lotion. It's wonderful. We'll massage it into you everywhere."

"I heard you with Pietro in the music room last night."

A tingle of fear rushes up Agnola's chest and throat.

"Don't worry. I'm glad you've found a better spot than the storeroom. And you needn't fear: I didn't put my ear to the door."

Agnola goes to the fireplace and leans against the marble for support. She looks at Dolce. This is surely leading somewhere.

"But . . ." Dolce pauses. "Pietro was laughing. Both of you were laughing." She sits on the bed. The bed skirt is crimson silk. The coverlet is crimson silk. Dolce's colorless skin seems lost in a sea of blood.

She lies down. Her naked body is beautiful, no matter how much she might be failing. That body is any man's ideal. Except Pietro's. Pietro is hungry for Agnola's body. Pietro loves her.

"Is Pietro generally happy, Agnola? Or was it just a momentary pleasure?"

"I'm not sure what you're asking, Dolce. And I'm not sure you have the right to ask it anyway."

"I need to know. Please."

"Why? Why on earth would you need to know such a thing?"

"Agnola, if you tell me, I will tell you what I say to Mirror."

"Mirror? You mean the big mirror in the grand hall? You call it by name?"

"Yes."

When Dolce passes through the big hall, she never fails to look in that mirror. She mumbles to it several times a day, and often cries. She cries silently, but her whole body shakes. Agnola is convinced Dolce's deterioration is somehow tied up with that mirror. Yes, yes, of course, it's because of Bianca. But the mirror is twisting Dolce, turning her inside out. Agnola needs to know what Dolce says to it. And surely the answer to Dolce's question is not harmful to Pietro. How could it be?

"All right. I agree." Agnola pats her own chest to calm herself. "Pietro is a levelheaded man. He's generally optimistic in spite of the ugliness of the world."

"What ugliness? Did something ugly happen recently? Did something happen over the last few days? Since you went to the afternoon party at the Pisoni palace?"

"No. Nothing new."

"Are you sure?"

"I think so."

"Nothing sad?"

"Sad? What are you asking me, Dolce?"

"How's the dog business going?"

"He fetched a lapdog from the trainers just two days ago. For the Pisonis' youngest daughter, Camilla. You know her. The one with all the ringlets. The little beauty."

"She's not that beautiful."

"She will be someday. Anyway, she said she wanted a puppy at that party, so I recommended Pietro, of course. Camilla is apparently thrilled with the dog. Pietro's happy."

"And his dog trainer friends, they're happy?"

"I don't know them."

"But Pietro didn't say they were sad about anything?"

"No. Nothing like that. Why do you ask these things?"

"Another failure. I feared as much." Dolce holds her hands up and shakes her head at them. "Weak. I can't do anything with these hands anymore. I was strong once. I could have pulled laces tight enough to crush ribs."

"What are you talking about?"

"I owe you only one answer." Dolce sits up. "I ask Mirror if I'm beautiful, if I'm the most beautiful one."

Oh. Such a simple and stupid thing. Agnola should have bargained for the answer to her other burning question. She's been a fool.

"Do you want to know what Mirror answers? No."

"But you are beautiful," says Agnola.

"Mirror is never wrong. And you have confirmed that."

Agnola grits her teeth. This discussion makes her angry against her will. "I don't understand. You never seemed to care about this before, and now . . . now it's all you speak of."

"We all have our peculiar ways, Agnola. Are mine that different?"

"Yes, they are, Dolce. They disgrace you. They diminish your soul. Vanity carried to such an extreme, bah!"

"It's not for the sake of vanity. It's for the sake of love." Dolce closes her eyes. She's silent.

"Are you drowsy? Have you been taking monkshood in the daytime?"

"Monkshood?" Dolce's eyes shoot open. "Who has monkshood?"

"That's what the physician gave us all, to help us sleep after . . ."

"No. He called the medicine something else . . . wolfsbane."

"It's the same thing. He warned us to use it sparingly, and just at night. It's dangerous."

"I know about monkshood, Agnola. I learned about it as a child."

"Don't overuse it."

"I haven't." Dolce hugs herself. "Indeed, I haven't made the use of it I should have. My hands are weak and useless, but monkshood is strong poison. And I know the right amount. This is a better way by far."

Agnola goes cold. "What do you mean?"

Dolce looks at her sharply. "Did I speak out loud? Don't pay attention."

Agnola sits on the edge of the bed. "Why didn't you come with me to the Pisoni party?" she says softly.

"I had things to do."

"Where?"

"What do you mean, where? Household chores . . ."

"Don't lie to me, Dolce. I know you were gone the whole day. You said not to disturb you, but I came into your room before I left, to check on you. You were gone. And Antonin was gone. You told me to have the Contarini women bring me to the party because you needed to send Antonin on an errand, but that wasn't true. You had Antonin take you someplace."

"You're right."

"Where did you go?"

"It's private."

"Tell me."

Dolce puts a hand on Agnola's shoulder. "I'll tell you, and in exchange you'll do me another favor."

"It's better if we just talk to each other openly. Like we used to do. Like sisters."

"Sisters do each other favors. And I need a favor, Agnola."

"What kind of favor?"

"Another disguise."

"I thought you liked the peddler outfit."

"I did. Now I want something else."

"What?"

"A daily dress, but fine. Like we would wear most days. And not in any usual color of Venezia dresses. Maybe in orange."

Orange? How like the Sforza women of Milano; Dolce will look ridiculous. Even more ridiculous than she looks now. "Do you know what a figure you cut, in the nude, but with gloves?"

Dolce pulls off her gloves. Her nails are split. Her skin is raw and red.

"Oh! What's happening to you?"

"Gloves hide a multitude of sins, no?"

"I'll call the physician."

"No, Agnola. He's useless."

"There are other physicians, Dolce. I can ask for recommendations. I can—"

"I'm taking care of it. I'm going for . . . the cure. My cure."

Agnola frowns. The mineral baths, of course! She should have investigated them, taken Dolce to them herself. "Antonin takes you?"

"Partway, yes. I walk the rest of the way."

Agnola's mouth goes dry. "It's dangerous for you to walk the alleys of Venezia."

"I don't. I go elsewhere. And that's all I'll say. For now. I've been honest with you, Agnola. I love you. Please, will you get me an orange dress? Quickly."

"It will take time to choose material and have the tailor come here and—"

"No, no, I don't care about all that. Have someone make it fast. Make it larger than me, and I'll stuff it where I need to. It will disguise me better."

A clunk comes from outside the door. "Thank you, Carlo." It's the voice of Lucia La Rotonda. "May I enter, Signora? Signorina?"

"Come in," says Agnola.

Lucia La Rotonda enters. She blanches at the sight of Dolce's shedding skin. "I made a giant pot. In case the signora wanted to bathe in it."

"That was considerate of you," says Agnola.

"Agnola, dear," says Dolce, "you can leave me in the capable hands of Lucia La Rotonda. You have an errand for me. Please hurry."

Agnola kisses Dolce on her paper-dry cheek and leaves. Outside the door she hesitates. And she happens to see Dolce hold her hand to her mouth, then look at it. On her palm is a tooth. *No. Oh, please no.* Agnola flees.

CHAPTER 37

Giallino

The pup trails behind Giallino, a little too far. He slaps his leg. "Come on, catch up."

She runs to his heels, tail wagging like a maniac.

He scoops her up and gives her a good rubbing up and down the tummy and back, behind the ears, under the chin. He kisses the top of her head and plops her down again. "Stay close. You could be the right doggy for the next little missy who comes along. Just stay close."

She looks at him intently.

This is good. Eye contact is the most important thing. It's what makes all of them so good with the dogs, especially the hunting dogs. They stand eye to eye, and the dogs get the message right off. Alvise is best at it, because he can stare down the most belligerent dog. He'll put his nose to the dog's nose and lift a warning lip, but it's mainly his steady eyes that do the trick. That's why he's in charge of the hunting dogs. But Bini's getting better at it all the time.

Giallino tried to work with the hunting dogs at first, but he hated the fact that no one but their trainer was allowed to pet them. Still, he loves this business. He loves living a free life, tramping through the woods in winter. Not having to do ridiculous antics to make a bunch of louts laugh. He's a skilled worker, independent, in charge of himself, and still part of a group. He's been here for only a matter of months, but he's as committed to these men as if he had grown up with them, though, of course, he has no idea what that would really feel like. Giallino was taken from his mother when he was an infant; he never had a family.

A family. That's what Neve called them last night. "The family in the woods."

When she said it, a shiver went up his spine. It made him sit tall. Because it's true. They've created their own family, and they've welcomed him into it.

Neve is part of the family now, too. Though they know she will leave someday.

Tommaso says he loves her. He says he'll win her.

But he won't. None of them will. Not because they're little and she's big, but because she's their sister. And they protect her. That's what brothers are supposed to do. You don't need to have grown up in a family to know that.

Her father will come home in the spring. At first it seemed like spring would never come. . . . Neve interrupted everything. It was impossible to do the simplest things, like change into a nightshirt, without considering where she was. Now spring seems just around the corner. Giallino's lips tremble. He presses them together hard.

The pup licks him straight up the face.

Giallino laughs. He was staring at the pup this whole time, but he'd forgotten about her. Neve hates to be licked by dogs. She says their breath stinks.

He walks. There's no reason to be sad. It's still January. The Dolomiti mountains are snow-covered. And Pietro said those mountains in Russia, whatever they're called, will be impassable for months. Neve's not about to disappear tomorrow.

A squirrel zips across his sight up ahead.

The pup stays at Giallino's heels. Good for her. It's possible she didn't see the squirrel, but Giallino doesn't think so.

He walks from tree to tree, making sure he comes within arm's reach of the trunks. Some of them must reek of fox or wolf. But the pup stays at his heels. She doesn't have to follow every scent, that's good. It could be her nose is defective. But if it is, that's fine, too. She won't get distracted from her owner by all the lovely odors of the household.

And he's never heard her growl.

Yep, this is a good pup for a young missy. Even a girl younger than eight.

He picks up the pup and hugs her. "Time to go check on Neve. Let's run." He puts her down and runs. The pup stays right at his heels. Better and better.

Thump! Then several smaller thumps.

Giallino spies a gray-brown stag through the trees. A big one. Giallino is sure he couldn't touch the animal's shoulder even standing on tiptoe. He scoops the pup into his arms and watches.

The stag is looking down with shock on his face. He has only one antler. Oh, of course, now Giallino sees it; the animal has just cast an antler. The stag walks up to the shed antler gingerly and sniffs. Then he licks it in obvious amazement.

Giallino suppresses a laugh. What a mystery the world must be to animals. Is it hard for him to balance now, with all that weight gone from his head?

And now Giallino recognizes the opportunity. Bini told him Neve loves venison. They're not supposed to hunt big game, but one deer—who would notice?

He slowly sets the pup at his feet. She sits, absolutely silent, waiting to see what he wants. Good pup. He reaches for the bow he carries slung on his back. No one walks in these woods without protection; Alvise has taught them the basics.

He pulls out an arrow, sets it in place, aims, shoots.

The stag flashes a look at the slipper-soft sound of the feather and leaps away, with the arrow lodged in his side. What a pity. He'll run a long time before he falls. Giallino couldn't keep up with him. It's a mistake to go hunting without dogs to chase down the prey. The beast is wasted. That's so wrong. Giallino would never kill an animal for sport. He did it for all good reasons, but it didn't work out.

He goes and picks up the antler. It really is heavy. But he needs to hurry now, so he holds it out to one side as best he can and runs. The pup stays at his heels. Tears roll down his face as he runs; he can't think why.

CHAPTER 38

Sebastiano

The woods are quiet this morning. Silent, really. The sound of Luminoso's hooves is the only noise. Riding along like this, with no goal, just enjoying the chilly air, comforts Sebastiano.

He looks up through the high, bare branches of the chestnut trees to a leaden sky. Maybe it will snow. The end of January is unpredictable. He likes that. Life needs more adventure.

He smiles ruefully. To think of changes in the weather as adventure—what a pitiable soul he's become. He's only twenty-three, he has everything ahead of him.

A crow flies overhead. Now a second, a third. Even in the pale light, they give off a green sheen. He should put his gloves on, but he doesn't trust gloves when he's riding. The leather can cushion the feel of the reins in his hands so much that he may pull too hard without realizing it. Luminoso has a soft mouth. Sebastiano trained the stallion himself; they are a team. This morning is cold, though. And he's enjoying a gentle ride. What harm could there be? He takes his gloves out of his jacket and pulls them on.

Caws break the tranquility of the woods. Sebastiano squeezes his thighs and Luminoso presses forward. The caws get louder. The birds are squabbling over something.

He follows the noise. A raucous, flapping black cloud covers the ground in front of him. Luminoso whinnies and prances in place. Sebastiano urges him forward and shouts at the birds. They rise again, screaming at him.

An arrow protrudes from the hindquarters of a stag. The carcass has been ravaged by something other than birds, something that ripped it apart. Probably boars.

Sebastiano dismounts as the crows scream and Luminoso neighs and stomps back and forth. Sebastiano pulls at the arrow. A crow dives at him. Another. They're coming fast, in a mob. He yanks with all his might and the arrow comes free. He runs for Luminoso, batting the birds away with his arms. He puts the arrow through a loop on the pommel, throws his leg over the saddle, and rides off.

Luminoso's thumping hoofbeats are drowned out by the sound of Sebastiano's heartbeat. Crows dive in spring and summer if you're near their nest or young. Everyone knows to just go the other way. But those are pairs of crows. This was an entire flock—who knows, maybe fifty birds—and they acted together. Sebastiano touches the back of his neck and then looks at his hand. Blood. He knew it.

He shakes. He was in danger—a murder of crows could overtake a full-grown man. And he's furious at whoever shot the stag. This is his property. No one has permission to hunt. He relaxes his legs and Luminoso slows to a walk.

It must have happened within the past day or so.

Who would come out here now? It's Carnevale in the city. And anyone he knows would have asked his permission.

This arrow wasn't made by the local fletcher. Did a stranger pass through? But what stranger hunts a deer? A traveler might pick off a rabbit and eat it over an open fire. A deer, never. You couldn't finish it off, you couldn't properly take it with you. No one would be that wasteful.

Maybe the dwarfs know something. They go through these woods frequently, training their dogs, but Sebastiano has had no reason to seek them out. His father used to claim the best lapdogs as the landlord's due so he could give them away as a grand gesture. Sebastiano doesn't even like lapdogs. They have bad breath. In any case, he'll go to the dwarfs' cabin.

He shifts in the saddle and squeezes his knees. Luminoso trots again, and the sound of the crows fades. A terrible sense of loneliness overcomes Sebastiano. He would love someone to tend to his neck, to rub his shoulders. Not a servant. Not at all.

The little curl of chimney smoke directs him now. Little curl from a little roof from a little cabin. It's an odd place, but the dwarfs built it themselves and they never ask for anything. As he nears, dogs bark. He's surprised. Usually in midday the dogs are scattered through the woods, wherever their various trainers have decided to practice with them that day. Well, good, he's lucky; he won't have to wait till evening to ask about the dead stag.

Sebastiano dismounts and ties Luminoso to a sapling. He grabs the arrow, then booms out a greeting as he reaches a hand to open the door.

It doesn't budge. It must be bolted from within.

"Hello in there," calls Sebastiano.

No answer.

"Hey! Open up. I need to talk to you."

Still nothing.

"What's going on?" He walks around the cabin. All the

shutters are closed. He jiggles them. They hold fast. "I know you're in there," he calls. "You can't bolt a door from the outside. Answer me!"

Nothing.

He pounds on the door with his fist. It's absurd that he should be thwarted like this. "This is Messer Simoli. Your landlord. I demand that you open up right now."

"How do I know that?" comes a voice. A woman's voice. Or a girl's.

So far as Sebastiano knows, there are only seven people who live in this cabin, all of them men. "Who the devil are you?"

"That's what I'm wondering about you."

"I told you who I am."

"Aren't you really Dolce in disguise?"

"Who the devil is Dolce?"

"My mother. My stepmother."

"Do I sound like your stepmother?"

"Don't be ridiculous."

"You're the one who said it."

The girl is silent.

Sebastiano crosses his arms. The wind has picked up a little. He's chilled. "Shall we start over? My family name is Simoli. My given name is Sebastiano. May I know your name now?"

"No."

"That's uncooperative of you. Highly."

Silence.

"Listen, I'm not your stepmother."

"Do you work for her?"

"I work for no one."

"So you just live off other people, is that it?"

"No." Sebastiano frowns. "I oversee this estate. I'm sure I do far more work than you do."

"Why would you say that?"

"I can hear it in your voice. You're Veneziano nobility. You probably spend your day playing the harp."

"Stop that!"

"Stop what?"

"The harp is a beautiful instrument."

"I agree."

"So why did you say that?"

"To upset you. You upset me."

"I didn't mean to insult you."

Sebastiano's feet are getting cold. He stomps in place. "I think maybe I've been away from people too long."

"You live alone?"

"With servants."

"Servants are people."

Sebastiano clears his throat. "What I meant is that I've been away from society too long. I'm losing my social graces." It's true. "I apologize."

"Why have you been away from society?"

"Things happen. Things you can't plan for."

"Ah." Her voice catches.

Was that a sob?

"I'm cold," says Sebastiano.

"I can't let you in. So go away. Get back on your horse."

"How do you know I came on a horse?"

"I'm not deaf."

"Right." Sebastiano sinks to the ground and pulls his knees to his chest. He feels a little warmer. In his left hand he still clutches the arrow from the stag. He turns it over and over. "Have you gone to Carnevale parties this season?"

"I'm barricaded in a cabin in the woods. Haven't you noticed? You seem a bit daft."

Sebastiano's eyes smart. She's certainly as rude as he's been. He doesn't owe her any niceties. "I made a mistake not to take part in Carnevale this year."

"Why do you say that?"

"It would have done me good. Perhaps even to get flat-out drunk and flirt with beautiful women, stealing a kiss here and there, or maybe more. I've gotten lucky at Carnevale in the past." Sebastiano knows he shouldn't be talking this way to a girl. But she's irked him, and this kind of talk warms him a bit. "All my friends count on getting lucky. It's like one giant secret that everyone shares; pretending it's a secret protects everyone's virtue."

"Hypocrisy," says the girl. "I hate it."

"Agreed," says Sebastiano.

The girl is silent for a bit. Then, "You could still go to Carnevale. The festivities continue till Martedì Grasso."

"Indeed I could. I have friends in Venezia who would take me in. But all of them have daughters who now, more than ever, look at me as an eligible bachelor."

"Are you?"

"Yes, I suppose."

"Then they look at you right."

"Not really. I don't feel eligible, you see. I've been solitary since summer, and I'm getting used to it."

"Are you a widower?"

"No. It was my father who died."

"I'm sorry. And . . ." She pauses. "Your mother?"

"I grew up missing my mother. She died in childbirth with a baby girl, who also died."

"So you were little."

"No. I was already twelve. So I grieved for the loss of both of them. I still do, though I miss my father even more now."

"My mother's dead."

"I know."

"How?" comes the sharp question.

"You don't have a stepmother if your mother's alive."

"Oh."

"Now who seems a bit daft?"

"I'm sorry I said that," says the girl. "Let's stop."

"Agreed. How old were you when your mother died?"

"Little. She died in childbirth, too. Along with my infant brother. I envy you being able to miss your mother. I remember almost nothing of mine."

"What rotten thing did you do to your stepmother?"

"Nothing! Why would you ask such a nasty question?"

"You're barricaded in this cabin, as you say. Against her, I gather. So she's angry at you. Did you run away?"

"I was swept away."

Sebastiano stands abruptly. "What? Did the men of this cabin steal you?"

"No, no. They're my heroes. They're helping me. They're keeping me safe."

"Safe? From your stepmother?"

"Yes."

"Where's your father?"

"Traveling."

"Where?"

"Far."

"Where?"

"Russia."

"What on earth would make someone travel to Russia in winter?"

"He's gathering books for his library. He left in autumn, and got snowed in. He'll be back in spring. He'll come for me. In the meantime, I stay inside."

"That's a long time. . . . What's the worst your stepmother would do to you, anyway?"

"Kill me."

Sebastiano shakes his head, though the girl can't see him. "People kill boys sometimes, to remove potential heirs. I've heard of that kind of wretched behavior. But who kills a girl?"

She's silent.

"Please answer me."

"I'm not a liar."

"I'm not calling you a liar. I just don't understand."

"I'm staying here till Papà comes for me."

Sebastiano paces in a circle. "It's not right that you should be in this cabin till spring. My house—"

"Don't think about it. Anyway, no sensible person invites a girl he doesn't know into his home."

"I'm not sensible. I'm lonely. There, I said it."

"Well, no sensible girl accepts such an invitation."

"I wouldn't harm you."

"The only thing I really wish I could have," says the girl slowly, "is a view of water. From our balcony, I could see a long stretch of the Canal Grande. I miss that so much."

"You can't see water from my house. But—"

"Stop. I don't even know who you are, really. Besides, it sounds like you have enough trouble taking care of yourself."

"Why do you say that?"

"You said it yourself. You need to do something, anything, to get yourself lively again. If it's not Carnevale, then something else. What else do you like to do in winter?"

"Well, my father, he was a noisy man. Quick to laugh, generous, and always on the lookout for beauty. We traveled, particularly in winter. It was the best part of life, traveling the world with my father. Everything was glorious seen through his eyes."

"I traveled with my father too."

"A girl?"

"I told you, I'm not a liar."

"Sorry. It's just that I've only ever heard of one girl who traveled with her father. In fact, I knew her, briefly. We traveled together, the four of us, to a monastery. It was right after my mother died. The girl's mother had also died not long before."

"So you commiserated?"

"Hardly. She was three. Maybe four. Argumentative with her father—my father disapproved, but I thought she was fun."

She's silent. After a long while, she says, "That's it, then. Travel is the answer."

Sebastiano rubs the back of his neck. "Listen, I'd like to help you."

"Why?"

"I'm not sure. Maybe because this is the longest conversation I've ever had with a young woman, just the two of us talking. It feels . . . intimate."

She's quiet. Did he offend her? "I don't know why I speak so openly with you. I didn't mean to upset you."

"Don't apologize. I know what you mean. I know exactly what you mean."

His breath speeds up. "Let me help you."

"You can't."

"At least tell me who you are."

"Never. I don't really know if anything you've said is true, you see. I don't know why you came to this cabin out of the blue."

"Because of the stag. Someone killed a stag on my land. I

brought the arrow with me. I wondered if the men here had seen anything."

"The stag? Oh, no! That's my fault."

"You shot the stag?"

"Don't be foolish. I don't hunt. But Giallino came across the animal yesterday. Bini had convinced everyone that I love venison after some stupid remark I made, so Giallino shot it. But it got away. I'm so sorry. The last thing I want is for these men to get thrown out because they violated their agreement with the landlord." Her voice breaks. "They are good men. The stag is my fault. Please forgive them."

"Are you crying?"

No answer.

"Don't be afraid. I won't punish them. In fact, I'll bring you venison, cooked a special way. I swear. Don't cry."

"I'm not crying out of fear. I'm crying because Giallino was so sweet. They're all so good."

"Well, that's no reason to cry."

"Sure it is. Go now. Go on your travels. Go before I believe you're sweet and I open this door and die."

CHAPTER 39

Biancaneve

Biancaneve lays the squirrels on their backs in a line: six of them. She skins one and keeps the pelt. Alvise has promised to show her how to make new gloves and hats for all of them once there are enough pelts. Actually, Biancaneve knows quite a bit about sewing. But she accepted Alvise's offer because she could see it made him feel generous. They all like to help her these days. She skins two more squirrels and throws a tail on the pile of pelts. She's good at this.

There's a loud rap on the shutters. Her heart jumps. It's been two days since Sebastiano was here. He has probably gone traveling already. It's foolish of her to hope. But if it is him, she's decided to tell him her name, to see if he recognizes it. After all, when he was twelve, he and his father went traveling with a girl and her father—and the girl's mother had died recently, and she was only three or four. Biancaneve cannot remember traveling with anyone but Papà. Still, she does have an isolated memory of riding in front of a big boy on a wonderful, fast horse, and the boy being ever so fun—and she has no idea who he was.

She goes to her bed and reaches under the pillow for the arrow Sebastiano left outside the front door. She twirls it in her fingers. Sebastiano was quick at sparring. That was interesting. The men of this cabin all dote on her now; Sebastiano was a welcome change. It was exciting to talk with him. The flutter in her stomach right now is due to nothing more than a hope for diversion from the routine. "Who's there?" she calls.

"That's not the right response," comes Tommaso's voice.

Biancaneve shoves the arrow back under the pillow. She goes to the window and opens a shutter. "Hi, Tommaso."

"You're not supposed to answer. Don't you know the rules yet?"

"Of course I know the rules, Tommaso. If I don't answer, then you have to keep knocking, and eventually you shout out your name, and I say I'm fine. But it's cold. Your knuckles get raw. So I figured I'd spare you some pain."

"Me? Just me?"

"Well . . . Tommaso, of course I want to spare you pain. You're very sweet and dear to me. But I want to spare everyone pain. Don't you want everyone to have safe knuckles?"

Tommaso frowns. "I don't know if I care."

"Well, I do. Thank you for checking on me."

"Don't open the shutters to anyone else."

"All right."

Tommaso peeks in the window. "You've skinned only half the squirrels."

"Don't worry. You'll have plenty for dinner."

"Want me to help?"

"No. I like doing it."

Tommaso picks a thorn off his jacket. "Don't answer next time."

"See you at dinner." Biancaneve closes the shutters. She finishes the squirrels fast, cuts them into pieces, and throws the meat into the bubbling pot.

Rapping at the shutters again.

"I'm not here," calls Biancaneve. "Does that satisfy you, Tommaso?"

"I'm not Tommaso," comes a quiet voice. Biancaneve can hardly hear it.

"Who are you?"

"I'm lost."

Biancaneve trembles. "Go away."

"I don't know which way to go." It's a woman's voice. Refined. But not Mamma's. Still . . .

"I can't help you. I have no idea where anything is."

Sounds of sobbing.

"Don't cry," says Biancaneve. "Please don't cry. I'm not allowed to let anyone in."

"I don't care about coming in. I just want a little encouragement. And maybe a cup of something warm to put in my belly. I've been walking for hours."

"Walking from where?"

"I'm not sure. My cousin lives nearby, toward Treviso. I'm visiting. I was with a group of hunters who went off after a bear. It's hard to talk through the shutters. Won't you open them?"

If she keeps a hand on each shutter, she can close them quickly in an emergency. The woman might be strong, though. "No."

"Well, all right. At least this stump is good to sit on. I need the rest."

A stump? There's only one stump, for splitting wood. It's far from the window, far enough that if someone made a rush for her, Biancaneve would have plenty of time to close the shutters. She opens the shutters just a crack.

A stocky woman in a bright orange dress sits on the stump. It's a fancy dress; she doesn't belong here. The peddler-woman disguise was more convincing. If this is really Mamma, she's doing a worse job than before. And hunting a bear? Really, now. Suddenly fury rises in Biancaneve's chest. "So what did you do when they went after the bear?"

"I told them I'd wait. And I did. I waited and waited. But they didn't return. It was hours. Finally, I started after them. And here I am."

"You should have gone back where you came from," Biancaneve says sharply.

"I wish I had."

"It was stupid to set off into the woods."

"I've been telling myself that for the past hour."

How can you argue with someone who keeps agreeing? Biancaneve looks hard at the bedraggled woman. Her dark hair is in clumps. She has fat cheeks, reddened in the style of the nobles. She doesn't look anything like Mamma. But Mamma is clever. "What would you like to eat?"

"What do you have?"

"Tell me what you want."

The woman sniffs the air. "Do I smell cabbage? I love cabbage."

Mamma hates cabbage. And tears glitter on the woman's cheeks.

Still, Biancaneve is almost sure Mamma cried when they were sitting on the *fondamenta*. She cried as she drugged Biancaneve. And the eyes of the old peddler woman—her eyes spoke of tragedy even as she pulled on the bodice lace. "I'll put a cup of broth on the sill and close the shutters," Biancaneve says. "Don't come near till I've secured them shut."

"That's hardly hospitable of you."

"It's the best I can do."

"You act as though you're afraid of me."

"I am," says Biancaneve.

"Oh, how awful, to be afraid of a lone woman lost in the woods."

"The last lone woman lost in the woods tried to kill me."

The woman's face shows horror.

Biancaneve closes the shutters. She fills a cup with broth, then opens the shutters the tiniest bit. The woman is still on the stump. "Here." Biancaneve puts down the broth and closes the shutters again. She listens.

After a few moments, the woman's voice comes. "It's good, that broth. Thank you. I put the cup back on the sill." Her voice sounds distant again.

Biancaneve opens the shutters. The woman is sitting on the stump and the cup on the sill is empty. "I'm glad you enjoyed it."

The woman opens a pouch and pulls out a silver toothpick. She cleans her teeth. Oh! She's missing a left front tooth. No one could fake that. This couldn't be Mamma! Relief floods Biancaneve. How harsh she's been to the poor woman. "Do you need anything else, dear lady?"

"No, I better be on my way." The woman slips the toothpick back into her pouch. "I feel better. You must be a fine cook."

"I'm learning."

"If you eat, you should cook."

"That's right," says Biancaneve. "We should all help in the chores of life."

The woman laughs. "I didn't mean it so seriously." She tilts her head. "You have beautiful hair."

"Thank you."

"I have nothing to pay for the broth with. But I do have a comb." She pulls a silver comb out of her pouch. "It's old and in need of polishing. But I'd be pleased if you'd accept it as my thanks."

"Don't be absurd. A cup of broth is nothing compared to a silver comb."

"A cup of broth and a few words when you're hungry and tired and alone in the woods—that's worth a lot. Please accept it. I have another at home anyway. Close the shutters and I'll put the comb on the sill."

"All right." Biancaneve closes the shutters. "Did you do it?"

"Yes." The woman sounds distant again.

Biancaneve peeks. The comb is on the sill and the woman is back on the stump. It's a simple comb, but really very nice. Biancaneve likes the curved handle. "Pity that I don't have a horsehair switch to clean it with."

"You can use pine needles, if you must."

"Or maybe squirrel tail. I have plenty."

"That sounds like a good idea." The woman shakes a warning finger. "Boil the tail first so you kill the vermin on it." Then she brightens. "Anyway, there's no hurry on the tail. I cleaned the comb just the other day. Go ahead, comb your hair. Or let your mamma do it."

"I don't have a mamma."

The woman grimaces. "I'm sorry to hear that." She looks infinitely sad. "Alas. I wish I had a daughter so I could comb her hair." She seems to be holding back tears. "I could comb yours, if you like."

"You're so kind." Biancaneve forces a smile. There's something painful in the woman's face. Did she lose a daughter? Fear pricks at her for a moment. But this woman is older and missing a tooth; Mamma is too caught up in beauty to pull out a tooth, no matter what. Biancaneve looks down at the charming comb again. "No. You should leave now."

"Cautious." The woman nods approval. "What a dear and good child you are. May I at least watch?"

Biancaneve pulls the comb gingerly through her hair.

"Such wonderful hair," says the woman.

Biancaneve combs harder now. That's the right way to comb. She digs in and combs and combs. It's so good to be doing this, after months of being unkempt. She'll look like herself again, even if inside she's all ajumble still. Comb, comb, comb. It's as though she can feel the glossiness grow.

Oh! Intense heat bursts through her skull. She looks at the woman in amazement.

The woman stands and waves, and weeps.

CHAPTER 40

Giallino

Giallino walks swiftly with the new pup at his heels. Pietro took his favorite one away—the little prize. He misses her. This new one isn't as promising. It takes many more repetitions to get anything through this one's skull. Giallino's annoyed. He rushes; he should have gone back to the cabin a while ago to check on Neve.

And there's the cabin. One set of shutters is open. Giallino half understands. With the hearth fire and the candles, the cabin can get smoky and smelly and stuffy. But facts are facts; The Wicked One wants Neve dead. Neve should wait till they're all home to air the cabin out. He breaks into a run and calls, "Are you crazy? Close those shutters!"

He reaches the window and looks in. No Neve. Then he sees her, on the floor, just under the window. The windowsill is too high for him to vault. For the first time in his life, Giallino curses his short arms. He runs to the door. It's bolted from the inside. Of course. He runs back to the window, nearly tripping over the pup, who has caught his panic. The pup barks. "Neve!" he shouts. She doesn't move.

He rolls the chopping stump to the window, climbs onto the window ledge, and jumps inside. He puts his face to hers. "Neve, Neve, wake up." Her bodice lace is that same old thing. He slips a finger under it easily. Some new trick, new disaster. "Neve," he says in her ear. "Don't do this! Don't leave us!" And then he sees it, a silver comb in her hair. Neve doesn't have a comb. She's been using her fingers. He pulls it free.

Neve moans.

The sound nearly brings Giallino to tears. "Neve. It's all right, Neve. I'm here now. You'll be fine."

Her eyes open. They look glassy.

Giallino runs for a cup of broth.

The pup yips from outside the window. "Wait," he calls to it. "I'll be right there for you."

He kneels beside Neve and drips just the smallest bit of broth into her open mouth. Her eyes are closed again, but she moans louder than before. Slowly, slowly, Giallino drips the whole cup into Neve's mouth. Slowly, slowly, she swallows it all. That's what she needed, yep.

She rolls her head from side to side. "My head is numb. My chest tingles." She struggles to roll onto one side and curls into a ball.

Giallino pats her back tenderly. "You'll get better fast, Neve. You'll be fine."

The pup whines.

Giallino goes to the window and reaches out. He manages to catch the pup. She licks his face frantically. He puts her down inside the cabin and kneels beside Neve. "Neve?"

The pup comes running over. Giallino blocks her. The last thing Neve needs is a lick.

Neve's eyes open. She tries to push herself up, but she collapses with another groan. "I think . . . I'm going to be sick."

Giallino rushes for a bucket and races back. She retches into the bucket over and over. Then she falls onto her back again.

He should splash out her mouth, give it a good cleaning. He looks around.

The pup sniffs at the comb, licks the teeth. In an instant, she contorts. Giallino grabs her.

Poison.

How can they win against The Wicked One? There are hundreds of ways to kill a person. How can they stay ahead of her?

Giallino hugs the stupid little pup to his chest and rocks on his heels.

CHAPTER 41

Agnola

"I hate this." Dolce looks at Agnola. "You shouldn't have dragged me here. These women are sick."

The water is the temperature of a warm day in midsummer; it doesn't let off steam or make one uncomfortable. It's beautifully comforting. If only Dolce let herself, she'd enjoy it. Agnola enjoys it.

Today makes a full week they have been at the Abano hot springs. The first morning they drank a rust-colored liquid that made them spend the rest of the day and night racing to the toilets, then back to bed for an absurdly deep sleep, then off to the toilets again. Then five days of drinking nothing but spring-water. Yesterday the bathing therapy started, so life turned enormously better. But Lucia La Rotonda doesn't get to bene-fit, for Dolce keeps sending her away for special ingredients for dinner.

"Do you think we should send Lucia La Rotonda home?" asks Agnola. "She's not having a good time. She never gets to sit in the baths."

Dolce splashes Agnola. "I just said I hate it here. Lucia La Rotonda's cooking is my salvation." She points at a woman across from them. "You know what she said?"

Agnola swats Dolce's hand down. "Don't point. It's rude."

Dolce slides under the water and comes up sputtering and wiping the water from her eyes. "She told me that there's a much nicer bath in Caldiero, near Verona. It's large and airy. You don't have to bring your own cook because the patrons are excellent cooks."

Agnola sighs. This small bathhouse is gloomy. "So why did she come here?"

"The Caldiero bath is outdoors. They allow patients only June through August."

"Well," says Agnola, "I hope you're cured long before summer." Then she remembers. "Oh, Marin will be back by then. You can go with him."

"What's the point of going with your husband when they separate the men's baths from the women's? Unless, of course, all your matrimonial pleasures lie in bed."

Agnola looks quickly at Dolce, then away. Did she hear Pietro with her?

"I know you had a visitor last night. I'm happy for you. I just like to tease you."

"I don't like teasing. And I won't talk with you about . . . certain things."

"All I want to know is whether Pietro is in good health."

Agnola's heart warms at this surprise. "He came only to visit me."

"But how is he, in body and in spirit?"

"Good. Those apples on our table this morning, he brought them from up north. They store them year-round because they're therapeutic. They clean poisons out of your system."

"Poisons?" Dolce strains toward her. "He used that word?"

"Someone he knows got sick and apples are making her better."

"Apples," says Dolce, as though to herself. "Apples thwart me?" She sinks back. "Can't I do anything right?"

Agnola is at a loss when Dolce says nonsensical things like this. And as often as not her outbursts lead to crying. Already, Dolce's bottom lip quivers. "This water is the best therapy, though," Agnola says quickly. "It's good for joint pain and runny noses and swelling and weeping eyes and infertility—"

"Nothing will cure my infertility."

Agnola could bite her tongue. Why on earth did she say such a thing? "I'm so sorry."

"I know. You don't have a mean bone in your body."

Agnola isn't so sure. She gets annoyed with Dolce. "Anyway, these waters have special curative minerals, good for all skin ailments."

"I can taste the iron and salt," says Dolce. "Let's see if it's helping." She holds up her hands and peels a nail off, just like that.

A spasm shoots up Agnola's back. "You're very ill, Dolce. We're here to make you better. Please, Dolce. You have to help yourself."

"I want to go home."

"These baths—"

"Please. I'm exhausted. Defeated. You can see the baths do nothing for me."

"We haven't completed the full regimen."

"It won't change anything. All I wanted to do was make everything right by the time Marin returned. But I can't, it's too hard. My heart isn't in it anyway. Sometimes I know what I must do. Other times I know I must do the opposite. I hate it. I give up."

Agnola leans forward to argue. But Dolce shakes her head. "Let's go home today. At home, I will follow whatever regimen you set for me. You'll help me, won't you, Agnola?"

"You know I will." Agnola looks around and sighs. "You're right. It's squalid here. The sides of this pool are filthy. The water, scummy. They say it's therapeutic, but it's plain old algae."

"Algae?" Dolce's eyes widen, her mouth opens in a circle. She stands. "Algae in hot water. Is this water red?"

"Slightly."

"I thought it was green. How blind I've been. Of course." She walks along the edge of the pool as though in a trance, feeling under the water with one hand.

"What are you searching for?"

"Mussels."

"You can't eat shellfish that grow in dirty water. They're toxic."

Dolce holds up a small mussel with a look of triumph and whispers, "It's fitting . . . like a circle closing. From my mamma to my daughter." She looks at Agnola thoughtfully. "You're right about Lucia La Rotonda. She needs to enjoy herself before we leave. She will bathe with you this morning and go into the mud bath, too, while I will fetch ingredients for the evening meal."

Agnola has been biting her tongue at Dolce's crazy words, but these last ones . . . "What? You can't go about the countryside unescorted."

"I'll hire an escort. All the women hire escorts. Who knows what services they supply? I could be as satisfied as you." Dolce laughs. "Then we can travel home tonight with the future stretched out ahead of us, all ours."

Agnola's head hurts hideously now. She's sick and tired of dealing with Dolce.

Suddenly, Dolce wraps her arms around Agnola. It's like being held by a chain of bones, she's grown so thin. "I'm sorry, Agnola."

"Really?"

"Really. Escorts. I don't know what comes over me, what makes me say things like that. I'm so sorry. I get . . . lewd . . . and vicious. I don't even know who I am. I wish everything were different, everything were how it used to be. Sometimes the only feeling I have is regret."

Agnola is sure that's true. Contrition softens Dolce's face. This is how it always is. Dolce will be hateful—there's no other word for it—then she'll suddenly realize and she'll be mortified at her own behavior. "It's all right."

"It will never be all right. But I wish it could be. I wish I could be someone else. Tonight let's cook the meal and serve Lucia La Rotonda. Let's make her favorite dishes. You and I can be partners, like we were with Bianca."

"I'd like that. It's a sweet idea."

"Do you think I was ever truly sweet, Agnola?"

"I've known you sweet. Right now you're sweet."

"No, I'm not. For I'm aware of what I've done and what I must do."

"What does that mean, Dolce?"

"Do you think my mamma loved me?"

"Of course she did! What a question."

"Thank you for saying that. You have no idea how much I wish it were true. Without that, I'm broken forever."

CHAPTER 42

Biancaneve

Biancaneve bites the side of her finger.

"What's the matter, Neve?" Giordano is looking at her over the work in his lap.

She's been leaning against the wall facing him, but she thought he was so absorbed in his carving that he wouldn't notice. She looks at her finger. It's bleeding. "Nothing."

"Tell me. Did you hear something?"

"No, not at all." Biancaneve looks around the room for an excuse. "I was just wondering if maybe instead of waiting until the evening to cook this octopus, I should do it now, and we can eat it cold later. I'm afraid it might turn funny, you know, off, if I don't cook it soon."

Giordano looks at her doubtfully. But he should believe her, because Pietro brought the musky octopus yesterday. He stopped in Padova to buy a basket of those apples and this enormous octopus, caught in the Adriatic.

Giordano gives a quick nod, stands, and stretches. "Go ahead and cook it. Then we can heat it again before serving and add those dried red peppers and oil and garlic. It'll be perfect. While you do that, I'll take a quick look outside."

"I didn't hear anything, really." How can she say she half wishes she did? She never even told the men that Sebastiano had visited. How can she now say she hopes he visits again? And, really, she shouldn't be thinking about Sebastiano. That was two weeks ago. She may never talk to him again. "Nothing."

"I believe you. But sometimes people sense things. I saw the look on your face. Maybe you don't even know what you sensed. I'll be right outside. Keep my carving knife at your side, it's sharp. And if anything happens, you shout."

"I will."

"If anyone knocks at the door or shutters, you shout."

"I know the rules, Giordano."

"Then why do you have such a hard time following them?"

Biancaneve deserves it, she knows. With everyone else in her life, she's been bold. With these men, she's apologetic.

Biancaneve turns her back so Giordano can't see her face and bends over the bucket of seawater. She pulls out the octopus. It's frigid, that water. The men kept the bucket outside overnight and it still hasn't warmed up.

"Bolt the door behind me."

Biancaneve slaps the octopus onto the table. She wipes her hands on a cloth, crosses the room, and lifts the bolt. It's heavy, but it easily slides into place. Instantly she feels relief. She's glad, really, that Giordano is making an inspection of the area. She hasn't been calm since that comb nearly killed her and sickened the pup.

Usually Biancaneve fights off anxiety with hard work and conversation. There's always a man with her these days, right in the cabin. They can talk, and these men have histories so much richer than she ever could have guessed. The things they've witnessed could put into prison some of the most important men of the kingdoms of Ferrara, Sicilia, and Milano. If those places have laws anything like that of Venezia. Apparently, nobility misbehaves in horrendous ways. Blackmail. Rape. Murder. All these crimes, committed right in front of a dwarf. Dwarfs don't count as witnesses in the nobility's view.

Biancaneve can't see how anyone who talked with these men for five minutes would not realize their intelligence, their sensitive feelings.

She goes to the table. Her eyes fall on Giordano's carving. It's almost complete. He's making her a comb from the antler of the stag that Giallino shot. She tears up.

Heavens, she's being silly today. Crying because others are kind to her? And letting her mind wander to that Sebastiano, who might not even be who he said he was. She pulls the octopus toward her and cuts off each tentacle close to the base. This octopus died for them. She cries again.

A bang comes at the door. "It's me, Neve. Giordano."

Biancaneve wipes her eyes. She lets Giordano in and returns to the octopus. "My mamma—my stepmother, I mean . . ."

"It's not your fault," says Giordano.

She swallows. "What are you talking about?"

"Call her The Wicked One, Neve. That's what she is. It's not your fault. You said it the first day we met you. Believe it."

"That only makes it worse, Giordano. It hurts so much, it's like eating glass."

"Sit down, Neve."

Biancaneve sinks onto a stool. "Don't speak ill of her. Please don't do that. She was a good person. Somewhere deep inside, that good person still lives. She cried when she watched me use the poisoned comb. Oh, Giordano, everything has gone wrong."

"You're all right here."

"Of course I am!" She reaches across the table and grabs his hand. "I didn't mean to sound ungrateful. What's gone wrong is her. It's as though some awful thing inside her has grown and taken over. Somehow something bad, as bad as anyone can imagine, got planted in her."

"What do you mean?"

"She does strange things. She talks to mirrors. Or, rather, to one mirror."

"That's not so strange."

"It's the way she does it. Not like you and me. She makes them."

"Really?" His eyes cloud. "Who taught her?"

"I don't know. She learned as a girl."

Giordano pats Biancaneve's hand. He seems distracted.

Biancaneve sits across from him, still as a stone, until she feels almost calm. Then she stands and goes back to preparing the octopus.

"You know," says Giordano, without looking up from his carving, "I knew a girl who made mirrors once."

Biancaneve chooses an onion to chop. "Really?"

"She was a big person. Like you."

Biancaneve's head feels strange. She remembers being with Mamma that night on the *fondamenta*. She remembers Mamma talking about foot-fishing with a man. She can almost hear Mamma saying his name. She strains to listen to her memory. *Giordano.* Could it possibly have been this Giordano?

"The girl was troubled," says Giordano, half to himself. "But it wasn't her fault. She was isolated. Treated cruelly. Called a monster. Her mother should have let her be adopted in Venezia so she could grow up among big people—that's what everyone else did when they had a child like her. I always wondered what happened to her. She disappeared one day. Her mother died and she just disappeared."

Biancaneve drops the onion.

A rap comes at the shutter.

Giordano jumps to his feet. "Who is it?"

"I don't mean to disturb."

"Well, you do. Go away."

"I'm not a thief."

"Go away, I said."

"Then are you also saying I might have this?"

"What's *this*?"

"This, what's at my feet."

Giordano goes to the window, clutching his knife handle so the blade points down. He looks murderous. Gentle Giordano actually looks murderous. Biancaneve thinks of Mamma holding the knife handle the same way that day she attacked the oiled-paper windows. She follows Giordano. "Get back!" he barks at her.

But the voice from outside answers: "I'm nowhere near the window."

Giordano opens the shutters a bit. Biancaneve can see over him. There's a woman out there, not old, not young. Her shabby winter cloak covers most of her. Her kerchief covers the rest. At her feet is an apple. Her hands are bare and, oh, they're red and scabrous.

"Is this apple yours?" asks the woman.

"Who else's would it be?" snaps Giordano. "Apples don't just lie around in the middle of the forest."

"Someone dropped it."

"Giordano," Biancaneve whispers, "let her have it."

"No." Then to the woman, "Apples stored all winter don't come for free. Don't touch it. Besides, what are you doing here?"

"Scavenging. Have you no pity for those less fortunate?"

Giordano is the most generous of them all. Biancaneve can see the muscles in his neck slacken a little. "Those are for Neve. Special for her. To keep her healthy."

"Healthy? Is that beautiful girl behind you ill? She doesn't look it. You want to see illness. . . ." She holds up both hands, with the backs toward Giordano and Biancaneve, and walks forward. Biancaneve clutches her stomach.

"Please let her have the apple, Giordano."

"Please," echoes the woman.

Biancaneve knows this is Mamma. The disguise doesn't matter. The missing nails and scabrous skin don't matter.

"Half?" says the woman. "Half, then?"

"All right," says Giordano.

"That should make me half healed," says the woman. "After all, a whole apple heals wholly, right?"

Biancaneve trembles now. Her mamma—her first mamma— said apples healed.

The woman coughs. "I'll bring this apple to you, kind gentleman. You've already got a knife in your hand, I see."

"No! Don't touch it. I'll come get it and cut it." Giordano looks at Biancaneve. "Bolt the door behind me, just in case."

"Don't go, Giordano," she whispers. "It's Mamma."

"You recognize her?"

"No. But I know it. It's Dolce, reminding me that she's my real mamma now."

"Dolce?" Giordano's cheek twitches. "That's the name of the girl I knew. The one I was telling you about."

"She was a princess, wasn't she?"

Giordano's mouth hangs open.

"See? That's her out there."

"I don't understand. The Dolce I knew became your step-mother?"

"Stay inside. Let her have the cursed apple."

Giordano shakes his head. "I want to see her up close, see if she's the Dolce I knew." He opens and closes a fist. "Bolt the door." He goes out.

Biancaneve doesn't hesitate; she bolts the door and watches from the window. This is what doom must feel like.

Giordano picks up the apple. He cuts it in half. Then he stands tall. Biancaneve senses a change in him. It's as though he's meeting his maker. Maybe he recognizes doom too. "Which half do you want?" he says to the woman.

"Beggars can't be choosers."

"This time is an exception. Choose."

The beggar looks from one half to the other. "They seem the same to me. They smell luscious." She pulls a pair of gloves from a pouch, puts them on, then picks up an apple half. Then she pulls a cut orange from her pouch and squeezes it over the apple half.

"What did you do that for?"

"Orange keeps it fresh. This way I can eat slowly. Make it last all day if I have to." She brings the apple toward her face.

"No." Giordano takes it from the woman and hands her the other half. "This is your half. Take a bite. Right now."

But the woman has already taken a bite. She looks happy. She looks sublime, in fact. Biancaneve can sense how very proud she is of her cleverness; she foresaw how Giordano would try to trick her. She outsmarted him. "Thank you," says the woman. She wanders off, nibbling at the apple.

Giordano comes into the cabin holding the apple half. It glistens with orange juice. Good Lord, the aroma of it is pungent. And odd. Something's wrong about it.

"That was your Dolce, wasn't it, Giordano?"

"I can't be sure. The shape of her face, her nose and mouth and eyes, all that seemed familiar. But that woman was emaciated, missing teeth, and she looked at me hard, as though she couldn't really see me clearly. The Dolce I knew was young and beautiful . . . she should still be."

If her mamma really was the Dolce that Giordano knew, then she grew up among dwarfs. Those moments on the *fondamenta* are all rushing back at Biancaneve. Mamma said, "The heavens conspired against us." She said, "They made you steal my future, but then you stole my mamma. You stole everything."

Biancaneve has no idea what Mamma meant about stealing her future, but the rest of it . . . That story Mamma told her, about the woman whose child was different from everyone, that woman was Mamma's mamma.

"Tell me, Giordano. Ricci used to belong to the Loredan family. Pietro belonged to the Zeno family. What families did Giallino and Alvise and Baffi belong to?"

"What are you talking about?"

"Don't you know?"

"Of course I know. Baffi belonged to the Barbaro family, Giallino to the Dandolo family, and Alvise to the Orseolo family."

"And Giallino has been with you only this winter, right? He came most recently, right?"

"Right. But what has that to do with anything?"

"The last tiny mirror Dolce gave was to the Dandolo family. Oh, Giordano, she made mirrors for the families you belonged to. All who were slaves, she set free."

"I don't understand."

"How could you? I'm only beginning to."

Giordano's cheeks slowly sag, eyes wide and sad. "She worked with the quicksilver all along." He shakes his head. "She must have known she'd get sick. She saw it happen to Venerio. The beginnings, at least—when his hands shook and he'd fall all the time."

"Venerio, the mirror maker. Bini told me about him."

"He went mad, then died. Dolce did that . . . for us . . . and after the way everyone treated her . . . Only her mother was good to her."

When Mamma told that story about the woman and child, Biancaneve said the woman didn't love her child. Biancaneve had hurt her. Fiercely. She trembles. "I told you. She's mad, not wicked."

"You're right. There is no Wicked One."

Biancaneve can't think about this any longer or she will go mad herself. She didn't mean to hurt Mamma, to be her enemy. She breathes hard. This is not her fault. She sinks onto a stool. "This half of the apple is poisoned, Giordano."

"Probably." He sets it on the floor.

Biancaneve leans forward to look closely at the little bits of orange pulp that sparkle and smell so odd . . . but it's a familiar smell. A fish smell. Shellfish?

At the same moment Giordano stomps on the apple.

Spray flies into Biancaneve's face. She snaps her mouth shut in surprise, but she doesn't swallow. She mustn't swallow! She rushes for the wine, sloshes it around her mouth, spits it out the window.

Giordano is at her side. "Good God, what do you feel?"

"Nothing."

"I'll get rid of the damn thing. Bury it." Giordano wipes the squashed mess into a cloth and carries it outside.

Biancaneve sits on a stool and waits. She can't think of what else to do.

It begins as a burning around the opening of her nostrils, then her lips. Tingling in her face, arms, legs. She observes it happening as though it's someone else dying, not her. Now her head hurts. She staggers to a bed, dizzy, nauseated. She feels like she has no body, no weight, as though she's a feather floating in a current of air. And this air that she knows is frigid feels so very hot.

She can hardly hear Giordano's calls. She can't lift her head. She can't move. She can't breathe.

CHAPTER 43

Pietro

"Pietro!" Agnola runs to him. She takes his hands. "What's the matter?"

What can he say to her? Pietro's eyes meet Antonin's. The man's gaze moves pointedly to Pietro's hands within Agnola's. Antonin turns his head to the painting hanging on the wall. Pietro should pull away, but he's glad Agnola's holding on to him. He's glad her attachment to him makes her oblivious to Antonin. He is so much in love with this woman. How is it that he's gotten into the unbearable position of not being able to tell her all the things that have been going on? It's a wicked twist of fate.

"I need to see the signora," says Pietro.

"Why? What's happened?"

"I . . ." He has to tell the truth as much as he can. "A friend has died."

"I'm so sorry. Someone dear to you?"

"She's become dear." Pietro hadn't realized that before, but it's true. In his visits to the cabin in the woods, he has come to know Bianca . . . or Neve. . . . She was not the vapid thing he'd thought her to be. Not at all. She was strong.

"Do you want to tell me about it?"

"No."

Agnola looks bewildered. "But you want to see Dolce?"

"I need her help."

Agnola shakes her head. "Her help but not mine?"

"It's a matter of money."

"Money?"

"Please, Agnola. I need to talk with the signora."

She bends forward and speaks softly. "Every day she's worse."

Good. The world will be better without her. "I won't make her worse." In fact, she'll probably rally at the news. She's finally succeeded.

Agnola nods to Antonin. "Please announce our visitor. Pietro and I will wait in the music room."

"You don't have to accompany me." Pietro walks ahead. "I know the way. I'll wait alone." He goes quickly into the music room.

Agnola follows. "Don't you want me with you?"

"No."

"But why not? Pietro, you don't have to be embarrassed about money around me. How much are you looking for?"

"More than you have."

Agnola's mouth opens in surprise. She sinks onto a chair, clearly overcome. Nevertheless, she didn't sink onto the closest chair, the nicest one; she leaves that for Dolce. Pietro loves Agnola so much. He stands right in front of her. It would be easy to kiss her now. They just look at each other.

At last Agnola finds her voice: "What do you need it for?"

"Need?" It's Dolce.

Though Pietro knows now that she is crazy, he still feels disgust at the sight of Dolce. After all, what's the difference between illness and wickedness when it causes such evil?

She stands in the doorway with Antonin a moment, then lets go of his arm and takes her place in the best chair. "Who needs what? And, welcome, Pietro."

Her face looks happy. But it's coated with a thick layer of cosmetics. She's in disguise . . . again. Covering decay. The illness consumes her, like fire.

Dolce and Agnola are both looking at him.

Pietro makes a slight bow to Agnola. He hopes she'll take it as an apology. "If you'll permit me, I need to speak with the signora alone."

"I won't permit you. I'm not going anywhere."

"This doesn't concern you." Which is a lie. Pietro wishes he could take it back.

"Anything that concerns you concerns me."

Pietro grits his teeth. "I'm begging you to leave us, Agnola."

"Did you not hear me? I'm not going anywhere. I am your ally, Pietro. If anyone has sway with Dolce these days, it's me."

Dolce shakes her head. "Enough of this."

Maybe Agnola is right to stay; maybe she can help. Pietro just has to be careful, very careful, how he words things. He bows again, in acquiescence. "If I may, Signora, I've come to ask a favor."

Dolce looks at him, then turns one hand palm up and bends the fingers repeatedly, as though beckoning, to hurry him along. Her eyes radiate contentment. Pietro is not a violent man, yet in this moment he can understand crimes of passion.

"A friend of mine died last night."

"For certain?"

Agnola gasps. "Dolce, what kind of a response is that!"

"Forgive me. Is there more to say?"

"She needs a casket," says Pietro. "Immediately."

"Oh, Pietro." Agnola jumps to her feet. "I have enough money for that."

"A special casket," says Pietro. "An expensive one."

Agnola frowns and sits again. "Is this a noblewoman?"

"Yes."

"Well, if she's married or widowed, she should be buried in her husband's tomb, if he was a decent sort and provided for her. She was married, wasn't she?"

"No."

Agnola stiffens. "Then she should be in her family crypt. This is a family affair."

"The situation is complex. The family is . . . scattered. I am begging you, both of you, to treat her as you would your own family."

Dolce leans forward. "It is impossible to bury her in our family crypt."

"I'm asking for a casket. That's all."

"And you want a fancy one," muses Dolce, a gloved finger resting on her cheek. Her face grows solemn. "Yes, I will give you the money for that."

Agnola reaches across and touches her sister-in-law's shoulder. "You're very kind, Dolce."

Pietro's hands ball into fists. He has to clasp them behind his waist and breathe slowly and deeply to overcome his anger. "We don't want wood."

Dolce tilts her head. "We?"

"Her friends."

"Her friends? So you've come to me for what? A sarcophagus of alabaster? One white as snow?"

Pietro's eyes dart toward Agnola, but she is looking only at Dolce.

"Something much more precious," says Pietro. "Glass."

Now Dolce and Agnola both stare at him.

"Murano's best. White crystalline. Perfectly transparent. She loved it. She said she adored it."

"And she did," says Dolce.

Agnola tilts her head. "What do you mean by that?"

"Who doesn't adore white crystalline?" Dolce taps her gloved fingers together. She seems pensive. "A glass-topped casket. Like Sant'Eliodoro. I used to look through the casket at him when I was a child."

"Saints' coffins are gruesome." Agnola wrings her hands. "Why would anyone ask for such a thing? Did this woman die a martyr?"

"No." Dolce hits her hand on the arm of the chair with a thud. "Let's not talk about martyrdom. Death is dramatic enough." She turns her head and gazes out the window on the canal. "A white crystalline coffin lid." Her shoulders give a little shake.

"Not a lid. The entire casket. All six sides must be perfectly transparent."

"Who ever heard of an all-glass casket?"

"I have, actually." Agnola nods. "I just remembered. Simonetta of the Vespucci family. She was a noblewoman, from the kingdom of Genova. She married a noble from Firenze, and died young. Your age, Dolce. Twenty-two. She had consumption. They made a glass coffin and carried her through the streets of Firenze to the burial ground at the church. Thousands followed the procession. Everyone was in love with her."

"Why glass?"

"To see her. She was famous. She was the most beautiful woman in the world."

"It's not true."

"What's not true, Dolce?"

"She was not the most beautiful woman in the world."

Agnola's mouth twists. "Maybe at her time she was."

Dolce seems to relax back into her chair. "Maybe so." She looks at Pietro. "Is this why her friends want the coffin to be glass? So that they can look upon her beauty still?"

"Not her beauty. Her presence."

"Hmm. You realize, of course, that she'll change rapidly. Skin white as snow will grow ashen. Lips red as blood will dry up. Hair black as ebony will fade."

"White skin, red lips, black hair." Agnola's voice is thin. "You speak as though you know her."

"I do. We all do."

A little shriek of pain escapes Agnola.

Pietro feels suspended. What is Dolce doing?

"The perfect beauty is someone we all dream about." Dolce stands. "I will not pay for a glass casket just so you can watch this girl's beauty rot. . . ."

"Who said she's a girl?" asks Agnola.

"Girl, woman . . . you do her a disservice." Dolce leaves.

Pietro's eyes are on Agnola. Her face has transformed. He shivers.

Agnola stands. "Take the glass chest-bench. I'll tell Antonin and Carlo to carry it down for you." She follows Dolce.

"Wait, Agnola. Please."

She turns around. "Oh, Pietro." She just looks at him. "How could you?"

"I didn't do anything wrong."

"Whatever you did, it has destroyed us."

CHAPTER 44

Sebastiano

Sebastiano checks the sum in the ledger one last time, closes it, and pushes the ledger to the corner of the desk so it squares up properly. There's nothing left to do before traveling. He's used his time well these past couple of weeks. His bag is even packed already. So he might as well go. In fact, he could leave this afternoon. What's to stop him?

He's going to Firenze, to have a little pleasure. That's what he agreed upon when he talked with the girl in the cabin. She was so sensible. She made him recognize his own needs. And she listened to him. Not out of politeness—she was hardly polite. And not out of wanting anything from him. She was just a good listener.

And a good talker, too. Her voice plays in his head. Not too low—she's a girl yet. Besides, she talked about her stepmother in the way younger people do. She's under the woman's power. But definitely not a child.

A young woman living with dwarfs. She could be very little, like them.

What color is her hair?

Sebastiano walks down the stairs to the kitchen. It's empty.

Of people, that is. The table is covered with the carcasses of little birds. Quails and crows. The servants must be planning a feast in his absence. Everyone has parties during Carnevale. Sebastiano should have suggested a party himself. And when he didn't, his housekeeper should have brought it up.

Everyone has left him pretty much to his own devices since Papà's death. Probably out of respect for his mourning. But Sebastiano's mourning has to come to an end. He should go grab his travel bag and take off for Firenze. Instead, he walks empty-handed out the door and to the stable.

What color is the girl's skin?

What color are her lips?

Sebastiano saddles and bridles Luminoso. This is foolish, what he is about to do. But the idea of being foolish makes him happy. And maybe it isn't that foolish, really. He talked with the girl long enough to get a sense of her . . . longer than most men get to talk with a girl before they marry. And all he wanted was to keep talking, to know more. Everything about her. Why shouldn't they talk again?

He mounts and is halfway to the cabin when he realizes he should have gone hunting first. Arriving with a pot of roasted venison smothered in some delicious sauce would have been perfect. And that's what he promised her.

But he can't turn back now. He will not allow reason to prevail. He needs to hear that girl's voice as soon as possible. He needs to find out her name. He's gone over their conversation perhaps a hundred times. She said her father went off to Russia to get books for his library. She said she traveled with him when she was a small girl. She said her mother died when she was little. The only girl he ever heard of who traveled with her father was the daughter of a recent widower who was building a library. A friend of his father's. They traveled together once—the four of them. His memory isn't able to bring up the man's name. Sebastiano is almost sure that was the only time he met the man. But he remembers the feisty daughter's name because it contrasted starkly with her black hair—Bianca.

He doesn't believe the girl in the cabin is the same girl. Coincidences like that happen only in stories. But the whole thing gives him an excuse to return and find out her name so that he can attach it to her voice. And he must see her. He must. So this time he will stay till the men show up. This time the door will open. This time their eyes will meet.

The old poet Dante wrote, "*Lo viso mostra lo color del core*—the face shows the color of the heart." Sebastiano understands those words. The eyes are like a window into someone's soul. He's been asking himself the color of this girl's hair and skin and lips, but what he wants to know most of all is the color of this girl's heart. He needs to know it.

He urges Luminoso on faster. The dog cages appear. And, at last, the little cabin beyond. And what's that?

Luminoso slows to a walk. Sebastiano halts him beside a glass box. Someone lies inside it. His breath quickens. What's going on? He slips from the saddle and secures the reins loosely so that Luminoso can graze.

The box isn't just glass, it's the finest crystal, perfectly transparent. Inside is a girl. Her eyes are closed. Is it the girl from the cabin? Who else could it be? He raps on the lid. "Hello, hello in there."

No change. He looks for a way to open the box. No latch.

"Get back!" A dwarf comes out of the cabin, holding an ax high. "Don't bother her!"

Sebastiano stands tall. He has no weapon. But he will not step back from this girl. "I am Messer Simoli."

"I know who you are. Just stay away from——"

"Excuse him, please, Messer Simoli." Another dwarf pushes the one with the ax aside. It's Alvise, the one Sebastiano's father dealt with. He's their leader, and the only one whose name Sebastiano knows.

The others crowd out of the cabin now. Sebastiano counts: eight. That's one more than there's supposed to be. No women among them.

Alvise bows. "We're in mourning. So we may not be on our best behavior with respect to guests."

Mourning. Sebastiano feels a great pressure behind his eyes. He must talk slowly. He must not rush to conclusions. "I am not a guest on my own land."

"Of course not. I meant 'visitor.' "

"I am not a visitor on my own land."

The old gray-haired one steps forward. "Alvise can bumble sometimes. I am Giordano." He bows. "As Alvise said, we're in mourning. Ricci didn't mean to be rude. He just feels protective. We all do."

"In mourning"—Sebastiano looks at the glass box—"for her?" His skin turns to gooseflesh. He remembers the girl's parting words, about opening the door and dying.

"Neve," says the blond one.

"Bianca," says another. "That's her real name." He's the best dressed. Like a noble's servant.

Bianca! The little girl's name, long ago. Sebastiano's eyes go back to that fine nose, peaked lips, high cheekbones. Maybe he does recognize her. "She doesn't look dead. She's . . . lovely."

"Skin white as snow, lips red as blood, hair black as ebony." It's the well-dressed one. "She could have been a fine wife. To you, Messer Simoli."

"He's too old for her," says another.

"He's exactly the right age, Tommaso. And he would have protected her."

"Stop it, Pietro," says Alvise. "We did the best we could. It was your idea to bring her here anyway."

Sebastiano puts up his hands. "You, Pietro, you brought her here? So you know her family? Who are they?"

"She's dead now. Does it matter?"

"To those she left behind it does. She deserves a proper burial."

"Only her father would give her that. Until he comes, the glass coffin is where she'll stay."

"No." Tommaso grabs Pietro's arm. "You're not going to let her father take her away, are you? That's not right. She should be here, where we can see her."

"He won't be back till spring, Tommaso. We have her for now. He'll need a chance to say goodbye. He'll need to bury her in the family crypt. You'd want that for a father, wouldn't you?"

Sebastiano rubs his mouth, trying not to weep. Bianca's cheeks look fresh—he reaches to touch one. His hand hits the glass and his neck and face go hot.

"It's all right," says old Giordano. "We know. She looks alive. Nothing about her has changed."

"How long has it been?"

"She died last night. We put her in the casket not an hour ago."

"And you plan to leave her out here till her father returns in the spring?"

"Inside might be too warm," says Giordano. "The cold helps . . . to keep her like she was."

"Animals will come," says Sebastiano.

"Why should they?" It's the mustached one. "There's no smell."

"It'll seep out eventually," says Sebastiano.

Giordano shakes his head. "The glass top fits right."

Sebastiano looks at Bianca's hands folded on her chest. He wants to hold one. What a morbid desire. His nose flares in disgust at himself. But she looks so very alive. "Animals will see her. They can come up and look right in. They'll attack."

"That's a stupid thing to say." It's the rude one, Ricci. "What animal pays attention to something that doesn't move and gives off no smell?"

"Any passing stranger could . . . bother her."

"Out here?" says Ricci. "What passing strangers?"

Sebastiano stands tall. He puts a hand possessively on top of the coffin. "I'm taking her."

"What!" Ricci steps forward. "No you're not."

"I have a courtyard. It's protected from everything. You can come visit her every day. She'll be safe there."

"She's safe with us," says Tommaso.

"Pietro even said it," says Sebastiano. "I can protect her better. She might still be alive if Pietro had brought her to me in the first place."

"I didn't mean that," says Pietro. He looks around at the others. "I shouldn't have said that. No one could have saved her. Her stepmother is too smart."

"I knew her father," says Sebastiano. "My father was friends with him."

They all stare at him.

Then Ricci lifts a lip. "What's her father's name, then?"

"I don't remember. But I met him once."

"You just said you knew him."

"I was only a child. We traveled together—Bianca and me and our fathers—to a monastery to find books for her father's library."

Pietro lets out a loud sigh. "Ah, yes."

Alvise comes forward. "You can't have her, Messer Simoli. We protected her—or tried to. It's our right to watch over her coffin."

His words make sense. But Sebastiano can't keep his hands from opening and closing. A frenzy holds him taut. "You hunted on my land."

"What are you talking about?" says Alvise.

"You shot a stag. Two weeks ago. You left him for the crows."

"Who told you that?"

"Bianca . . . Neve . . . she told me."

"When?" It's Ricci.

"The day after you did it. I could bring all of you to justice. And I will, if you don't let me take the girl."

"You don't care about the stag." Ricci stomps in a circle around Sebastiano and the glass coffin. "You're smitten. Admit it."

Smitten. Is that what he is?

"Come and visit her," says Giordano kindly. "She's not going anywhere."

Sebastiano looks around desperately. "Is this the best spot for her? Do you think she might be better off on the other side of the cabin, where the dog cages are? That way if anyone came along at night and disturbed the coffin, the dogs would howl."

"Neve wouldn't want to be near the dogs," says the blond one.

"What are you saying?" says the mustached one. "She loved the dogs."

"Sure," says the blond, "but she didn't like them to lick her. She said their breath stank."

Sebastiano's heart leaps. He looks at Ricci. "Good Lord, man, you're right; I'm completely smitten. What kind of fool am I? But I am convinced, totally and utterly, that this girl should have been the one I married and built a family with and grew old with. I feel I've lost everything." Tears run down his cheeks. He's a blubbering idiot. He puts both hands on the coffin lid and leans till his face is just inches from the girl's. "I would have cherished you all my life."

"Listen," says Giordano in a thick voice. "Maybe the signore is right. Maybe Neve should be moved closer to the cabin."

"She liked the hens," says the mustached man. "We could place her near the coop."

Alvise and Ricci take one end of the coffin. Sebastiano and Pietro take the other. The five other men walk beside them. Sebastiano can't take his eyes from the girl's face. What? Did her eyelids quiver? Stunned, he drops his corner of the coffin.

But the glass doesn't break. Thank the Lord.

Alvise and Ricci and Pietro put down their corners. Everyone stares.

The girl's eyes are open. Her mouth is open. She pushes up against the glass with her hands.

The men are already lifting the lid.

The girl sits up and runs both hands along the rim of the coffin slowly, slowly. Her eyes register horror. She hugs her chest and shivers. She twists so she can look from one face to the next, as though she's making an inventory. Finally, she looks at Sebastiano. "Sebastiano? Is that you?"

"I love your voice."

"What are you doing here?"

"I came to be your husband, if you'll have me."

"Do you have any idea of . . . Are you mad?"

"You make me feel like the world is exciting. And we agree: dog breath stinks."

"Good Lord, you are mad."

"Perhaps. We can figure it out together."

CHAPTER 45

Pietro

Pietro stands beneath the high table in the Contarini family's palace. The cloth covering it hangs so low that the tassels at the four corners touch the floor. It's perfect. No one can tell he's there and he can still see the tips of the ladies' shoes as they come close to lean over the map spread out on the table. He will recognize Agnola's shoes. *She must not wear new ones. Please. This has to work.*

The voices are noisy. Women at these parties have a habit of talking over each other, multiple conversations going on, people participating in more than one at the same time. Such confusion has never bothered Pietro before, but it's hard on him now, as he strains to pick out Agnola's voice. Where is she?

The women sound happy and not at all interested in the map, really. Map rooms like this one are for the men, not the women. But Signora Contarini is proud of her husband's new acquisition, so she's invited her afternoon party to crowd into the room and exclaim over it. They understand; each woman dutifully says it's marvelous, sometimes speaking even as they step to the table, before they've had a chance to look at it.

Agnola must be here. He knows she was invited. Pietro studies the shoe tips.

At last. He closes his hand around her ankle, firmly. He doesn't dare move his hand upward; he doesn't dare even linger. But, oh, good God, how he wants to. He snatches his hand back under the cloth.

No sound from above. Agnola doesn't speak. He couldn't have mistaken her shoe. And even if he had, he couldn't have mistaken her ankle. He loves that ankle. Besides, if it were someone else, she'd have screamed.

"Wonderful," comes Agnola's exclamation at last. Her shoes stay a moment. Then they disappear.

The women leave the room maddeningly slowly in a haze of high, rapid voices. Pietro comes out from under the table. Agnola is last. She hesitates in the doorway.

"Come back," Pietro says. "We need to talk."

She drops her head. Her back is to him, so he has no way of guessing what she's thinking.

"Please. It's important."

"It wouldn't look right for me to be caught talking with you privately."

"Should anyone ask, you could say you're negotiating a gift for a friend. A surprise puppy. Shut the door."

"You've thought about this."

"I've thought of nothing else."

Agnola shuts the door and turns to him. Her face is solemn and rigid.

Pietro's heart melts. "I love you."

Agnola winces.

"She lives."

Her eyes flash anger. "Don't you dare keep saying that!"

"It's true. She almost died. I thought she was dead when I

asked for the money for the glass coffin. But she didn't die. And now she is safe. Dolce cannot get to her."

"Where is she?"

"Safe. I told you."

"A child who must hide from her mother cannot be called safe. Her whole life is in ruins."

"She's stronger than that. After every one of Dolce's attempts to kill her, she adapted."

"Dolce tried more than once," says Agnola in a reedlike voice. But it's not a question. "Tell me where she is."

"On the mainland."

"What kind of answer is that? The mainland is huge. Why should I believe you?"

"It's true."

Agnola's face goes red. Her eyes glisten. She folds her hands together and holds them under her chin. "Where is my precious girl?" she whispers. "Where, exactly?"

"At the Simoli home."

Her mouth drops open. Then a smile forms slowly. "Good Lord, I've heard of them. But I don't know where their home is."

"The woods near Marteago. They know your family."

Agnola blinks. "The Grimani family owns land there. They summer there. It's not far." She lifts just the tip of one shoe and slaps it down. "Take me there."

"I will."

Her cheeks go slack. "You lied to me."

"No. I withheld information."

She gives him a baleful look.

"It's different, Agnola. I had to."

"You let me suffer."

"I wish I could have spared you that. But you are open,

Agnola. And Dolce catches everything. She would have looked at your face and known."

"I have kept you secret, our love." Her hand goes to her mouth. "No. She figured that out." She wrings her hands. "What part did you play in it all?"

"The part of the wretch. I will tell you all, every detail. But I never harmed Bianca. And had I not played my role, she might be dead now. No, she would be dead. Most assuredly. Dolce is determined."

Agnola pulls on her fingers. "This is a tragedy."

"Yes. But only Dolce need sink forever. The human soul can rise after terrible destruction, Agnola. You know that. Bianca is rising above it even as we speak. Sebastiano courts her and she responds. In only a week I've seen her change. A blush comes to her cheek when he enters the room."

"Sebastiano?"

"Messer Simoli. You'll like him. He's a fine young man, and charmingly unpolished. They traveled together as children with their fathers."

Agnola drops her hands as if in defeat. "You know so much, I know nothing. In this moment I feel like a . . . child. I've been frightened and stupid. The spinster who's as foolish as she is homely."

"Far from it. You are the most constant woman I've ever known. You have stood by Dolce in her ravings, despite your grief. You see whatever good there is in people. You put that first. You are full of love. No one is more beautiful than the fount of love."

Agnola puts a finger on her bottom lip, that lip Pietro loves to nibble. Her eyes look tentative.

"Love me, Agnola. Please."

"How can I resist?"

CHAPTER 46

Agnola

A gnola stands at the high table in the library. She turns the pages of the tome slowly. She does not read, but she appreciates the flow of the letters and the decorative paintings. She runs a gloved finger along the page. Marin doesn't like them to touch the pages with bare hands because over time they will leave marks. And it is important to follow Marin's guidelines in his absence. He's coming home to personal sorrow. At least his library will be intact.

Agnola is looking at a choir book Marin bought from a collection in Munich that originally came from the church of San Bartolomeo in Venezia. She stops at a painting. Vines twist around the outer frame of the central picture, with a profusion of flowers in yellow and red among deep green leaves. In the middle sits Maria the Virgin with the baby Gesù. They are surrounded by dazzling gold. The mother's eyes don't look down at the infant, but out at the viewer, at the world. And they brim with pain, as though even then she sensed the agony ahead. What courage it takes to love someone you know is doomed.

The choir books in the old church of Santa Sofia are not so elaborate. It's an old building, in severe need of repairs. But Agnola goes there every Sunday and she'd never think of going anywhere else. Pietro says a humble church is the only church that has a chance of being honest.

But then, Agnola has come to realize that almost no one has a chance of being honest.

Footsteps clack along the hall. Agnola goes to the library door and watches as Antonin enters the music room. After all that talk about the music room being Bianca's domain, Dolce has taken it over. Doesn't she realize that's an open admission that she has been assured Bianca is dead? Is she so far from sane that she doesn't feel the need to hide her efforts? She has never mentioned the disappearance of the glass chest-bench, either. She doesn't pretend she has been robbed; her behavior says it really belonged to Bianca.

Every morning Dolce strums unmusically on the harp and weeps. Then she stands by the window and stares at the canal for hours on end. She goes through her day with perhaps a total of twenty words to others. She is like a crab, all folded in on herself.

Still, Agnola feels no pity. She feels fear: Dolce must never learn Bianca lives.

From here, Agnola can't make out what Antonin is saying. She moves quietly into the hall until the voices become clear.

"Messer Sanudo? Again?" says Dolce. "All right. Show him in."

Antonin leaves the music room and heads for the main staircase.

Agnola goes hot all over. Fate is handing her an opportunity. She can't hesitate.

She runs after Antonin and catches him by the sleeve at the

top of the stairs. "Please, Antonin," she whispers. "You must delay him. Say the signora needs time to dress. Take him into the courtyard for a while."

"The courtyard is cold."

"But sunny. It's a sunny day. Have Lucia La Rotonda make him a hot drink and bring him *zaleti* while he waits."

"We have none."

"What do you mean? She made many the other day, just to please Dolce."

"The signora had her throw them out. She says they were the lost signorina's favorite biscuit."

A perversion of a penance perhaps, since *zaleti* are Dolce's favorite, too? Crazy Dolce. "Then whatever biscuits she has. I don't care, Antonin. We must delay him. Find a way." She squeezes his arm. "It's crucial."

"As you wish, of course." He goes down the stairs.

Agnola rushes to look under Dolce's gilded bedstead. She has no idea what size a flask of quicksilver would be, so it might be hidden anywhere. Nothing. She kneels in front of one chest after another, feeling through the folded clothing, then the sheets and pillowcases. Nothing, nothing.

She gets to her feet and looks at the wardrobe on its carved lion paws. *Please, please, let it be here.* The heavy doors swing open. Stacks of books rise in two towers. This is where Marin keeps the ones he plans to restore.

And, there, in the corner, is an iron flask. Agnola doesn't open it. She doesn't know what quicksilver looks like anyway. And what else could it be?

Now, where can she put it?

She could throw it off the balcony, but someone might see.

Where will Messer Sanudo fail to look?

She goes into the sewing room. The flask is short enough to fit under the lid of the yarn basket. She snatches up gold silk and wraps the flask in it, tying the cloth very, very loosely at the top with a bit of yarn. Then she stuffs in ribbons, padding the flask around the sides and up over the stopper. She lets the tip of one yellow ribbon hang out, as though someone was careless in putting it away. She sets this in one corner of the basket and arranges the yarn neatly around it. Her creation looks like a silk bag of ribbons.

Agnola goes out into the hall. She should go to her own room and wait, the picture of innocence. But the suspense of not knowing what Messer Sanudo is doing from one moment to the next is unbearable. She breathes deep and heads for the music room.

She had not been planning this. Or, if she had, she didn't realize it. But everything fits now. So far as Agnola knows, there is no evidence to support Dolce. Not one thing.

She knocks on the music room door and enters without waiting.

Dolce looks at her with surprise. "Did Antonin tell you to come in here, too? Are we to be interrogated together again?"

Agnola doesn't dare answer. She is new to lies. Her best course is to say and do as little as possible. She takes the chair beside Dolce's.

Antonin comes in followed by Messer Sanudo and two younger men, all three in black. They bow and Messer Sanudo introduces his companions. Agnola's chest squeezes painfully.

"Officials of the Republic," says Dolce, in a superior tone. She barely nods. "What is it you require this time, Messer Sanudo?"

"We've visited Torcello."

"Ah, my old homeland. Did you see a yellow wildcat?"

Messer Sanudo clears his throat. "I fear you do not understand the gravity of the charges against you, Signora. This is no time to talk nonsense." He takes a step forward. "The people living on Torcello know of no mirror making on the island. There are but a few families there, since the island has been reinhabited only in the last few years, so we questioned each of them. We were most thorough. There was, apparently, a number of unfortunates living there for a while. But they were evicted when the rightful owners returned to their homes."

"Unfortunates?" says Dolce. "You mean dwarfs?"

Agnola jerks to attention.

"Yes, in fact." Messer Sanudo sniffs. "How did you know that?"

"I told you, I lived there. I made mirrors there."

"You lived in a dwarf colony?"

"Yes."

Messer Sanudo takes another step forward. "We also went to Murano. The task was much more time consuming there. Did you know that nearly three thousand people are employed in glass making there?"

"I know little about Murano," says Dolce.

"We went into every factory, every shop. No one gets their mirrors from Torcello. Everyone on Murano makes their own. With a formula they invented."

"Today. But not eight years ago."

Messer Sanudo gives a loud sigh. "Signora, many factories make small pieces of glass. But no one on Murano makes these little pocket mirrors, though now they are talking about doing so. Apparently, every girl and woman of Venezia wants one."

Dolce smiles. "Vanity prevails."

"That leaves us with only your story. Do you understand? And your story makes no sense, Signora."

"Truth often doesn't make sense."

"Do you have anything that can corroborate your story?"

"Of course."

Messer Sanudo's eyes widen. He looks relieved. "You do? Well, show us, dear lady."

"I make the mirrors in a storeroom. If you look, you'll find the glass and tin and stone weights."

"Please lead us there."

Dolce looks at Agnola. "My sister-in-law can show you. She's familiar with that storeroom. You know what I mean, Agnola."

Agnola's neck and checks are afire. But she shakes her head, as though in confusion. "I'm not sure."

"Both of you can lead us there."

"Is that an order?" asks Dolce.

"I'm afraid it is, Signora."

"In that case," says Dolce with a smile, "who can refuse?"

They go down the stairs, a silent procession. Agnola's eyes feel glassy and dry.

They go to the storeroom, past casks of wine. Dolce's nest is there, the nest Agnola and Pietro frequented. Agnola has to close her eyes for a moment. Antonin has brought them all candles. The idea of dropping hers and simply setting the whole palace on fire flashes through Agnola's mind. She trembles.

"Where are they?" Dolce shines her flame in the rear corners of the storeroom. "Where!" She looks at Agnola. "What have you done with them?"

Agnola threw them in the Canal Grande. After Pietro came to ask for money for a glass coffin, Agnola knew Dolce was responsible for Bianca's death. And she knew Dolce had somehow gotten Pietro to play a role. She couldn't begin to guess how, but the certainty blinded her.

She went down to the storeroom and found Dolce's paraphernalia for mirror making. She tossed it all off the balcony. She didn't do it secretively or to thwart Dolce in her attempts to exonerate herself with Messer Sanudo—she hadn't thought that far ahead. She did it in the brightness of day, like a young girl making wishes. She did it to steal from Dolce the chance to make more mirrors, because mirrors had been the ruin of them all. She did it to protect them, though she thought they were all lost already.

And now it has come to this. As though she'd planned it. How strangely things turn out.

Agnola steps backward, away from Dolce.

Dolce comes at her, hands outstretched.

Messer Sanudo steps between them. "Signora, please contain yourself. Trying to transfer the blame to your sister-in-law may make things worse for you."

Dolce looks at him oddly. "Worse? There's still the quicksilver. Follow me."

And so the procession climbs the stairs again. They go into Dolce's room. She opens the wardrobe and her mouth forms a silent shriek. She looks at Agnola. "It was here this morning. Where did you put it?"

Agnola doesn't dare look away. She plays a statue.

"Search the palace," says Dolce, her eyes still on Agnola. "You'll find it."

"Go," says Messer Sanudo to the two other men. "You, take the next floor up. You, take this floor. I'll keep the ladies company."

There are four chairs in the room. Messer Sanudo looks at one. "May I?"

"I don't care what you do," says Dolce. She sits on the bed.

Messer Sanudo takes a seat. Agnola sits beside him and imagines the sewing room, sees one of the men approaching the yarn basket. Pulling at the ribbon that hangs out from the yellow silk sack of ribbons. Opening the sack. Her breath is so shallow, she feels light-headed.

The men return, look at Messer Sanudo, and shake their heads.

"How did you know?" Dolce looks at Agnola. "How did you know they'd come today? You did it today. I know you did. I polished that flask this morning, polished it and polished it. How did you know?"

"Signora," says Messer Sanudo, "your sister-in-law couldn't possibly have known we were coming. We don't announce visits like this."

"Visits like this? What does that mean?"

"Visits where we've come to take the criminal away. If we announced our visit, some might flee. Signora, you have secrets that threaten the health of the Republic."

"Health? You mean 'wealth.'"

"The wealth of the Republic is a large part of its health. You buy from a scoundrel. Your only hope is to give him up."

Dolce stands and walks to Agnola. "Do you realize what you've done to me?"

For an instant, guilt transfixes Agnola. Dolce is off to prison for a crime she didn't commit. But the instant passes, for, after all, Bianca lives. Pietro has taken Agnola to visit her. The dear girl lives. She even thrives. And if Dolce were free, she'd go after Bianca again. There's no question.

Dolce must be stopped. And the Dolce Agnola once knew, the Dolce who is gone forever, would want it this way. Agnola believes that. She has to believe that.

Agnola looks Dolce in the eye. "Bianca," she says.

Part VI

THE WAY IT ENDS

CHAPTER 47

Dancing

Pietro stands in the bleak, narrow corridor. Bars cross the window between us horizontally and vertically. "I can't fit my head through," I say, "but my hand goes easily. Is that why you're standing so far back? Are you afraid of me?"

"I've come with news."

"News before dawn? Come a little closer; it's hard to see you in this murky place." I try to sound encouraging.

"Agnola wanted you to know. Before we left."

"Agnola's leaving?" I grab the bars with both hands and press my face into an opening. Marin will come home to find everyone he loved so dearly gone. "She can't go, Pietro. She can't. Marin needs her."

"You're not in charge."

"Don't let her go. Marin is a good man. Tell her to remember that and behave accordingly."

"You're not making any sense. But I don't care. I'm just the messenger." Pietro's arms are crossed. He rocks a little on his heels. "We're going to the mainland. We'll be gone a week. To a wedding."

I'm half elated. "You and Agnola? You're getting married?"

"If she wants that. But that's a question for later. We're going to Biancaneve's wedding."

"Biancaneve?"

"That's what she calls herself these days. To celebrate her new life, and her past."

Snow White. My heart flutters. "So she did die? And then she lived?"

"She's different now. She doesn't want city life anymore. She's in love."

I let go and drop to the damp wood floor. She's alive. *Thank you.*

Pietro's voice comes through the window above me. "We'll dance at her wedding today."

"Bianca . . ." My voice is weak. "Biancaneve . . . she should wait for her father to return. He'll want to give away his daughter."

"I told you: you're not in charge."

"Have another ceremony when he returns. Everyone can dance then."

"I bear messages only from Agnola to you. She believes this information will soothe some part of you, and knowing that helps her sleep. Guilt weighs on her."

"Yes. . . . Deception is contrary to her nature. Tell her, these last few weeks, my world is no longer black. Dark shimmers at the edges whenever it wants, but sometimes I can see the center again. Tell her in those moments I know she did the right thing. Tell her I'm . . . grateful. And . . ." The dark encroaches. I try to push it back, but it swings across my face, smothers me. "Tell her I'll be dead . . . in weeks."

"Weeks? They haven't even set the date for a trial yet."

It's not the Republic who will kill me. It's my illness. I'm nearly dead already. "Do you know what they do to me to try to get me to tell them something that I cannot tell them? To reveal to them the name of someone who doesn't exist?"

"I've delivered Agnola's message."

"And she thinks that absolves her? Giordano knows I told the truth. I recognized him. I could call upon him if I wanted to!" I'm shouting, frothing at the mouth.

"Agnola knew you'd be like this. She said you even told her when you were at the baths together—you said, 'It will never be all right.' She wishes it were different. But it can't be. You're sick—and that makes you dangerous.

"Agnola has a giant heart, but, me, all I can think is, good riddance. We'll be dancing as you die. And the men who took care of Biancaneve this winter, they'll dance at the wedding. And they'll dance when she has children and whenever beautiful things happen to her. They'll know her forever. Sebastiano has given them the cabin to live in for as long as they want. So die, go ahead and die. Let this evil end with you." I hear his footfalls fade.

The darkness retreats.

My parting message to Agnola almost had dignity . . . it almost conveyed the best of me . . . until I ruined it.

There has to still be a best of me. Please, Lord.

Dangerous.

Something crawls up the front of my leg. I squash it through my skirt. Something else bites my foot. I pull off my battered boot and stocking and rub at the stinging spot. I have so many bites, all up my legs, my back, my chest, my head. My neck is lumpy. I cough all the time. I'm covered with weeping sores.

The woman to my left, the one who is always watching me, stands and comes over. She towers above me. "I can piss on your foot if you want. It takes away the sting. And it's hot, for a moment at least."

I point at the oozing gash on her ankle. "Piss on yourself," I say.

Some of the other women laugh. But no one laughs hard. No one has the energy. We are a withered lot. The food is too disgusting to eat.

A key clanks in the lock. "You." The guard points at me. "Come."

I pick up my boot and stocking and walk past the guard, who locks the door once I'm out. The stone floor of the corridor is cold on my bare foot. Something to focus on.

Biancaneve weds today. Biancaneve of the birds. Biancaneve the beauty.

I walk ahead of the guard to the end of the passage, to the room I know well. My interrogator awaits me. "Is it sunny out, Torture-Monger?"

"Too early to tell."

"I used to love the sun, you know. Now it sears my eyes."

Torture-Monger indicates a stool. "Sit, Signora."

"Is it a proper day for a wedding?"

"Any day is a proper day for a wedding if the man and woman choose each other."

"Well, aren't you a renegade."

"Signora, once more, I recommend that you cooperate. You look revolting, you smell revolting, your legs wobble as you walk."

"Are you blind? You may be right about my odor and my wobble. But I am beautiful still. Somewhere that other me exists yet—the beautiful one—the one Marin loves. And not just him. Agnola, too, and Bianca—Biancaneve, that is."

"Sometimes I think you are crazy. Other times I'm sure. But, Signora, oh, Signora, those cells—the well, as we call them—are not the right place for a person of your social standing. Cooperate. Give us the name of the thief. The one who stole Murano's mirror-making secrets. The traitor to the Republic."

"I know no such person."

"One name, and you will be moved to the cells on the top floor. They are cleaner, less crowded, without infestation."

"Colder, too, I hear."

"Lead roofs make them icy in winter, steamy in summer. But it's almost spring. You'll be brought to trial in spring. And if you cooperate now, you are likely to be seen as the victim of a scoundrel. A noblewoman, taken advantage of."

"But I'm not, you see." I look around the room. It's empty but for two stools and a table. "No instruments of mutilation today?"

"You don't know what instruments of mutilation are, Signora. What you've experienced thus far is like a father disciplining a child."

"You can't frighten me." I spit into my hand and hold it out toward him. Two molars sit there in a puddle of blood.

He draws back and gapes at me. Then he leans toward me. "Treason is punishable by the gallows."

"I am innocent of treason, but guilty of worse."

"Nothing is worse than treason."

"Blind and stupid, that's what you are."

"Let's take a walk." He half lifts me by the elbow, and leads me into a room.

Iron contraptions hang from the walls. If I looked, I might be able to guess what they're for. But I don't look.

"All right, lunatic, give me a smile, and I'll let you choose your method." He opens his hands and spreads them wide. "Boot or cuff?"

"I don't understand the question." I don't understand anything.

"Iron shoes or iron wristbands."

"Boot."

"Bad choice. You'll never walk again."

"I can hardly walk now."

"Spikes or fire? These boots"—he holds them up—"spikes poke in as I tighten the vise. These others, I heat them in the coals."

Along one wall is a fireplace. The coals spill out in a half circle and glow. There will be a great fire at the wedding. There will be roasted meat. "Who will eat the liver and lungs?"

"You will, Dolce."

Am I hallucinating? I haven't heard Marin's voice this whole time in prison. I turn around slowly, as slowly as I can, so as not to scare off whatever phantom might stand there.

"Excuse me, Signore," says Torture-Monger. "No one is allowed in this chamber."

Marin stands there. Real as the dank of this prison. "Messer Sanudo let me in. I am Messer Cornaro; the prisoner is my wife. Please extend us the courtesy of speaking in private. Messer Sanudo will be here soon, to give you instructions." Marin holds out a purse.

Torture-Monger takes it and leaves.

Marin looks at me with a ghastly pale face. His hair has grayed.

"The Russian winter has faded you, my husband."

"I am less ravaged than you."

I see myself in his eyes. Hideous. I turn my back on him again and sink to a squat, as small as I can. "Have you come to save me or witness my death?"

"I believe you were about to be tortured, not killed."

"Marin, speak to me."

"I hardly know what to say."

I keep my eyes on my feet. "Did you just happen home in time for the wedding?"

"Yes."

I look up at him. Could the Lord have bestowed this one mercy?

"And no. A messenger made it through the mountain passes to tell me that my daughter needed me. He set out in February, the most treacherous month. So I came back as fast as I could. I arrived two days ago, just by chance in time for a wedding I knew nothing of." He puts both hands to his forehead and rocks on his heels. "When I left, you were sick, but still loving. My daughter was safe. My sister was respectable."

"Agnola is still respectable."

"She has . . . Pietro." He drops his hands. "He puts her out-side Venetian society."

"You've never really cared about Venetian society, Marin. You proved that when you married me. She's happy with him."

"I hope you're right. It's all . . . My heart is breaking."

"Our daughter . . . is safe."

"Agnola told me you tried to kill her."

"Four times."

"You tried to kill our daughter." He is crying loudly.

My head rests heavy on my knees.

"Can you tell me why?" he asks. I shake my head. "Do you know why?"

I love Biancaneve. I love Marin. I love Agnola. Some days my mind seems to be reviving. I know what I have done. I know everything. I will never understand, but I know. My head rolls with tiny balls of iron that clink against each other all day, all night. That was me who did all that. That other me. "I went mad. Everything still . . ." I stop.

"So my wife is insane. That's what they all say."

"Why are you here, Marin?"

"When they told me what had happened and that you were in prison, I thought you were behind bars for attempted murder. Only this morning did Agnola confess to me."

"Why?"

"I found out she had sent Pietro here to tell you about the wedding, and I asked her why. . . . It all spilled out."

"And so . . . you rushed here to save me."

"I didn't rush anywhere."

"Of course not. Nothing can save me. The only ones who can give testimony about my mirror making on Torcello are Giordano and Bini and Tommaso. And their word would mean nothing to Messer Sanudo."

"My word would mean something to him. I can say you made them here in Venezia."

"Is that what you decided to do?"

"Not at first. Rage can win over grief. But then Bianca . . . Biancaneve . . . prevailed upon me. She wants you at her wedding. She pleaded. She said the world is too full of madness and despair. She wants no more mistakes. She begs that cruelty give way to kindness, charity, and love. Most of all, love. That's what our daughter said."

I hear her voice in those words. I could go to the wedding. I could see my daughter lit up with love. I could watch Agnola at

Pietro's side, brave against the cold tide of Venezia. I could even lean on Marin. It would be balm for my ragged soul.

She is right, that daughter of mine. Her plea is right. Let love prevail.

My head has strong moments; it is possible that it could heal.

But this body can never revive. *Thank you, dear Lord, for that much, at least.*

"She said something else, too," says Marin. "She told me what you did with the mirrors, for the slaves. They all know. She said that proves you are there still, the mother she knew, full of love. Are you, Dolce?"

I have never loved them more. But I won't answer Marin. He has a right to his rage. It will help him through.

I stand and look at the two sets of boots: the first with spikes, the second to walk in fire. I know they wait.

Fire and weddings, after all, they make a match.

Biancaneve didn't know what she asked for when she said she wants no more mistakes. My poor, dear daughter. *Let me be strong enough to make no more mistakes. Guide me, please.*

"I'm not much of a dancer. But our daughter's getting married. I won't dance at her wedding—I'd only be a blight, a reminder of the worst. Make her understand my absence is a gift of love. Tell her to smile that I am at least capable of this much. I'm going to dance here. Tell her my last dance was for her. You can turn your back if you wish." I step into the second pair of boots.

Marin clasps my arm. "I loved you once, Dolce. You loved me. Perhaps . . ."

"No, Marin. We could never trust me. Ask Agnola. That's what madness means, don't you know? Let me go, dear man, love of my life."

Marin's face crumples. He lets go.

I stomp through the coals. I stomp and stomp. I dance. My feet may be iron, but the rest of me is grace, the spirit of love, the essence of beauty. Biancaneve is alive. And so is my soul. This is how it ends.

Author's Note

Most instances of mercury poisoning can be treated by removing the source of the mercury and sometimes following up with medications, completely reversing the symptoms. But when mercury vapor is the source, a cure can be elusive even with present-day medications. Dolce, like others of her time, was misinformed about vapor. If exposure to mercury vapor continues, the body becomes infertile and declines in many ways, with deteriorating skin, teeth, nails, kidneys, eyes, and psychological well-being. Exposure like Dolce's would ultimately lead to insanity and death.

The comb in this story has been dipped in aconite, which is poisonous on contact. It can certainly be fatal, but Biancaneve didn't get a strong enough dosage to kill her. The apple half in this story was doused with orange juice mixed with the liquids of mussels infected with neurotoxins from algae and bacteria. These liquids cause paralytic shellfish poisoning, which can be fatal. Sometimes a person who has consumed infected shellfish will breathe so shallowly that they will be believed dead. If they don't die, when they recover, it seems they are rising from death.

Selected Bibliography

Adelson, Betty M. *The Lives of Dwarfs: Their Journey from Public Curiosity Toward Social Liberation.* Piscataway, NJ: Rutgers University Press, 2005.

Ajmar, Marta, and Flora Dennis. *At Home in Renaissance Italy.* London: Victoria & Albert Museum, 2006.

Aslan, Lokman, Murat Aslankurt, Cengiz Dilber, Murat Özdemir, Adnan Aksoy, and T. Dalkiran. "Ophthalmic Findings of Acute Mercury Poisoning in Primary School Students." *Journal of Clinical Toxicology* S1:010 (2012): 2161–0495. doi:10.4172/2161-0495.S1-010.

Azvedo, Bruna Fernandes, et al. "Toxic Effects of Mercury on the Cardiovascular and Central Nervous Systems." *Journal of Biomedical Biotechnology* (2012). doi:10.1155/2012/949048.

Brown, Patricia Fortini. *Private Lives in Renaissance Venice: Art, Architecture, and the Family.* New Haven: Yale University Press, 2004.

Cohen, Elizabeth Storr, and Thomas Vance Cohen. *Daily Life in Renaissance Italy.* Westport, CT: Greenwood Publishing Group, 2001.

de Cervin, G. B. Rubin. "The Evolution of the Venetian Gondola." *The Mariner's Mirror* 42, no. 3 (1956): 201–218.

de Chavez, Kathleen Payne. "Historic Mercury Amalgam Mirrors: History, Safety and Preservation." *Art Conservator* (Spring 2010): http://www.williamstownart.org/techbulletins/images/WACC%20 Historic%20Mercury%20Mirrors.pdf.

Deeds, Jonathan R., Jan H. Landsberg, Stacey M. Etheridge, Grant C. Pitcher, and Sara Watt Longan. "Non-Traditional Vectors for Paralytic Shellfish Poisoning." *Marine Drugs* 6, no. 2 (2008): 308–348. doi:10.3390/md6020308.

D'Elia, Anthony F. *The Renaissance of Marriage in Fifteenth-Century Italy.* Cambridge, MA: Harvard University Press, 2004.

Edgerton, Samuel Y. *The Mirror, the Window, and the Telescope: How Renaissance Linear Perspective Changed Our Vision of the Universe.* Ithaca, NY: Cornell University Press, 2009.

Johnston, F. (1963). "Some Observations on the Roles of Achondroplastic Dwarfs Through History." *Clinical Pediatrics* 2 (December 1963): 703–8.

Kalas, Rayna. "The Technology of Reflection: Renaissance Mirrors of Steel and Glass." *Journal of Medieval and Early Modern Studies* 32, no. 3 (2002): 519–542. doi:10.1215/10829636-32-3-519.

Labalme, Patricia H., and Laura Sanguineti White. Translations by Linda Carroll. "How to (and How Not to) Get Married in Sixteenth-Century Venice (Selections from the Diaries of Marin Sanudo)." *Renaissance Quarterly* (1999): 43–72.

Laven, Mary. *Virgins of Venice: Broken Vows and Cloistered Lives in the Renaissance Convent.* New York: Penguin Books, 2002.

Martin, John. *Venice's Hidden Enemies: Italian Heretics in a Renaissance City.* Berkeley, CA: University of California Press, 1993.

McCray, W. Patrick. "Glassmaking in Renaissance Italy: The Innovation of Venetian Cristallo." *JOM* 50, no. 5 (1998): 14–19.

McKee, Sally. "Domestic Slavery in Renaissance Italy." *Slavery and Abolition* 29, no. 3 (2008): 305–326. doi:10.1080/01440390802267774.

Melchoir-Bonnet, Sabine. *The Mirror: A History.* New York: Routledge, 2001.

Moritz, Fabienne, Patricia Compagnon, Isabelle Guery Kaliszczak, Yann Kaliszczak, Valérie Caliskan, and Christophe Girault. "Severe Acute

Poisoning with Homemade Aconitum napellus capsules: Toxicokinetic and Clinical Data."*Clinical Toxicology* 43, no. 7 (2005): 873–876. doi:10.1080/15563650500357594.

O'Bryan, Robin. "Grotesque Bodies, Princely Delight: Dwarfs in Italian Renaissance Court Imagery." *Preternature: Critical and Historical Studies on the Preternatural* 1, no. 2 (2012): 252–288.

Palmer, Richard. "'In this our lightye and learned tyme': Italian baths in the era of the Renaissance." *Medical History* Supplement 10 (1990): 14–22.

Ruggiero, Guido. "Law and Punishment in Early Renaissance Venice." *Journal of Criminal Law and Criminology* 69, no. 2 (1978): 243–256.

———. "The Status of Physicians and Surgeons in Renaissance Venice." *Journal of the History of Medicine and Allied Sciences* 36, no. 2 (1981): 168–184.

Shimizu, Y. "Paralytic Shellfish Poisons." In *Fortschritte der Chemie organischer Naturstoffe/Progress in the Chemistry of Organic Natural Products,* 235–264. Vienna: Springer, 1984.

Venerandi-Pirri, I., and P. Zuffardi. "The Tin Deposit of Monte Valerio (Tuscany): New Factual Observations for a Genetic Discussion." *Rendiconti Società Italiana di Mineralogia e Petrologia* 37 (1981): 529–39.

Verità, Marco, Alessandro Renier, and Sandro Zecchin. "Chemical Analyses of Ancient Glass Findings Excavated in the Venetian Lagoon." *Journal of Cultural Heritage* 3, no. 4 (2002): 261–271.

Wheeler, Jo. "Stench in sixteenth-century Venice." In *The City and the Senses: Urban Culture Since 1500,* edited by Alexander Cowan and Jill Steward, 25–38. Hants, UK, and Burlington, VT: Ashgate Publishing, 2007.

Acknowledgments

Thank you first and always to Barry Furrow, and to Brenda Bowen, Maggie Christ, Ivy Drexel, Sharon Friedler, Elena Furrow, Nick Furrow, Alice Galenson, Ashley Hoyle, Lorraine Leeson, Meg McWilliams-Piraino, Kate Nicholes, Nathan Sanders, and Rachel Sutton-Spence for comments on earlier drafts and troubleshooting details of plot with me. And a crystal-white thank-you to my constant cheer squad and editorial team, Alex Borbolla, Dana Carey, Sarah Eckstein, Teria Jennings, Alexandra West, Hannah Weverka, and, especially, Wendy Lamb, who said, "Why not Venice?" Many thanks, as well, to copy editors Heather Lockwood Hughes and Colleen Fellingham for their care and attention to detail, and to kid-ethic.com and Shannon Plunkett in the art department for the striking cover and interior design.

About the Author

Donna Jo Napoli has been publishing stories for children and young adults since 1991 and has about eighty books in print, including *Alligator Bayou, The King of Mulberry Street,* and *Daughter of Venice,* available from Wendy Lamb Books.

Donna Jo is a dual citizen of the United States and Italy, where many of her stories are set. She lives in Swarthmore, Pennsylvania, with her husband. Visit her online at donnajonapoli.com.